# SWEET CURSE

## KALI SWEET URBAN FANTASY, BOOK 4

## MISTY EVANS

Beach
Path
Publishing
LLC

Sweet Curse, Kali Sweet Urban Fantasy, Book 4

Misty Evans

©2010 - 2024

ISBN: 978-1-964028-07-1

Cover Art by Fanderclai Design

Formatting by Beach Path Publishing, LLC

*To all those cursed.*
*And to all those who are blessed.*

"The daimon throws us down,
makes us traitors to our ideals
and cherished convictions —
traitors to the selves we thought we were."
~ Carl Jung

# 1

*E*very blessing hides a curse.

I'm a demon, but I love humans. They're so... imperfect, creative, and...well, mortal.

Being what I am doesn't mean I'm perfect, obviously, only perfectly wicked. Because I'm one of the original vices Jesus cast out of Mary Magdalene back in biblical times, I'm cursed with virtue running through my blood as well. I'm constantly at war with my evil side, and now my horrible flaw of loving humans has landed me a new job—one I don't particularly like nor want.

After my boss, Damon, was slain, I was forced to take over his job as head of the Bridge Institute, an organization that keeps supernaturals in line with the human population. We "bridge" the gap between the two species—insert an eye roll here, but look, I didn't come up with the name—and I'd gladly give up the promotion to have Damon back.

Protecting humans is what I do. With supernaturals, I take revenge. Being a vengeance demon has its perks, but as I said, every blessing hides a curse. I can't exact vengeance for myself, even when I've been wronged by, say, a certain half-Chaos demon, half-human male.

Rad, the demon-human hybrid in question, walked beside me as I headed down an alley seeking a rundown tenant building on Chicago's South Side. It was nearing sunrise, the time most supernaturals were tucking themselves into bed, and I was on a mission for Lucifer hunting one of his fallen angels. Rad thought I needed help; I let him tag along for the eye candy even though he broke my evil heart several centuries ago, and I still wasn't sure I could completely forgive him. One of the downfalls of my demon side – I don't forgive and forget.

The former rock star has always been gorgeous, even back in the day in Rome when I first saw him in Queen Maria's court. Dark hair, full mouth, golden eyes...he mesmerizes me as much now as he did then. My weakness for his body is only compounded by what the sound of his voice does to my insides. Deep as the night is dark, fluid as the blood running in my veins, that voice propelled him to fame and fortune in the human world. Fame and fortune he'd recently given up to take over my job as the Bridge Institute's enforcer.

Training seven days a week and working at night, he's filled out his tall frame to maximum capacity. The muscles in his shoulders and back have formed many curves and indentions I enjoy running my fingers over. His stomach is a washboard, his chest firm and solid. His thighs are hard as steel beams...all the better for our adventures in and out of the bedroom.

"Four shifters behind us," he murmured. His trench coat flared behind him as he walked. He used its camouflage to palm a gun with one hand. In his other was a silver dagger.

The shifters had to belong to Mo, our perp and renegade vampire.

Shifters working for vampires? How unnatural. "Do not engage," I muttered back. "We're here for Lucifer's angel, not to start a turf war."

2

Chicago's South Side had as many supernatural packs as human gangs. Many were shifters, a few vampires, and plenty of demons. All of them were outcasts—renegades or runaways from their families or social groups.

I sniffed the air. The four shifters following us smelled like a mixture of wet dog and road kill. Hyena? Jackal? Rare in these parts. Probably imports from the southern hemisphere. I wondered how they liked Chicago's current bout of freezing spring weather.

I increased my speed just to see what the shifters would do. Rad followed my lead, and the four behind us did the same.

One lone streetlight illuminated the alley. Rad chuckled ominously under his breath. "They obviously don't know who you are."

I no longer wear my red cape—the calling card of Kali Sweet, Bridge Enforcer—because I am no longer enforcer, and the paparazzi had snapped my picture on more than one occasion when I'd been with rock star Radison Beaumont. They'd tagged me "Red Riding Hood." Cute, right?

I don't do cute. Never did, never will.

Since I couldn't afford the media attention, I'd given up the cape. For me, it was easier to avoid the spotlight. Rad not so much; leaving behind his famous status had been difficult. Luckily, neither the media nor Rad's fans had ever gotten a clear shot of my face, so once the red cape was gone, so was I.

Except for the Red Riding Hood posers all over Chicago. Many of Rad's fans now wore red capes in some freaky camaraderie/cosplay shit.

Behind us, the shifters made snorting noises. One of them whined low in his throat.

"Maybe they *do* know it's me," I said, "and want to find out if I'm all that, like everyone claims."

Another chuckle from my sidekick, low and confident, the

sound sending a thrill up my spine. "Either way, I don't believe they're going to play nice."

I didn't want to play nice. I wanted to dispose of the jackals, find Lucifer's angel, and return to the Institute. I had a pile of work waiting for me. Dozens of supernaturals depending on me.

In a nutshell, Damon's job sucked. I should have given him more credit and less of a hard time when he was alive and well.

But the archdemon had taught me well. I couldn't lead the supernaturals living and working at the Institute if I couldn't use discretion. And discretion was definitely needed to retrieve Tabriss VondeVeer from the clutches of Big Mo Jennings.

Besides, Lucifer wanted this rescue done quietly. Making a mess of the guys behind us would call attention to our mission —attention from humans *and* other supernaturals.

Footfalls echoed, the jackals' larger-than-life shadows hovering on the brick walls of the alley buildings. No discretion here. They weren't even trying to be stealthy as they tailed us.

Filtering through the alley's malodorous bonanza, my nose caught the scent of oiled metal—*guns*—and sharpened steel— *knives*. The knives emitted an unusual fingerprint odor—an alloy traditionally used to make fighting blades.

I fingered Volante, my whip coiled at my waist. She was an extension of me and my inner demon, able to read my magic and rarely needing direction. "Those guys have to belong to Mo, right?"

We'd made it to the end of the alley and prepared to circle behind the building to a bedraggled backdoor with a single light over it.

"Does it matter?"

He knew it did. Big Mo was a freak in the supernatural world. A very rare pairing of vampire and Dread demon. Dreads were like human MMA fighters—big, beefy, tough as nails. In their demon form, they had red skin and ram-like horns. Humans sometimes mistook images of them for the Devil.

Human girls mistook Mo for a handsome older guy who liked *Twilight* movies and wanted to give them a thrill acting like, well, a famous actor in the starring role. He and his outcasts were very 21st century, using social media to find these teenagers and convince them to fulfill their fantasies of sexing it up with a vampire.

His meals consisted of human females between the ages of fourteen and twenty-one. He drank their blood—at its reproductive and extremely potent peak—to keep his magic as powerful as possible. Tabriss happened to be seventeen and probably the most potent female he'd ever encountered. Her blood wasn't only reproductively rich; it was mixed with angelic mojo.

I threw a glance over my shoulder. The jackals were leering at my ass. *Such dogs.* I had expected Mo to have security, but not this kind.

Rad sensed my internal conflict, wanting to take out the muscle but not incite a fight with Mo. "He's violating every rule in the Bridge Mandates, Kali. We should light his ass up."

"All in good time. The Institute has enough to handle at the moment." *I* had enough to handle. "And Mo can call up a band of renegades that could do more harm to humans than what he's already got. I don't want a war with him. Not yet."

"You sure this isn't about him being a half-vamp and you not wanting blowback on your Master?"

Alexandru, Chicago's head vamp, was not *my* Master. Not in the traditional sense of the word. We'd shared blood and I was Queen of the Chicago vampires by a horrible fluke, but I was a demon, not a vamp, although I did appreciate the extra juice it gave me. Rad was just jealous of my relationship with Dru.

His jealousy worked for me – it meant he was still in love with me.

I motioned him to walk past the building's entrance. There was no need to let the jackals alert the Dread demon that we were there. At this point, they probably thought we were two lost supernaturals, and they were looking forward to having a little fun with us. "Can you create a distraction?"

Rad gave me a look, suggesting I needed a refresher course on his skills. A tiny gust of wind, strong and purposeful, lifted the ends of my hair. The gust turned into a steady breeze. Paper, cardboard, and other debris in the alley whipped past my feet. His magic sent a tingle of lust through my veins.

"How big?" the Chaos demon asked.

He did come in handy. "Big enough to make them turn tail and run."

"Snap your shields into place."

I touched my ring finger and thumb together on each hand, raising my magic into an invisible protective bubble. In the next second, the wind morphed into a gale, gusting strong enough to roll a dumpster down the alley. It flowed around my magical bubble, and I watched as the dumpster came to life and bore down on the jackals.

They'd formed a line to stalk us, the leader a few steps ahead of the others in his alpha spot. Now, the three of them scattered as the stinky dumpster zeroed in on them. Shouts rang out but were consumed by the wind. They ran; the dumpster gave chase. Their group and the hulking metal canister rounded the corner and disappeared.

Watching them scatter made me smile. Watching Rad, in all his chaotic demon glory, made me lick my lips.

He'd raised his hands slightly from his sides, the wind roaring around him like the caress of a lover. It lifted his hair, as it had done mine, and pressed his clothes against him. His weapons were still in his hands, but they seemed to be resting there, shimmering and trembling in his palms. A look of euphoria touched his face. He'd been training all right. He was beautiful in his power.

Too bad his display of magic was over so fast.

The wind died. Rad cut his gaze to mine. His golden eyes glittered with an internal, supernatural light. One that said he was master of the night. "How was that, boss?"

I hate it when he calls me boss. He did it for the same reasons I had once taunted Damon with the term, especially when he and I disagreed about policies and procedures. But this time when Rad said it, there was a subtle underlying tone that surprised me. Not smart-assed. Not flippant.

Sexy. Earnest.

*He wants my approval.*

I gave it to him, counting on getting something in return once the mission was over. "Remind me to reward you for your outstanding service when we get back to the Institute, enforcer."

He gave me a mocking bow. "I do so enjoy being your subordinate."

Employee, blood slave, lover. Anyone else in those positions would have been under my subjugation. Rad never entirely was. I suspected love had something to do with it.

*Love.* A confusing human emotion. Demons weren't supposed to experience it, and yet many of us did. Even Lucifer Morningstar himself.

But he wasn't a demon. He was Fallen.

I eyed the building, ready to finish the mission and deliver Tabriss to Lucifer's waiting arms. I sensed no magical wards, no invisible trip wires or cameras. Apparently Mo wasn't worried about attracting trouble. "Let's get this over with."

Rad checked the end of the alley, making sure the jackals

were truly gone. By the time he came back, I'd disabled the three layers of locks on the door, both mundane and magical. Laying my hand on the brick building, I called on all my magic to get a feel for what—and who—lay inside.

Demon power rises from the earth. As I summoned mine, I felt a warm vibration surge up my legs, play tag with my spine, and flow down my arm and into my hand. The demon inside me reveled in the rush.

"How many?" Rad asked, watching my back.

Dark magic zinged along my nerves. Demonic magic. "Six or seven of Mo's males. Five are vampires. The others are demons, but low-level ones."

"The target?"

"She's in there. I sense a dozen human females, at least one that is Fallen."

"Weapons?"

I concentrated harder. I could smell metal, steel, gunpowder. Demons didn't need weapons, per se, but we all like our toys. Volante snaked over to and up my arm, quivering in anticipation of the potential bloodshed. "The usual. No silver, though."

"Bonus."

Bonus was right. I opened myself to the emotions of the entities inside. Pain was the most prevalent – the enslaved females were full of it. Fear and horror mingled with the pain.

On the flip side, the demons were...content. Recently fed and high on their captives' blood, they seemed to be resting in a way that suggested they'd had a satisfying meal.

Even low-level demons enjoy human blood. Since these had enjoyed a recent dose, their magics would be more potent. Not nearly as strong as mine, but I needed to anticipate their increased abilities.

And if Mo had just fed, he'd be one hopped-up Dread.

"You find Tabriss," I told Rad, removing my hand and

quietly opening the door. "I'll take care of Mo and his goons if they wake."

He nodded, whisking past me and into the building. Just as he passed the threshold, I felt a new energy, an aura I never expected. "Wait!"

I reached for him, but it was too late.

## 2

The ghost dog was the size of a hellhound and equally vicious. Because it was a phantom, its coloring was vague and blended in with the dark interior, making it difficult to see.

Except for its bared teeth. Infused with Mo's magic, it was as dangerous as any real dog. More so since the magic gave it an advantage despite its dead state.

It lunged for Rad's thigh, intent on taking him to the ground where its sharp teeth and snapping jaws would have an advantage. In its corporeal body, it had probably been a fighting dog. One Mo had raised from the dead to defend his property. It was a vicious, soulless entity, its only goal to maim and kill.

Rad had his silver knife in hand. I grabbed Volante from my arm. The ghost dog's razor-sharp teeth shredded through Rad's coat and pants, sinking into his skin. Rad didn't so much as cry out, plunging the knife into its head.

I snapped the end of my whip at it, making contact with the hellhound's ribs. The dog froze in mid-bite, then disappeared, its ghostly atoms scattering into a million pieces.

Silver didn't destroy specters, only interrupted their energy form. "He'll be back," I whispered, readying the whip for any more unsuspecting attacks. "You all right?"

Rad eyed his pants and the torn and ragged skin underneath. His voice lowered to a murmur. "Nothing a little of your blood won't cure."

He lifted his eyes to mine. Light from the alley reflected in them. *A little blood and a lot of sex*, those eyes said to me.

"Do you ever think of anything else?" I teased.

He wiped off the knife on his other pant leg, a sticky substance from the ghost dog's head glowing softly on the fabric. "Not usually."

Shaking my head, I scanned the entryway and beyond. No alarms had sounded, no voices echoed from the rooms off the long, narrow hallway. The supernaturals were sleeping, and their midnight snacks were in blood-drained comas.

Keeping Volante at the ready, I crept through the house and changed my original plan. I stationed Rad at the basement door and made my way down the rotted wooden stairs to the dank, cold underground holding cells.

Not just cold, *freezing*.

The smell was the first thing that hit me. Dying humans have a distinct odor like meat just beginning to go bad. When they've been drained of blood over and over and kept at such cool temperatures, the smell is less stomach-turning but still gross.

I flipped on lights and saw a dozen females strung up by their hands, their faces as ghostly as the guard dog at the door. Bite marks and burns covered their naked bodies.

Revulsion filled my chest. I checked pulses. Four were dead. Three so far gone, they wouldn't live another day. Tabriss was alive, probably thanks to her angelic origins, and the other four were also alive and in better condition. Recent *Twilight* addicts added to the group.

Humans were gullible by nature. Human teenage girls, the

worst. Playing on their fantasies was too easy. It all made me want revenge in a bad, bad way.

Unhooking Tabriss, I lowered her to the floor; her frail body weighed less than a hundred pounds. She lay prone, eyelids fluttering as if trying to open but failing. Her hair was matted and fresh bite marks showed on her neck. Piercings covered her ears, nose, and eyebrows. Several tattoos decorated the pale skin over her left breast, right hip, and on the tops of both feet.

It wasn't my style, but soothing nonsense words flowed from my mouth as I gripped her hands and sent a dose of magic into them. My magic won't heal, but it's powerful stuff. I figured it might jumpstart her angel mojo and give her a boost of self-healing.

Her body convulsed slightly. Her eyelids fluttered once more, but she was a pint low in the blood department, and it would take more than a surge of magic to get her on her feet.

Which brought me to a quandary. My blood was the most powerful on Earth. As one of the original vices, I wasn't just a demon. Jesus had morphed me into both vice *and* virtue... something I'd only recently learned. Add to the fact I had very old Master vampire blood running in my veins, and I was a supernatural freak of epic proportions.

My blood could literally raise the dead.

Technically, I had three blood slaves, one of which was Rad. Demons who work for the Bridge Institute aren't allowed to have blood slaves, nor did I want any, so my predicament was unusual and undesired. No way was I adding another to my list.

But Tabriss was a fallen angel. What were the rules regarding angels and demons sharing blood? Had to be a huge, whopping no-no. Would my blood help or hurt her more? Wouldn't angel blood trump anything else?

She moaned softly and squeezed my hand. So light I almost missed it.

A sudden surge of need rose in me. In my head, I heard Damon's voice. *Protect her. Help her. She belongs to you.*

Huh? I shook my head, clearing my voice. She didn't belong to me; she belonged to Lucifer.

But the hot need to protect her refused to be suppressed. My temples pounded with it; my chest tightened. My fingers stroked her hair, touched her piercings. *Mine.*

Satan's balls. In the overall scope of things, I was already screwed. Why not ensure my damnation?

Taking a small knife from the inside of my boot, I slit my wrist. As blood seeped from the wound, I held it to her mouth. Her cracked lips didn't move, so I opened them to let the blood in. After a minute, she reflexively swallowed. Once, twice, three times.

Rad's voice, low and quiet, floated down the stairs. "How's it going down there?"

Tabriss's eyes opened. She looked directly at me.

*My God.* Her eyes were lavender. Just like...

*No. Not her.*

The old pain tore through my chest. I couldn't go there. That was three hundred years ago, and I should have been there to save her. I'd failed then, but Tabriss was here and now. Her, I could save.

"I'm Kali Sweet." I ignored the way my magic wanted to wrap itself around her. "I'm going to get you out of here."

Her head came up off the floor, lips latching onto my wrist. She pulled deep, and a zing of energy flew up my arm. Her tongue licked in between sucks, and I felt the warm metal of a tongue piercing. The tiny ball rolled over my open cut, smooth in comparison to her rasping tongue.

Heat flooded my chest, a flash of bright light exploded inside my head.

"*Merde,*" I whispered to no one in particular.

Rad's voice came again. "Kali?"

Tabriss took a final tug, sucking my blood in a rush. Then she released my arm, laid her head back, and stared at me through her lashes. She was panting, and so was I. A silvery blue glow shone around the edges of her pupils.

"Can you stand?" I asked.

My blood rejuvenated her enough she could sit, but when I drew her to a standing position, she stumbled trying to put weight on her legs. Since I had no idea how long it might take for her to recover enough to walk out on her own, I lifted her and threw her over my shoulder in a fireman's hold. "We're coming up," I murmured to Rad.

She didn't fight me carrying her up the stairs. There, I turned her over to Rad, hustling him toward the back door while keeping an ear and an eye out for potential threats.

The house stayed quiet. The ghost dog didn't reappear. At the door, I gave Rad instructions. "Get her back to the Institute and give her to Di. I'll contact Lucifer as soon as I leave here."

"You're not going with us?"

Discretion was meaningless if it meant I had to leave the surviving females in the basement. I couldn't do it. "I'll catch up as soon as I can. I won't be long."

Rad smiled. "I knew you wouldn't leave the others behind."

Oh, I was leaving them behind. But I was also making sure Mo's enterprise was temporarily put out of business. I removed my coat and put it on Tabriss. It was big on her but did the trick to cover her nakedness and most of the marks. "I'll see you back at the Institute."

"I'm not leaving you here to take on Mo and his bastards alone."

I could wipe Chicago off the map if I turned my inner demon loose, but it was cute he was worried about me. "I'm not fighting them head-on, just putting a stop to their dealings for the time being. Trust me, I don't need backup."

Rad didn't quite believe me, but Tabriss moaned, and he relented. Sort of. "Promise you won't do anything stupid."

I don't make promises, and I don't like being coerced. Or having someone imply I make stupid choices. Turning on my heel, I went back inside, Volante in one hand and my cell phone in the other. The door shut softly behind me.

"I'd like to report a crime," I said to the 911 operator when she answered. "I live over on Keeler, and I think my neighbor is a serial killer."

# 3

The fallen angels, or simply Fallen, of Lucifer's heavenly army were buried in the Lost City of Angels – a place I'd never been to, and which happened to be on a separate plane of existence.

A few, like Tabriss, had been reincarnated as earthly beings. In human form, their magic was buried deep, constantly fighting to get out. They didn't know about it or understand how to control it, causing them to fall into lives of violence, drug use, and prostitution. Upon his death, Damon had gone to hell like any self-respecting demon and now worked for Lucifer, searching for Fallen and bringing them to me at the Institute to rehabilitate.

"Another one?" Kirill, the Institute's resident doctor and Bridge board member, paced Damon's office. Which was now *my* office. I still thought of it as Damon's, though. He'd be back once he'd served his time with Lucifer. At least that's what he'd told me. "That makes forty in the west wing alone."

Forty. "That's a significant number in biblical numerology, isn't it?"

"Why?"

"Maybe that's it. That's the end. Forty Fallen, and we're done."

"You think so?"

He was as hopeful as I was. We looked at each other for a moment, both of us remembering the old days and longing for the Institute to get back to normal.

"Unfortunately, no. Lucifer once told me that there were a thousand. I suspect he was rounding down."

"Holy hell." Kirill rubbed his pudgy face. "Surely we don't have to find all of them."

I knew better than to assume anything. I used the phone on the desk to page Neve, my human friend and current office manager.

She answered begrudgingly, not even saying hi. "Di has Tabriss resting comfortably. I've notified Damon she's in our keeping since you forgot to contact him and Lucifer earlier."

I hadn't slept or eaten yet. I hadn't even had time to feed my blood slave or make him live up to the promise I'd seen in his eyes earlier. From Neve's tone, I had the feeling she hadn't slept or eaten either. "Thank you," I said, "but what I called for was to ask if you'd seen Salmad anywhere this morning."

Kirill shot me a funny look. Neve's voice belayed she was also surprised I would ask for the priest. It's rare. Very rare. "He's in the chapel."

"The chapel? *What* chapel?"

"The new one. The one he converted from the old torture chamber."

It was my turn to be surprised. "I didn't authorize that. What if I need that torture chamber?"

"*Kali*," Neve admonished. "We don't torture people. Or supernaturals."

I wasn't in the torture biz anymore. Not since I'd left Queen Maria's enslavement. Still... "I have three prisoners who could all use a little encouragement to do what I ask. He can't just go and turn the torture chamber into a fucking chapel."

My arch nemesis Queen Maria, Rad's ex-fiancée, Parker Burkett, and Victoria, a vampire-witch who'd raised Lilith from hell, were all guests of the Institute for their crimes against humans and supernaturals. I might have been out of the torture business, but I wasn't above giving them a dose of their own medicine if need be. "Outside of Lucifer's minions, those living here are mostly demons. What do we need a chapel for?" I added.

She sniffed. "Well, I think it's a good idea. Spirituality is a blessing. One can never have too much of it."

Said the woman who carried talismans from every religion she came across, from crucifixes to Celtic circle jewelry. Neve believed in being safe. "Just send Sal to Damon's office, will you?"

"You mean *your* office?"

Whatever.

I disconnected and looked at Kirill. "A chapel? Really? You okay'd that? Cuz I sure as hell didn't."

He looked chagrined, but only slightly. "It's keeping the priest out of my hair. Yours too. You should be glad I told him to go for it."

The office door opened. Maddy, our resident teen vampire who changed moods as fast as she went through my extensive designer clothes collection, strolled in. She wore my favorite red bustier and skinny jeans.

The bustier gaped here and there, but the huge eye of Horus necklace adorning her neck distracted me. "What's up, Mouse?"

She held up her cell, then tossed it on the desk in front of me. "You made the news."

"*Cazzo.*" The last thing I wanted. The little bit of publicity my red cape and Rad had generated had nearly given me a stroke. "What this time?"

A video of a local newscast played on the screen, a tall woman in a pink coat and a microphone looking into the camera with a somber face. Behind her was Big Mo's building, enveloped by yellow crime scene tape and knee-deep in cops and FBI agents. *"...police report eight women have been recovered. They have not released their names as of yet, but I'm told by an inside source, all eight are from a pool of women who went missing earlier this year."*

"Eight?" I said. "There were twelve. Eleven, not counting Tabriss."

The reporter went on. *"Four men have been arrested."* Photos of the men flashed across the screen. The four shifters from the alley.

*Merde.* "Mo got away."

"You didn't take him out?" Kirill asked in disbelief.

I should have. I *knew* I should have. "I was trying to be discreet and not stir things up with his gang. I have enough on my hands at the moment. I can't handle more. The *Institute* can't handle any more. Calling in the cops seemed like an effective way to see the women were rescued and Mo put on ice for a while."

But Mo wasn't on ice, and he'd taken at least three of the victims with him.

*Damn.* I punched the desk.

"You rescued Tabriss," Maddy said, trying to put a positive spin on things. "Lucifer will be happy, Damon will be happy, and you and I can look for Mo tonight. Rad will help. Cole, too. I bet I can even get Brianna to join us."

A hunting party. This was exactly what I'd been trying to avoid. "Damon should have never asked me to go after Tabriss. He should have done this job himself since she was so important."

Why *was* she, I wondered? He'd refused to divulge that information, but I'd known it the moment I saw her. The moment I touched her. I'd never had that type of reaction to a Fallen before.

Damon was in charge of tracking down the angels, a deal he'd been forced into by Lucifer, but one he was good at. In fact, there wasn't anything Damon wasn't good at from where I stood, and I'd known him for several hundred years.

When Damon unearthed the angels from the City or discovered where their human incarnations were on earth, he brought them to me. The Institute housed them, introducing the human ones to their true powers and rehabilitating those who'd been buried in the City as a favor to Lucifer.

Not that I could have said no to the king of Hell and not ended up a shish kabob, but I owed the Devil for helping me stop Armageddon a few months back.

Being in another's debt never sets well with me. Being in Lucifer's debt is a *nightmare*.

The request to rescue Tabriss had taken me off guard. At first, I'd refused, risking Lucifer's anger. Then Damon stepped in and made the request personally from him. Tabriss was special, a crucial integer in restoring universal balance, blah, blah, blah.

Used to be I could say no to Damon without blinking an eye. These days, after witnessing his earthly death, not so much. The grief, fear, and anger I'd felt had been overwhelming...too human. The vengeance I'd wanted to take on the killer...well, let's just say it was a good thing I didn't follow through.

Because Rad had been the one to cut off Damon's head.

It had taken some serious self-analyzing and zenning-out for me to forgive him.

On Maddy's phone, the reporter continued to list details about Chicago's latest serial killer and the women he and his buddies had abducted. At least the details the cops were giving out.

Kirill rose from the couch, strolled to the door. "Damon knew you were the right entity for the job. Maybe he wanted you to go after Mo and rescue the other females because he couldn't. Ever think of that?"

Always a touch pompous, the demon knew what buttons to push.

"That wasn't his directive," I argued. "If he wanted me to act as Bridge enforcer, he should have said so. I was acting as director. Acting the way he would in my place."

Kirill shrugged. "Quite possible. You never know with Damon."

Wasn't that the truth? "What should I do now? Go after Mo? Or leave it be?"

"If Mo finds out it was you who turned him in to the police, he'll be gunning for you. Get him first, you have less to worry about."

I would never have *less* to worry about. Not as long as I was in charge. "I hate this job."

"Stop whining. Damon designated you to be in charge for a reason. He knew you'd make the tough calls, and they'd be the right ones, so do the damn job. You don't have to like it."

He walked out.

O-*kay*. I looked at Maddy. She shrugged, snagging her phone from my desk. "What got under his scaly skin?"

Kirill wasn't scaly, but his aura generally was due to the fact he dabbled in spreading some pretty damn awful diseases. Pestilence, the Red Horseman, had been his boss. Finding himself a demon without a purpose, he might have been a teensy bit jealous that Damon put me in charge and not him.

I rubbed my tired eyes. "Why are you up at this time of day?"

"Couldn't sleep."

The tightness in her face told me there was more to it. And in Maddy's world these days, everything had to do with a certain shifter. "Lover's spat?"

She made a rude noise in the back of her throat. "He's seeing someone else. A shifter, like him. She's a dog, for Christ's sake."

"Literally or metaphorically?"

"Huh?"

Another of my blood slaves, Arman, had fallen in love with Maddy around the holidays. Vampires and shifters are like oil and water, and she'd pretended not to see his blatant puppy love since she considered a shifter beneath her. But Arman's a charming kid with a shy smile and skater-boy tendencies. After a while, that charm and seemingly undying devotion got under Maddy's cold skin.

Unfortunately, by that time, Arman had given up on her.

"Is she a shifter dog, or is she a dog for stealing your boyfriend?" I clarified.

She did a mock shiver. "Both. She's a Chihuahua. All big eyes and ears and little body. I mean, what could a were-cheetah see in..." —she wrinkled her nose— "*that?*"

"Love is blind."

Her gaze snapped to mine. "He *loves* her? Did he say that?"

One pile of dog shit stepped in? Check. "I haven't talked to Arman in weeks. I have no idea how he feels about her. I didn't even know about his new romance until you brought it up, remember?"

"Oh." She flopped down on my sofa, working the gum in her mouth like she was chewing a bullet. "I hate him."

"No you don't, and you know he's nuts about you. The Chihuahua is a tool. He wants to make you jealous, so you'll appreciate him and want him the same way he wants you."

"Really?" She thought about it for a moment. "You think I still have a chance?"

"Stop mooning over him. Find a pretend boyfriend. See who caves first."

A slow grin spread across her lips. "Look at you, giving relationship advice. Things are good with Rad, huh?"

*Brat.* "How about you round up that group to hunt Mo tonight, and in the meantime, get some sleep."

The grin broadened. She saluted me, rising from the couch. "Sounds like a plan, oh great and wondrous Oz."

I mentally swore at her back as she left. The Oz moniker wasn't far from the truth. Every day, I had to work harder at appearances. Harder at pretending I knew what I was doing. Smoke and mirrors weren't usually my thing, but there was this deep, driving need to do this right. To not screw up.

For Damon.

I sank deeper into his soft leather office chair, exhausted physically and mentally. Forty Fallen.

*I could be done.*

That was my hope. Only a little longer and I would go back to my old job.

The exhaustion took over, and I closed my eyes.

# 4

We live in a world of opposites...light, dark, good, evil. In the dream world, things are not as clear-cut. What is classified as good on the plane of earthly existence may be evil in a dream. Or perhaps, as in the dream I was having, one entity contains both light and dark, love and hate.

Damon came at me from the shadows, his archdemon energy pure evil. The look in his red eyes, as well. "Choose," he said.

My feet stumbled backward, and yet his energy drew me toward him like a magnet. My voice was thick and garbled. "I want to, but I...can't."

His aura took on a weird dynamism. His energy morphed into something akin to Lucifer's. "Choose!" he demanded.

"Leave her be." Rad, behind me and off to the side, held a golden sword. "She's done enough."

Damon moved suddenly in front of me, arms going around my waist. "There is no such thing as *enough*. He is coming. You must choose."

His magic enveloped me, comforting, even though it was

dark and dangerous. My demon surged, reaching for it, for him. "Please don't leave me," I whispered. "I need you."

In the distance, I heard a female laugh. I searched the shadows for her but didn't see anyone.

Damon held me locked against his chest. Tears formed in my eyes. I wanted to hug him, but my arms wouldn't cooperate. They hung limp at my sides.

"Wake up," he commanded. "Wake up and prepare for his arrival."

His lips found mine, pressing against them with ferocity. I couldn't resist. I kissed him back, parting my lips to give him access to all of me.

"Kali," Rad's voice floated to my ears from far away. His ocean scent teased my nostrils.

Damon's magic dispersed, and Rad's chaotic energy wrapped itself around my demon, protective and calming. Damon's lips morphed into his. "Wake up..."

I opened my eyes to find Rad crouched beside me, his face close to mine. His golden eyes were clear, a tiny crease showing between his brows.

I lay on the office sofa, the room aglow with afternoon light. Licking my lips, I avoided Rad's gaze, sure he could see into my thoughts. I hated dreams because I had no control inside them. No way in real life would I kiss Damon willingly. No. Way. "What...what happened?"

"You had a nightmare." The crease deepened. "You were calling for Damon."

Nightmare.

Damon's kisses, even if I *was* dreaming, were hardly nightmare material, no matter how guilty I felt for enjoying them.

*It was just a dream!* I rubbed my eyes and face, trying to shake off the lingering remnants. "He was telling me to choose."

"Choose what?"

"I'm not sure. He told me someone is coming. I need to choose."

Rad's hand cupped the side of my face. His thumb rubbed my jawline. "You've been having an awful lot of nightmares lately."

For nearly three hundred years, the only nightmare I'd had involved Rad shoving a silver knife into my heart. When I was seventeen, he left me at the altar—or at least that's what I'd believed until six months ago when he reappeared and told me what really happened that night. Reality had truly felt like a knife in my heart, thus giving my subconscious fodder for the nightmare.

Since Rad's reappearance, those nightmares had vanished... up until Damon had died by Rad's hand during our fight with the Four Horsemen of the Apocalypse. Now, even though Damon was technically alive in Hell, he showed up off and on in spectral form and he came to me in my dreams, sexier than ever.

And just as deadly.

I knew it wasn't the real Damon in my dreams. Yes, my former boss was an archdemon, and yes, he was the most demanding male I'd ever worked for or with, but there was no way he would actively enter my subconscious and seduce me.

"Most demons don't dream," I sighed. "I wish I didn't."

Rad's face was still tantalizingly close. He stroked my hair, dropped his gaze to my lips. "You're not most demons."

The heat in his eyes warmed my blood. His energy stroked my demon, still comforting. She purred, rubbing herself against his magic. She preferred him out of control and wanton, so she stroked him back, demanding and seducing, trying to get him to cut loose.

His demon didn't bite. All he did was tilt his head and lick his bottom lip. She refused to relent, and I was too strung out to tame her. A second later, his magic grabbed her hard and bent her to his will, but instead of growing angry, she once again purred.

"You're so controlled these days," I said, suddenly panting. I traced the crease between his brows with a finger. "So skillful and...disciplined."

He continued to lean over me, his muscled chest pressing firmly into my side and left breast. The crease disappeared. A smile danced at the corner of his lips. "I've had a very, very good teacher."

When he'd become the Bridge Institute's new enforcer, he'd done an average job of bringing criminal supernaturals to heel. Average, in my book, wasn't good enough, so I'd taken it upon myself to give Rad private, *ahem*, lessons in how to handle rowdy supes. Nothing I enjoyed more than playing the dangerous supernatural and schooling Rad in the ways of being an enforcer.

"I'm impatient and demanding," I said, teasing his lips with mine.

His smile widened. "And exceptionally skilled."

I had the feeling we weren't talking about his enforcer training anymore.

He dipped his head and teased my lips with his tongue, his teeth. Less controlled, but still in charge. He sucked and nipped, consuming me in a way that was too hard and too possessive.

I loved it.

I fought him a little, pushing back and making him work for it, even though, secretly, I was totally turned on by this new, demanding side of him. Around everyone else, I always had to be the tough one. My friends, coworkers, and the other demons, vampires, and supernaturals who looked up to me expected me to be tough and strict. They respected me and took orders from me. Pollyanna would have been eaten in short order.

I made difficult decisions every day, meted out discipline and punishment as needed. Brought justice to those who couldn't fight for themselves. I had to be the calm, cool, unemotional leader of a ragtag group of humans, supernaturals, and now angels, 24/7.

In Rad's arms, I could be who I really was...a female demon who loved hard, lustful sex and needed stress relief on a daily basis. Outside of the bedroom, anyone who tried to control or manipulate me was in for a rude awakening, but here, with the male I loved, I could let down my guard and enjoy the extremely explosive nature of our attraction.

Rad's aura went from assertive to aggressive. His kiss followed suit. He plowed his hands through my hair and traced the curves of my body, squeezing, massaging, stroking.

I arched into him, pressing my puckered nipples into his chest. I shoved my tongue into his mouth and moaned in satisfaction when he climbed on top of me.

My demon scratched at his control, egging him on. The scent of an ocean storm and sin swirled in the air. I rocked my hips into his and laughed as he pressed back, a rock-hard bulge spreading my legs and hitting the mark between them.

He bit my bottom lip, nipped my chin, nuzzled my neck. One of his hands reached for the edge of my shirt, tugging it up to expose a breast. His mouth latched on through the thin material of my bra, and he tongued my nipple through the fabric. A minute later, I was divested of everything but that bra, and Rad was working his way down my stomach. I was so lost in the throes of lust that I didn't hear the door to the office open.

My fingers dug into Rad's hair, my body curving up under the heat of his lips.

"Kali," Neve's voice said, sounding far away.

And then a deeper, demanding male voice said. "Kal-*i*."

My eyelids flew open, my body going rigid. Panting, I raised my head.

*Oh, hell in a handbasket.*

The archdemon of my nightmares was standing in the doorway, one seriously damning scowl on his face as Neve hastily retreated from showing him into the office

# 5

"*D*amon?" I squeaked.

Rad froze between my thighs. "You've got to be kidding," he murmured against my skin.

My hands flew around, pushing Rad off, only to realize I was naked except for my bra. I jerked him back, using him as cover.

"What are you doing here?" I asked Damon, refusing to meet his eyes. Since he'd gone to work for Lucifer, I'd only seen him up close and personal a couple of times. "Did we have a meeting?"

He crossed his arms, refusing to look at Rad as Rad surreptitiously picked up various pieces of my clothing and handed them to me. "You do realize that is a vintage LaNouva you're ruining."

"Uh..." It was an ugly black sofa, *that's* what I knew. "Nothing's ruined, and you should learn to knock."

"I believe this is *my* office. Neve buzzed you, and when you didn't answer, she was kind enough to help me find you."

Oh, yeah, that was definitely annoyance burning in my stomach now. Rad moved to stand in front of me, providing a

30

screen. I stood on the sofa in question and jerked on my skirt, looking over Rad's shoulder. "*Your* office? This office belongs to whoever is running the Institute. That would be me since you forced me into the job. You want the office back? Then tell Lucifer you're done hunting Fallen and *take it back*. We have forty angels now. That should do it."

He was immobile, stoic, more physical than ghost. Then, a small smile broke over his lips. A smug gleam appeared in his eyes. "It's good to see you." His aura brightened, and my brain warmed as he pushed a thought at me. *And so* much *of you.*

A growl of irritation escaped my throat. He'd been able to communicate with me mentally since he planted his *psukhe* seed in me during a very nonsexual kiss. Talk about invading my personal space. I wasn't exactly the warm and friendly type who loved to share her thoughts and feelings with anyone. Far from it. I kept my thoughts and emotions under tight guard.

Raising my mental defenses, I gave him a hard glare.

*Don't get emotional. Don't take it personally.*

Rad helped me off the couch. "What's up, Damon? Why are you here?"

The smug gleam in Damon's eye departed. He turned serious once more as he gave Rad the stink eye. I couldn't blame him there since Rad had been the one to take off his head. It saved mankind, but *still*. "I'm here for Tabriss."

"We only just found her this morning." I straightened my shirt, the bra cup underneath still wet from Rad's mouth. "She was drained nearly to death. She's not ready to go anywhere."

"Ready or not, I must speak with her."

His tone irritated me as much as his earlier invasion of my mind. The protection I'd felt earlier for her reared its head. "She doesn't know she's Fallen and needs time to recover from her injuries. You can't just spring it on her in her current state and expect she'll be understanding."

His forehead tensed as if he were perplexed about my resistance. I was perplexed about it as well. "Is she in the infirmary?"

Rad placed his hands on his hips. "Kali said you'll have to wait."

Damon didn't acknowledge him, keeping his attention on me. My brain warmed, but I kept my defenses in place, blocking him. His eyes narrowed. "What did you do?"

He couldn't have known I'd shared my blood with her. "I followed orders, like always."

Breaking away from the stare-down, I went and sat in his office chair and shuffled a couple of files. "I saved her from dying at a renegade vampire's hands. That's what you told me to do."

Silence descended, and I felt his eyes devouring me, his magic poking at my defenses, looking for a way in.

Rad sensed what he was doing and moved to block his line of sight. "Kali will let you know when the angel is ready."

A weird feeling bloomed in my stomach. Warm and comfortable. I didn't need Rad's protection from Damon, yet I liked that he was once again taking charge.

Dark magic rose in the room, antagonistic and leaden with testosterone. Male demons are similar to humans when it comes to showing assertiveness and virility. Damon finally met Rad's gaze, and their magics collided like two giant ocean waves, tingling my skin and sending a rough-edged shiver down my spine.

Before the Mexican standoff went further, I suppressed my demon and rose from the chair to my full height. "You gave me the power to run this Institute, Damon, and that's exactly what I'm doing. It wasn't my choice to take in Lucifer's angels, but I've done it, giving them the care and training they need to once again become the fighting warriors who will face Michael when the time comes. Therefore, it's *my* call. Tabriss is not ready for you to speak to her or to take her from here until I deem her so." *Mine.* "Until then, you and Lucifer will stay away from her."

Surprise colored both Damon and Rad's auras, though neither moved a muscle.

Damon's surprise instantly morphed into an anger that matched mine. Slowly, he uncrossed his arms, his mouth tight. "She is critical to our plans, Kali. Critical to your health and well-being."

"*My* health and well-being? Is that a threat?"

He paused. I felt him trying to push thoughts into my head. When he couldn't get past my defenses, he simply said, "Handle her with care."

The instant he left, the hot burn of adrenaline coursed through my veins. My hands shook, my knees felt like Jello-O. I plopped down in the chair. What the hell had just happened? Why was I having such a strong reaction to Tabriss?

Why did I feel like I needed to protect her from Damon and Lucifer?

My tight muscles and hyper nerves held no answer, but I wondered again if giving her a taste of my blood had created some sort of weird bond, like a blood slave and master.

*No.* I'd felt the drive to help and protect her before I'd shared my blood.

Didn't matter. What was done was done. No turning back, and I wouldn't ignore my instincts to protect her.

But Damon's willingness to give up that easily made me more nervous than the stand I'd just taken. If he found out I'd shared blood with Tabriss, his anger would know no bounds.

I'd face it head-on. Especially now that I knew Tabriss wasn't simply another warrior in Lucifer's army. What she was, I had no idea. All I knew was that Damon's words about her being special rang true.

"Nice bluff," Rad said, facing me.

"I wasn't bluffing." Retrieving Volante from the top of the

desk, I let her coil around my arm and retrieved several other weapons from the bottom desk drawer, tucking them into various hiding places under my clothes. "And there's no way Damon would accept an order from me."

One of Rad's brows lifted in question. "You think he's headed for the infirmary?"

I left my boots lying on the floor. "I think he's already there."

# 6

*I*nside the white, sterile walls of the infirmary, Tabriss, Kirill, and Damon squared off. The three of them formed a triangle, like combatants in a cage.

Damon's smoky wood scent was thick. A flowery, hibiscus aroma lay underneath, spiking with every move Tabriss made as she inched away from him. Her eyes darted to me, then off to my left and up, landing on Rad's face.

"You," Tabriss said to Rad. The tightness in her face eased a bit. "You saved me."

Her soul bubbled underneath her human heart, its magic trickling out toward him. Her too-thin arms and legs stuck out from the hospital gown, making her look like a cartoon character.

Her gaze shifted back to me, and recognition dawned in her eyes. "And you." She licked her lips, her lavender eyes locking onto my wrist. "You..."

My blood surged, my magic rushing with it. "Helped," I finished for her. No reason to mention sharing blood. "How are you feeling?"

"Like shit."

Kirill had doctored her wounds and gave her a human blood transfusion and IV fluids. She was no longer as pale as she'd been when we found her, but there were still dark circles under her eyes. She wavered slightly every time she moved.

"That's understandable. You were near death when we found you."

"Who are you people?"

Damon started to answer. I stepped forward, cutting him off. "We're going to help you recover from your ordeal. Is there any family or friends you need to contact?"

I wasn't going to let her call anyone, but I wanted to know if there was someone out there looking for her.

Her gaze darted around, and her non-answer told me what I needed to know. "Where are my clothes?"

As suspected, she didn't immediately latch on to calling a friend or family member. That was good. For us, anyway. If no one was looking for her, we'd have an easier time keeping her isolated until she came to understand who and what she was.

"You were naked when we found you, but we'll find you some comfortable clothes. You're about my height. I've got jeans and a shirt that should fit. Are you hungry? How about I bring you some food as well?"

"You can't..." She swayed and grabbed her head with one hand and the wall with the other. "...keep me here against my will."

Sure we could. I sent a small burst of magic at her, causing her to feel dizzier and weaker than she already was. "You feel strong enough to leave on your own?"

Her back hit the wall, her knees buckling. She slid halfway down, fighting it all the way. I smiled at the fight in her, admiring it. But her tired, anemic human body couldn't hold her. Her butt hit the floor.

Laying her head in her hands, she was quiet for a long

minute. I could feel her resistance fading fast. Damon's attention was fixated on her. Kirill and Rad watched me.

Slowly, so as not to startle her, I took a few steps closer and bent down. "You're safe here. I'm not going to hurt you, and I give you my word: I won't let anyone else harm you either. The male who did this to you will be punished and stopped from doing it to others." At least, I hoped so. "You need food, clothes, and a place to recoup from your experience. This is that place. The Institute is a safe haven for humans like you, and you're going to meet others who've been in similar circumstances."

I was getting good at this speech. I wished I didn't have to give it at all.

"Humans *like me*?" She laughed, and then her breath hitched as she fought back tears. "What day is it?"

"Thursday, March fifth."

"What year?"

Odd. Mo needed a fresh supply of female blood every thirty days or so, but I'm sure being his blood donor probably felt like an eternity. Either that or she'd lost brain cells along with blood cells. "What year do you think it is?"

She gave me a scalding glance from under her eyebrows. Her gaze zeroed in on my leather bustier and skirt. "From the way you're dressed, I'm either in a bad horror flick or back in the 17th century. Although your skirt is too short for that time period."

*Back* in the 17<sup>th</sup> century?

*Wait, did she just dis my wardrobe?* "You're familiar with the 1800s?"

She ignored my question, focusing on her own again. "What *year* is it?"

Rad stepped to my side. "You don't know?"

Her eyes zeroed in on his legs, moved up his hips to his chest, taking their sweet time. She finally looked at his face. "Aren't you that rock singer?"

A tight sigh. "Not anymore."

Was that disappointment I heard in his voice?

Tabriss had a wistful look in her eyes. "I saw you at a concert last summer. You were amazing."

He was amazing all right. And he knew it.

"I love performing live. *Loved*," he corrected, giving me a sheepish glance before saying to her, "I'm glad you enjoyed the concert."

She shook her head slightly, trying to refocus on the present. "Who did you say you were?" she asked me.

I felt rather than saw Damon leave. I patted her hand, helped her rise. "Let's get you dressed and fed. When you're feeling better, we have a lot to talk about."

## 7

*S*itting at my former boss's desk that evening, I glared at Salmad, the *vitium*, and current pain-in-my-ass, perched in a chair across from me. "You want me to *what*?"

Salmad adjusted his priest's robes. He was the sin of *acedia*, Sloth, wrapped up in the vice's counterpart *industria*. His magic put up a defensive shield against the aggravated energy coming off me. "Close your eyes and tell me what you see."

All I needed was to fall asleep again. "If my eyes are closed, I can't see anything."

He sat forward, his face all righteous. "But you can, Kali. As a vice and virtue hybrid, you have a direct connection with the divine, with your past, present, and future. If you close your eyes and meditate, images and symbols will come to you. The other *vitiums* and I have been doing it daily."

The seven *vitiums*. All of the vices back together, living it up in Chicago and recently stopping the biblical Apocalypse. Fun times.

Five of them live and work with me. The sixth, Maria, is the one chained in the warded prison cell below the Institute. Blessing or curse? I haven't decided if having them all so close is either or both, but Sal's latest entreaty made me lean toward curse.

"Doing what exactly? Conversing with God? Hate to break it to you, Sal, but having a link to the divine is *not* on my bucket list."

No need to link to the divine when I had plenty of heavenly creatures living at the Institute. Too many, in fact. Yes, the Fallen were a quiet faction, but damaged. Very damaged. Their energy screamed of desperation and longing. Their convoluted auras gave me migraines. Most were as conflicted about good and evil, and its hold on them, as I was about being a supernatural hybrid.

"There are secrets stored up here," Sal pointed to his head. His hair had grown several inches since Armageddon and was white. I wasn't sure if that was his natural color, or if the Four Horsemen had scared him bad enough to turn it that color.

He scooted forward and tapped a finger on the desk. "Secrets that must be unlocked for the seven of us to continue cohabitating on this earth peacefully."

I glanced down at Michael's sword lying on the edge of the desk. Since the last Damon nightmare, I had kept it in reach in case the archangel came by for a visit. He would, but I didn't know when, and I had to keep the sword away from him.

Maybe that's what Damon had been warning me about. I wish I'd had a chance to ask him before he vanished that morning. *Armageddon, take two.* And with my luck, my buddy Lucifer wouldn't be around to fight off his brother this time. Saving the Institute and the Fallen would all be on me.

Definitely not a blessing.

I hated Lucifer for forcing Damon to work for him. Damon should have been behind the desk listening to the priest's theories. I may have been doing my best, but I was a poor substitute for the archdemon, and truth be told, I missed him, even though his last visit had been annoying.

And embarrassing.

"It's been months, Sal. Everything's been quiet. As quiet as can be expected, anyway." We still had plenty of supernaturals in Chicago breaking Bridge rules and harming humans. Like Mo. "Maria's contained down below and the rest of us are cohabitating pretty well, considering."

Considering we were all half original vice, filled with powerful, dark magic. Demons, in general, don't get along well when forced to eat, breathe, and fight together. The *vitiums* were ten times worse, even with a helping of virtue to balance things out. I am *superbia*. Pride. *Superbia* and *humilitis*. It is our virtues that tame our vices, but each of us had days when we couldn't stand to be around the others. Most had lost control of their demon-selves at least once in the past few months. I was the most adept at keeping mine on a leash, thanks to years of conditioning and training under Damon's tutelage. The others hadn't been so lucky.

Sal sat back and looked disappointed. "The other shoe, Kali. It will drop."

Of course, it would. We were all waiting for it, but what exactly would *it* be? Michael's return? Maria breaking out of her dungeon prison in the basement?

"We need to understand our origins," Sal went on. "There is a shift going on in the current culture—a shift in beliefs. You and I only exist because our culture believes in the Christian version of angels and demons. Think of all the lost cultures whose stories were never written down and whose followers are now extinct."

"What in Satan's name are you talking about?"

"We are real because our culture made us so. But every three-thousand-point-two years, there is a cataclysmic turnover. Faiths dissolve, and new ones take their place. Religion is rewritten again and again, although it brainwashes its followers to believe that it has existed since the beginning of time. Civilizations die, and new ones spring up in their place. We are at that juncture now."

I sighed mentally. I didn't have the time or brainpower for this.

Sal read the disbelief on my face. "The symbols and images the *vitiums* can see when we concentrate are like a code. We unlock the code, and we'll know how to save ourselves from certain destruction."

Maddy came through the open door and plopped down on Damon's couch with her cell phone, fingers flying over the keypad. She wore a T-shirt that read, "*Forget princess. I want to be a vampire!*"

She didn't say anything, and Salmad fished around inside the sleeve of his robe, withdrawing a rolled-up piece of paper. He stood and smoothed the paper out on my desk. "I've been cataloging the images that come to each of the others and myself. Symbols and letters not of this world, Kali."

His scribbles looked like Da Vinci's crazy drawings and ramblings back in the day. Not that I was around then, but Maria had several works of his in her court library, and I'd read them with fascination. A genius, Da Vinci took crazy to a whole new level. "Have you been watching *Ancient Aliens* on NatGeo again?"

Maddy looked up, total sincerity on her face. "There's documented proof they were here, Kali."

*Ah, jeez.* I pointed to the stacks of files on the desk. "And these are documented proof that if I don't get back to work, neither of you will have a roof over your heads in the near future."

Sal snatched up his paper. "Tomorrow, we'll meet in the chapel for a meditation session."

"Yeah, about that chapel..."

"I have converted part of the north tower into a place of serenity. The Fallen need to reconnect with their spirits, and the rest of us need to balance out the demanding boot camp you've put us all in."

Boot camp?

He didn't wait for me to argue, gathering his robes and *whooshing* out the door in an air of *vitium* anger. Seemed like that's how everyone left my office these days.

A cloud of vexation hung over me. Chapels, meditation, ancient symbols...like it wasn't enough I was living under the same roof as angels, now Sal was shoving spiritualism down my throat.

Maddy returned to texting. "Tabriss is sleeping peacefully, and Di's keeping an eye on her. Tabriss was asking for you, so you better make time for her this afternoon. Oh, and I sent Neve home to get some rest."

Di—Aphrodite—was the perfect supernatural to help the Fallen. Being the goddess of love, she exuded calm and acceptance. "Thank you."

"On another topic, Brianna says you're not responding to her calls or texts. She's not helping bring in Mo tonight until you talk to Dru."

"Brianna is not my mother. She is one of my vampire subordinates and not a very respectful one at that."

"This isn't about her. It's about Dru. She's really worried."

Brianna had a serious obsession with the Master vampire. "When *isn't* it about him?"

Pausing, Maddy pointed a finger at me. "True, but things are weird at the House. Like *weird*-weird. You should call Bri."

I restrained a heavy sigh. "Define weird."

"Dru hasn't been out of his bedroom in days, and the House vampires are all twitchy. Bad mojo if you ask me."

Bad mojo with vampires usually meant something was up with their blood supplies or politics. As queen, it was my duty to find out what was going on and fix the problem. Like I needed yet another issue to claim my time and mental resources. "I was just there last week and everything was normal."

Normal for vampires, anyway.

"Yeah, not so much now." She smacked her gum, fingers flying again. "Might have something to do with that thingie Dru got on Monday."

"Thingie? Could you be more specific?"

"Bri called it a nun-something. Nunti..."

"*Nuntius?*"

"That's it."

*Nuntius* was Latin for message or messenger, depending on how it was used. "What was the message?"

She waved a hand. The ring on her index finger was huge. And expensive. "Some princess from the old country is paying him a visit. He's being summoned to act as host, but scuttlebutt is, he's engaged to her."

"Engaged?" That was certainly news. The same drive to protect Tabriss now made me want to head to the House. "To a vampire princess?"

I watched Maddy's ring reflect light from my desk lamp. "Is that my ring, by the way?"

She shrugged. "Well, duh, who else would he marry besides a *vampire* princess, and yes, the ring is one you never wear." Her eyes widened with forced innocence. "I didn't think you'd mind."

As per normal, she'd helped herself to my things, and also, as per normal, it made me feel like she was my little sister. "I didn't realize there were any."

"Rings?"

"Vampire princesses. And promise you won't lose that ring, okay? It was a gift from a friend."

"Someone famous?"

Only an incredibly talented late 19th-century impressionist who'd been given the ring by a lover in exchange for a painting. A painting with a lot of nakedness in it. He'd been terrified her husband would find out about their affair, which he had, so the painter gave it to me as payment for saving his backside from the woman's werewolf husband. "No, just a friend," I lied.

Maddy was fascinated with the rich and famous, even the dead ones. She made a frowny face and gave the ring a second appraisal.

"Tell me more about this princess," I said.

"Princess Irina Dragon-something arrives tomorrow, and Dru is supposed to throw this big party and have everything in place for her. Apparently, he's not happy about her visit and is hiding in his room like a spoiled brat."

Dru was pompous and had the entitled-vampire-Master cliché down pat, but hiding from something – especially a female – wasn't his style. "I'll call him later."

My phone buzzed with a text.

*Time for our lesson, mon coeur.*

Lesson. Right. I'd promised Rad a lesson. Now, all I needed was a clone.

Rad had taken to calling me "my heart" in his native French, and those two words eased my stress. I knew of other things he could do to me to ease my stress during our lesson. *Two minutes,* I typed back.

Maddy slouched farther down in the sofa. "We should go to the House so you can see what I'm talking about. It's ugly. And then you can get the full scoop on Princess I. I sent you the link to her Instagram account. She's rocking the whole royalty-bitch thing. Designer this, Maserati that. You know the type."

Said the Undead girl wearing a priceless emerald on her finger.

I didn't have time to visit Dru, but I was extremely curious about this princess and his supposed engagement. A little hurt, too. He'd never told me he was engaged, but maybe if he married her, she'd agree to be queen of Chicago's Undead. "Good idea."

"It is?"

Rising, I snatched Michael's sword from the desk and headed for the door. "After I'm done handing Rad his ass, we'll go see Dru."

She jumped up from the sofa. "Awesome. On both accounts."

The gleam in her eye told me she was going to follow me to the training room. "Where are you going?"

"With you. I want to see you kick Rad's butt."

We left my office and I hit the button on the elevator. "These are private lessons. I don't like an audience."

"Because you ravage him afterward?"

Actually, I ravaged him before, during, and after. Naked fighting was a fun pastime.

The elevator opened and we stepped inside. I punched the down button with the hilt of the sword. "I teach him some of my tricks. Tricks I don't want everyone to know. Makes me less effective in the field."

"I'm not everyone."

"You certainly aren't."

She sent an accusing glare my way. "What's *that* supposed to mean?"

Fifteen-year-old vampire drama coming up. "You're special, that's all. Found a new boyfriend yet?"

"I'm working on it." Her face softened a bit as the elevator descended to the basement. "Are you being sincere about me being special or just trying to get me off your case?"

Smart, this one. "Do you know any of my friends, other than you, whom I allow to raid my clothes, shoes, makeup, *and* jewelry?"

A smile. More gum smacking. A shoulder nudge—Maddy's version of *you're cool*. "I am special, huh?"

The elevator doors opened. Like sisters, we marched side-by-side to the training room's doors. I threw one side open. "Yes, you are, but I still don't —"

The loud hum of voices engulfed us. So did enough magic to lift the hair on the back of my neck.

In the stands, vampires, angels, and assorted supernaturals stared down at us. Rad stood in the center of the floor, bare-chested and weaponless, sporting a cocky smile.

"Uh, about that private lesson..." Maddy eyed the crowd of onlookers.

A group of Fallen females sat on the bottom bleachers, doe eyes locked on Rad. Since he'd come to live at the Institute and work for me, he'd acquired a clique of female followers. Can't say I blamed them, but annoyance and possessiveness burned in my chest every time they were around.

"Yeah." I glared at the Chaos demon, snapping my defense shields into place to block out the energy sizzling the air. A tingle of jealousy fired up under my skin. That damn smile of his told me he'd orchestrated this show and had something up his sleeve.

I was exhausted and needed sleep. And a few minions to take care of everything.

On my arm, Volante shuddered in anticipation. Michael's sword glowed. I let Volante's handle slide into my empty palm as I gripped the sword in the other hand a little tighter. "Looks like the lesson plan is about to change."

## 8

They say death is the great and final equalizer. For humans, that may be true. For supernaturals, death is just another stage of our existence. Violence is our equalizer.

I had no desire to hurt Rad, only teach him a lesson. By putting me on the spot in front of the Institute's employees and visitors, he was forcing my hand.

The training center fell deathly quiet, everyone expecting me to attack. For half a second, I considered the best approach...whip or sword?

And then I realized the best way to "attack" was to do the opposite of what those looking on expected. The opposite of what my lover, pretending to be my enemy, anticipated.

So I dropped the sword and released Volante's handle. Pointing a finger down, I gave her the silent command to unwrap herself from my arm and coil on the ground.

She obeyed, leaving me weaponless. At least to the crowd's eyes. A collective gasp went up, but outside of Maddy and Cole, a Warrior demon who was my bodyguard and the best self-defense instructor around, who stood in one corner watching me with interest, no one knew I had throwing stars on a service belt around my waist and several daggers inside my boots.

Not that I planned to use them.

Rad, now suspicious, narrowed his eyes. His smile, however, didn't falter. He loved a challenge.

Throwing a little sway into my hips, I walked toward him and returned his smile. As I slunk up to him, I touched his cheek with a finger. He stood stock still, the only movement the bob of his Adam's apple and the darkening of his golden eyes with lust. "I thought it was going to be just the two of us," I murmured under my breath.

"There are Fallen who keep coming to me for advice on fighting supernaturals," he replied, keeping his voice low and cutting his eyes toward his female groupies. "I invited them to watch our lesson to avoid having to give any private tutorials and ending up with my ass in trouble."

Circling him, I ran a fingernail over his waist, up his spine, and across his shoulder blades. He shuddered ever so slightly. "Oh, your ass is still mine after this, Beaumont, but I guess we might as well give them what they paid for."

I faced him, lowering my defense shields and going up on tiptoes to kiss him. Deep. Hard. Full of promise.

Parting his lips with my tongue, I wrapped my arms around his neck and rubbed my breasts against his naked chest. His free hand came up and gripped me behind the neck, returning my kiss with enough heat to make my knees weak.

The magic in the room went into overdrive—normal for demons, vampires, and others prone to embracing the seven deadly sins. The angelic mojo, on the other hand, cooled, dropping the actual temperature in the room by a good thirty degrees.

*Jealous, bitches?* Check.

Because of his Chaos magic, Rad's energy was frenzied and

tumultuous on a good day. Combined with his half-human energy, his magic became unruly any time he became emotional. So, although he'd learned to tame that chaos, this time, he didn't try to control it.

The air in the room swirled around us. The commercial light fixtures hanging from the ceiling swayed. The reinforced concrete walls hummed as the iron rods inside them vibrated.

My body wasn't immune to Rad's magic. Of its own volition, my spine arched, pressing my hip bones into his pelvis. My stomach pushed against his.

His aura went red with passion, and the instant I felt his body switch from fight mode to sex mode, I struck.

"Vengeance is mine," I whispered against his lips.

My defense shields snapped into place. At the same time, I crouched and whirled in a circle, sticking out one leg to take him out at the ankles.

He fell. On the way down, he stuck out a hand and sent a gust of wind at me, knocking me onto my back and sliding me across the floor despite my shields.

He'd definitely been paying attention when I taught him to focus his chaotic magic into a direct hit.

Laughing, I held out my hand, and Volante jumped into it, wrapping her braided leather body around my arm. The wind picked up, becoming a swirling tornado, and lifted us into the air.

Air born. A weird sensation for a demon who draws her magic from the earth. I'd flown in airplanes and always enjoyed the experience, but planes are made from steel and other earthly components, hence supporting my body and allowing me to connect with their stored energy.

The wind currents Rad created cut off my supply. They spun me around above the ground and acted like a magical bubble, keeping me off balance. I flung out my hands, trying to find my equilibrium, but only caught more air.

The force carried me higher. My magic stopped and started, righting me, then shorting out and causing me to go feet up. My protective shields failed.

The demon inside fought for control, and with every disconnect of magic, I grew more out of control, careening back and forth, somersaulting in the air.

So this was his trick. Interesting. Annoying but interesting.

I couldn't remember an opponent outside of Maria lifting me off the ground before in this manner. And when she'd done it, it had taken a lightning bolt from the heavens to knock me back down.

Various options for counteracting the wind ran through my mind. None seemed feasible. Wind created from air magic was no easier to control or short-circuit than wind from Mother Nature, and it could be just as devastating.

Unless you took out the demon causing it.

I couldn't reach Rad, couldn't get close to him under the circumstances. Couldn't even build up enough of my own magic to break through the bond holding me. How could I have left myself so vulnerable? In three hundred years, I'd never considered what might happen if I were cut off from the earth and my source.

"Give up?" Rad called from across the room. He was once more on his feet, that damning grin wide on his face.

*If you can't fight 'em...* My demon hated the idea, but it had merit in this situation.

"Yes." I stopped fighting the currents. Forced my muscles to relax and give in. I allowed myself to be swept up by the wind, losing myself in it. If I hadn't been so annoyed, I would have laughed again at the pure pleasure of it.

*Freedom. This must be what that feels like.*

Rad slowed the wind and floated me to the ground. I stayed relaxed and limp. My eyelids fluttered closed, and I heaved a relieved sigh as the floor—and the ground deep underneath it —welcomed me back.

When the Chaos demon leaned over me and said, "Never thought I'd see the day when I could best the great Kali Sweet," I raised a hand and punched him in the groin.

# 9

The groupies cried out in surprise as Rad buckled, grabbing his balls and making a strange noise in the back of his throat. On his knees in front of me, his gaze went fuzzy.

I grinned before I jumped to my feet and pushed him sideways. Easier than cow-tipping, I tell ya.

Maddy threw her fists in the air and started hooray-ing. Many of the other supernaturals and those Fallen who didn't follow Rad around with puppy-dog eyes also cheered. I caught Cole's eye and he winked.

Then I leaned down, placed one hand over Rad's and cupped him. I sent a magical caress to his injured male parts, and as a bonus, I sent a second wave of soothing magic into his mouth via my tongue. His senses picked up on it, carrying the magical medicine to his brain, and his body melted under my touch.

Once I was sure he was no longer in pain, I rose and quieted the audience. "When faced with an unexpected or unknown enemy, become meek, seductive, anti-confrontational. Your enemy will lower their guard, and that's when you strike. Any questions?"

One of the Fallen in the front row practically spit nails at me. "Is he unwell? Have you damaged him?"

Rad rose and faced the female. His smile was now sheepish, but he laid a hand on my back and ran his fingers up and down my spine. "I'm good. No worries."

I'd be the judge of that. "And this concludes our lesson for today."

Quick and efficient. Now I could get back to work.

Conversations rose as the audience filed out. I gave Rad a questioning look. "Where did you get the idea to disable me that way?"

Moving slowly, he retrieved my weapons and handed them to me. "I remembered how Maria's ghost lifted you off the ground the first time you fought her. I wondered if I could manage the same and, in effect, disable at least some of your powers. If it worked on you, it would be an effective weapon in the field."

Rad's humanness required him to be more creative as the enforcer. I nodded, pleased he was taking his job seriously. He'd shown me a weakness I hadn't realized I had. "Good idea. Definitely effective. Before sunrise, I promise to reward you for a job well done."

"Before sunrise? What about right now?"

If only. I'd pay thousands of dollars for a clone. I really would.

I handed him Michael's sword as his groupies flocked around him. "Return this to the office for me. I'm going out for a while. Meantime, there are three files for you on the corner of my desk. Supernaturals breaking Bridge laws."

Maddy sidled up next to me. "Are we going to the House?"

Rad sent a wave of chaotic energy up my spine. His way of saying, "Hurry back." Shivers ran over my skin and I smiled to myself, walking out of the gym. "Might as well get it over with."

Outside, the sun was almost done setting, throwing shades of pink and purple over the gray Chicago skyline. Lake Michigan was dark and waveless, almost too still. Maddy and I hopped in my TT Cruiser and headed north for the House.

Either Brianna sensed us coming, or Maddy texted her. When we arrived, she met us at the door. Her blond hair was in its usual high ponytail, not a strand out of place. Her red lips were straight out of a Maybelline ad.

"You look like hell," she said by way of greeting.

"Always nice to see you too," I answered.

"Why didn't you answer my calls?"

"I thought it was obvious that I don't like talking to you."

Our antagonistic relationship was rather enjoyable. Secretly, we respected each other, but we both refused to admit it. I didn't have to pretend to like Brianna, and she didn't pretend to like me.

Honesty—always the best policy.

She smiled, relishing our tit-for-tat game as much as I did as she escorted Maddy and me into the foyer. The heels of my boots clacked on the marble floors.

"If you bothered to grace us with your queenly presence once in a while," she chided, "I wouldn't need to call you."

"I'm running the Bridge Institute and caring for Lucifer's Fallen. Take your petty bitching to Satan if you dare."

Another smile. *Touché.* She pointed straight up. "Our Master is up there."

*Your Master, not mine.* "What do you know about his vampire princess?"

"She's a fraud. There is no such thing."

That gave me pause. "Is that so?"

A brief nod caused her ponytail to bob. "Vampire history is full of bloodlines claiming to be royal. Not true. The only royal line was Vlad's. He created our Nation, and he only had sons, including Alexandru, who carried the genetic abnormality. Those sons only created other vampires by biting them, and there were no original female vampires who could birth Undead babies. This *princess* was made, not birthed from royal loins. *If* she's even a vampire."

Birthing, loins, *yeesh*. Made me want to get back to Sal and his meditation initiative. "So she's a fake. Why is Dru so worried?"

A wall of magic hit me. Undead magic. Sensual and demanding.

Maddy and Bri felt it too, turning in unison to face the House Master standing at the top of the stairs.

"Because I must still marry her," Dru said, descending from the second floor. Several days' worth of beard shadowed his jawline. A wildness danced in his eyes and his usual impeccable wardrobe was disheveled. "Unless, of course, you kill her for me."

"It's the 21st century. If you don't want to marry her, don't."

A group of vampires emerged from the back of the house, talking and laughing and heading toward the front door. All were dressed in black, all equipped with weapons hidden under their coats. When they saw me, their lighthearted banter ceased. The lead male nodded at Brianna, bowed to me. "My queen."

Those with him followed his lead, showing me respect, even though their Undead magic clouded the air with distrust and dislike. In unison, their attention traveled to Dru and the musky magic filling the air thinned.

"We're off to patrol," the leader announced. "North and west. Team two will take east and south. If Mo is in our territory, we'll find him."

"Very good," Dru said. "Notify me immediately once you've located him."

"Shall we take him dead or alive, Master?"

"Dead. Eternally."

"Mo?" I interjected. "You're going after Big Mo?"

Dru lifted an eyebrow. "Aren't you?"

"Well, yeah, but..."

Maddy rocked on her heels, hands deep in her pockets. "I sort of told him what happened."

"As is your duty, young vampire." Dru sent me a nonverbal warning not to disagree. "I assumed your enforcer would be out looking for Mo tonight, Queen. I have two teams who will assist."

I hadn't assigned Rad the job because I wanted to lead the hunt. I itched to have Mo under my fingertips and make him experience at least a fraction of the pain and fear he'd instilled in the females he'd hunted and killed. "The Institute will handle it."

"Meaning *you*?" Dru turned with a subtle roll of his eyes and started back up the stairs. Over his shoulder, he said to the leader of his Undead soldiers, "Spare no quarter and bring me Mo's head."

The leader of the group shot a glance my way. The House Master and Queen held equal authority in vampire dynamics, but Dru held the respect of all of his subordinates, while they merely paid homage to me because he demanded it.

But I am their queen, like it or not, and I'm a vengeance demon who could end them with a touch of my fingers. They may not respect me, but they fear me, and I can live with that.

As Dru disappeared back into his rooms upstairs, I held the leader's eyes and murmured, "If you find Mo, text me and take him alive. He and I have unfinished business."

The male hesitated for a second, an argument on his lips. The female on his left nudged his rib with an elbow before the argument came forth, and he simply bowed his head and took his group out the front door.

Bri gave me a condescending glare. "You shouldn't under-mine the Master."

"And you shouldn't sleep with him."

Her glare sharpened. "I'm his blood slave."

"You're also his bodyguard. A bodyguard must stay unemo-tional and unattached or she loses her edge."

"Is that why you no longer use Cole as your bodyguard lately? Because he's in love with you?"

Cole wasn't in love with me, and his friendship had been one of the strongest and longest-lasting of my life. I didn't take kindly to her accusation or the tone of her voice.

"Your failed relationship with the Warrior demon is not because of me, Brianna. You're Dru's blood bitch. Cole hates vampires, but he put that aside for a long time for you, which means you're something special to him. You threw that back in his face when you continued fucking your boss and letting Dru use you as his personal snack behind Cole's back."

Maddy hitched a thumb over her shoulder. "I'm just going to go...um...file my nails or something." She disappeared into the bowels of the House.

Brianna was a cold bitch, but the truth registered in her eyes. She looked away, the hateful glare dissolving and a hitch shortening her breath. "I stopped sharing Dru's bed while I was with Cole, but he broke off our relationship anyway." Her gaze dropped to the floor. "I don't know why, but I suspect it's like you said—he hates vampires and that's the one thing I can't change."

Now I looked at the floor. Things were more complicated between them than I'd realized, and Cole and I hadn't had a good heart-to-heart in months. Not that we shared chic-flick moments, but we'd been friends and coworkers long enough, we did occasionally stick our noses in each other's business. This time, however, I'd been too busy with my new position as director to butt into Cole's love life.

I was not Brianna's friend, but she seemed genuinely upset about the loss of her and Cole's relationship. If we were correct, though, that Cole could no longer get past her Undead state, there wasn't anything to be done about it.

Words of wisdom escaped me, so I awkwardly patted her shoulder. Then I climbed the stairs to find out why Dru wanted me to kill the vampire princess for him.

## 10

*I* smelled Di before I saw her.

My best friend, Aphrodite, sat in Dru's office, thumbing through paperwork on her lap. Today's fragrance— *au naturel* for the Goddess of Love—was champagne and strawberries. Usually, I didn't notice her scent because I was surrounded by supernaturals with much heavier, more substantial odors. They tend to drown out anything light and dainty.

Inside the House of Chicago's Undead, however, Di's elegant, sensual perfume clashed with the scents of old blood and grave dirt. I moved into the room, and she looked up. "What are you doing here?" I asked.

Dru skirted his desk to sit down. "I've hired Sweet Investigations to help with a little...vampire problem."

Sweet Investigations was my pride and joy—the business I'd set up nearly thirty years ago on my own. Because of my recent promotion to head of the Bridge Institute, I'd handed the reins of SI over to Di, who'd been running the office for me.

"What vampire problem?"

"The one you brought back from Rome has proven to be... rebellious. He's causing trouble with the new Alpha."

"First of all, I didn't bring him back, he showed up on his own." I knew I should have killed that SOB when I had the chance. He'd been too cocky for his own good when he challenged me to a fight in the arena at the European Bridge Institute. "Secondly, what's he done to the shifter leader?"

A wave of Dru's hand. "Nothing for you to worry about. It's being handled. And eventually, you and I will get back to that little deal of ours, won't we?"

Exalting the Undead Nation over the other supernatural factions in Chicago. That's what I had offered Dru once in order to gain his help manipulating Lucifer. "How could I forget?"

He looked at Di and smiled. She smiled back, rose from her chair with the file in her hand, and brushed past me with an air kiss. "I'm on it."

Her sweet scent trailed out the door with her and her magic swung it shut.

Dru's attention stayed riveted on the door as if he could still see her...and he liked what he saw.

The blood in my veins rebelled. I glanced at Bri, who stood off to my side and was staring holes in Dru's head. Yep, that's what I thought. Brianna had been "made" by Dru, and the vampire bodyguard was in love with her maker, regardless of how she felt about Cole. I wasn't in love with him, but my body burned with jealousy anyway. He and I had once shared a very intimate kiss that had turned into a couple of rounds of beating each other up. Along with that, the blood he'd shared with me to save my life was both a blessing and a curse. I wished I knew a way to remove it, but I didn't. Worse, the vamp Master now had his eyes on my best friend.

Sure as hell, this was going to get ugly.

Snapping my fingers to get his attention, I decided to ignore the unwelcome tingle in my system. I would talk to Di later and make sure she was warned about Dru's intentions. "Tell me about the vampire princess."

His focus shifted to my face, but his aura still held the remnants of lust. Di did that to most males, both human and otherwise, but I'd never seen a vampire Master as strong as Dru fall prey to it. Another rush of blood told me he wasn't under her spell. He planned to put her under *his*.

Huh. *Good luck with that.*

"There is bad blood between my family and hers, but she is no vampire princess."

Bad blood seemed like an ironic statement coming from a vampire. "What is she?"

"A nightmare."

"I get it. You don't want to marry her, so again, I say, *don't*. Problem solved."

He shook his head, toyed with a paperclip on his desk. "Not *nightmare* as in a terrible dream. A nightwalker. A succubus."

Ah, jeez. Demon mares.

*Mare* in "nightmare" did not stand for a female horse. Rather, "nightmare" was the common human term for bad dreams, but the cause of those was a demon. Night horrors was more accurate. Supernaturals called them nightwalkers, and some were genuine *Succubae* or paramours—demons who took female form and had sex with humans in their sleep. Welcome to the land of Queen Maria.

Supernaturals were generally immune to all but the strongest of these sorts of demons, but I'd recently run into a very strong nightmare in Europe who'd once tormented Damon. Any demon that could enter an archdemon's mind and terrorize him was one to be wary of; sounded like I might have another one to keep an eye on.

Dru tossed the paperclip aside. "My mother killed Irina's mother in the late 15th century in a very bloody battle. Irina's family sought revenge, and things were ugly for a long period of time for the Undead Nation. We had no defense against the nightwalkers. They turned our Nation into raving lunatics, exposing us to humans and forcing us to go underground during the Early Renaissance. In an effort to stop the carnage, my father cut a deal with Irina's *gens*. She became an honorary vampire princess, and her blood was sealed with mine in a salt *constringo* ceremony."

"You're kidding."

"I would not joke about such a thing."

"You're in deep shit then."

A *constringo* was a binding ceremony used by demons, vampires, and other nefarious supernaturals through the years. The two subjects were drained of blood to the point of death. That blood was mixed with salt—a binding agent—and powerful magic before the blood was administered back into their bodies.

"That's why I need you to kill her. It's the only way to break the blood-salt bond."

Dru and I were bound by blood, but this went beyond that. Upon either of our deaths, the bond would dissolve. A salt-blood bond carried over into the afterlife. "Killing her won't change anything. You're bound to her for eternity."

His elbows thumped onto the desk, his head dropping into his hands. "She never wanted to be with me. She hates vampires." He snorted a humorless laugh. "But now, she's coming for me. I'm having all these dreams. She's inside my head...and I can't fight it."

I could relate since Damon was haunting mine. This explained the wild look in Dru's eyes, the disheveled appearance. *Raving lunatic, here we come.*

"Why now, after all these years?"

His head rose. His eyes met mine. "Because she wants you."

"Me?"

"She wants to take over my empire. That means taking both of us down."

My demon bristled. Volante trembled on my arm. I stroked her, my blood heating instinctively at the threat. I had no desire to remain queen of the vamps, but no one was going to strip me of the title.

Besides, I never run from a fight, and this fight sounded like the perfect stress reliever.

Rising, I smiled as dozens of potential ideas to neutralize the fake princess ran through my mind. Even in my exhausted state, I couldn't resist a good fight. If things went my way, I'd have Mo to torture tonight and Irina in a few days.

"Relax, Master. No one's taking over the Undead Nation on my watch. Irina can come after me any old time. I'll be ready for her. Meanwhile, I'll figure out a way to help you block your mind from her invasions. Sal or one of the other *vitiums* can help. That'll really piss her off."

He didn't look reassured. "Don't make the mistake of taking this lightly, Kali."

"She's messing with your head, Dru. You and I are two of the most powerful supernaturals on earth at the moment. We can handle her."

I hoped I wouldn't eat my words later because, really, when do things ever go my way?

# 11

*M*addy plugged in her iPhone to my car stereo and belted hip-hop tunes as we headed south again. After a couple of songs and her atrocious singing, my head hurt, so I unplugged her phone and turned on my favorite satellite radio.

Five Finger Death Punch soothed my nerves as we left the West Side. My cell rang, and I lowered the volume before answering.

It was Rad. "I found Mo."

"Mo?" I zoomed in and out of traffic, the night feeling like home even with the dozens of headlights breaking up the shadows. "You were supposed to be tracking the clown in the white van."

"Urban legend. All three of those files you left for me are, in fact."

"Urban legends are based on supernatural causes. The clown appeared in the early 1990s, disappeared, and now we have sightings again. We need to figure out who and what he is, and if he's tied to the kids who've gone missing on the South Side in the past six weeks."

"I'll get on that after I get Mo. He's at Chloe's."

Chloe ran a blood bank under our favorite club. She specialized in rare types of supernatural blood. "Buying blood?"

"Not sure."

I took an exit too fast, slamming Maddy against the door. "Hey!" she yelled.

"We'll be there in twenty," I told Rad. "Watch out for Dru's soldiers. They're looking for Mo, too."

"Why?"

"Dru wants Mo off the streets as much as we do, but it seems he thinks he's helping me by sending a crew out after him. I knew this would turn into a clusterfuck."

A long silence. I could feel Rad's aggravation through the phone. "Well, they'll be too late if they show up here."

"Wait 'til I get there. I'll help—"

The line went dead.

"Damn it."

Maddy grabbed the door and held on. "What?"

"Rad spotted Mo at Chloe's, and he's not waiting for backup."

She snorted. "He doesn't need it."

"Of course he does."

"No, he doesn't. You just won't let him do anything on his own. Kinda like me."

*Here we go.* "You're fifteen. I'm three-hundred and a handful. If you don't like my rules, you're free to move out of the Institute and live at the House. I'm sure Dru would love to put you to work there."

"I'm a vampire. I don't need rules to keep me safe."

"Being a vampire doesn't make you invincible."

"Neither does being a demon, but I don't see you following any rules."

I had rules, all right. One of them was *don't get emotional.* It was harder and harder not to with Maddy. She was like my younger sister and, after what we'd been through together in recent months, a close friend.

*You can't save someone who doesn't want to be saved.* I'd been trying to give her space and not hover when I sent her out on assignments. I still worried about her and reminded her every chance I got to be careful. I couldn't help it—the big sister in me turned surrogate mother whether she wanted one or not.

I wasn't all that happy about the situation, either, since I'm not the motherly type. I could blame it on my new role as director of the Institute and, unexpectedly, as the keeper of Lucifer's Fallen. It was my job to take care of a lot of supernaturals.

But the truth was, I'd felt a sense of kinship to Maddy from the first night she showed up on my doorstep. "I've lived a long time and have a lot more experience than you do," I reminded her. "I'm sharing my wisdom with you so you don't have to make the same mistakes I did."

Her phone was out, thumbs typing at vampire speed. "Like you said, I'm fifteen—sixteen in two months, by the way, if I were still human. I'm *supposed* to make—"

Without warning, a bright light exploded in front of the car, and we hit a wall. Not a literal wall, but a glowing, yellow wall of magic.

My head flew back, and Maddy's phone sailed into the windshield. Reflexively, my hand shot out to block her from hitting the dash.

The airbags exploded, blinding me as effectively as the glowing magic illuminating the car. Inertia sent the car spinning counterclockwise. I heard Maddy's head hit the passenger window and the subsequent crack. She hissed, fangs bared, as I held onto her arm. My inner demon roared as well—not at the rough treatment, but at the magic enveloping the car.

It sizzled along my skin, searing through my pores and into

my muscles. My blood boiled. As the car began to slow its crazy spinning, I touched my ring fingers and thumbs together, calling forth my protection magic.

Nothing happened. It was trapped inside my body, stalled. I tried again, sending all my energy into the act. My demon clawed inside my chest, insisting the only way to repel the magic surrounding us was by freeing her.

Gritting my teeth, I kept her caged and grabbed the steering wheel hard. I was a *vitium*. I had Master vampire blood inside me.

*Repel!*

The car slammed to a stop. On my arm, Volante shuddered, and my demon fell silent.

The magic glow didn't diminish, but the airbags deflated and I saw Maddy clearly. "You okay?"

Her head was bleeding. The smell of it permeated the air, calling to my blood to shield her from whatever was out there. This was another reason I felt protective of her—I was her vamp queen. It came with the title.

"What the hell was that?" she yelled, wiping at the blood trickling down her temple.

The eye-searing light, the magic eating its way into my bones could only be one thing. "Archangel."

Her eyes widened. "Shit."

I had a few more expletives to add. There was only one archangel who was after me.

*Michael.*

I touched my fingers and thumbs together again. Nothing.

*Thump!* Something fell on the hood of the car. The already smashed front end dipped, bowing to a heavy weight. The yellow glow receded enough I saw feet and legs through the windshield, but the rest of Michael's body was hidden in the angelic fog. I couldn't tell if we were still on the street or a million dimensions away from Chicago. There were no streetlights, signs, or other cars. The landscape behind the archangel had an iridescent tinge.

He stood on the hood. I imagined his giant arm punching through the sunroof and snatching me out of my seat. "Get out of the car," I told Maddy. "Run."

"I'm not leaving you."

"Maddy—"

"No!"

*Goddamn kid.* As her queen, I could command her to leave. I didn't. Michael wanted his sword back. I'd left it at the Institute under heavy wards. Wards provided by Lucifer and several others. Michael needed me to get it out so he wouldn't do me in just yet.

"Get off my car," I yelled.

The massive feet and legs didn't move. *Bastard.*

The tips of his wings came into focus as more of the angelic light ebbed slightly. He took one step off the hood and landed on the ground beside my door. In the next second, the door was ripped from its hinges and went flying.

"Hey!"

Inch by inch, the rest of his body came into view as he leaned down to look at me. He was a giant. God-like in his beauty and bearing. His wings fluttered as his ice-blue eyes met mine. "Kali Sweet. The devil's whore."

Truthfully, I've been called worse. "I hope you're going to wave your magic wand and fix my car," I said, shoving the deflated airbag out of the way and hauling my battered body out of the driver's seat to confront him. "My insurance doesn't cover damage by angels, *testa de cazzo.*"

He tipped his head, sculpted cheekbones and all. "When I finish with you, you will not have the ability to operate this machine."

He grabbed me by the neck, lifting me off the ground. Maddy yelled something, but the magic from his touch created a loud crash of thunder inside my head, drowning it out. I kicked and struggled, and for the effort, got a laugh out of the big guy.

This was it. I could see it in his eyes. Regardless of the fact he needed me to retrieve his sword, Michael was going to kill me with one good squeeze of his giant paw. I called on my demon. She sat frozen inside my chest.

I couldn't breathe. I couldn't even blink. Michael's hand on my throat was cold and crushing. His eyes, his aura, his entire presence overwhelmed my internal circuits. He lifted his other hand and placed it on my forehead. A kaleidoscope of colors and images exploded behind my eyeballs. Icy-hot pain scorched my cerebellum. A grinding sound bubbled in my ears —gears slipping and locking up.

Memories flashed, then ran like water through my mind. Lucifer had done this to me once. He'd looked inside my memories, searching for the truth of my origins. I didn't know what Michael was after but it couldn't be good.

*Lucifer!* I mentally screamed. If there was an entity who could save me, it was him. Of course, he didn't much like me, so I called for Damon too. *Help!*

The pressure on my throat increased, the pain making my eyes roll up in my head. Blood, warm and metallic, gurgled up from my lungs, into my mouth, and ran down my chin. I couldn't swallow or make a noise, even though every instinct cried out for me to fight, scream, and attack the monster killing me.

Choked to death by an angel. Hell if I was going to die that way. *Do the unexpected.*

Overpowering my will to fight, I forced my body to go limp. It wasn't all that difficult, considering. While my brain and instincts wanted nothing more than to fight, my body knew it was a lost cause.

My muscles refused to relax at first, desperate for oxygen,

but I made myself think of Rad. The ocean. The safety and security of his arms. *Peace.*

In my world, there would never be peace. Only death and then a new kind of Hell. Death...maybe it wouldn't be so bad. I could make Lucifer's life miserable down in Hell.

That thought actually cheered me. I would have smiled if...

*Whack!*

A lightning bolt of magic speared Michael's chest, sending him cartwheeling backward. I flew in the opposite direction, hitting the car and dropping to the ground like the limp hundred-and-twenty-pound weight I was.

For a minute, I lay completely immobile, gagging and sucking in as much air as I could get past my damaged throat. The blood in my veins immediately went to work, trying to repair the damage, and Maddy came into view. I could hear her talking to me, but I couldn't quite make out what she was saying. Her features were blurry, her voice in a vacuum. I couldn't even smell her normal vampire essence. Everything seemed to be less. Less vibrant. Less noisy. Less...*there.*

*About damn time*, I mentally yelled at Lucifer. *He nearly killed me!*

My magic sputtered, and after a couple of hard shudders racking my system, came back online, instantly slamming a bubble of protective energy around me. Weak, but at least it was something. With it, I felt a burst of Master vampire blood surge up my backbone and soothe my throat. The roaring in my head dimmed. At the same moment, the demon in my chest bellowed in rage.

Magic in place? Check. Demon pissed and ready for action? Check. Maddy safe and sound?

Well, she wasn't hurt. That was a start.

"You piece of..." I staggered to my feet, ready to go after the bastard archangel. Dizziness swamped me. My throat still felt raw, but I could make sound. Italian curses flowed out of my mouth so fast I could hardly make sense of them. *If only I had that sword.*

Could I use it against its master?

Moot point. Things still seemed dim and fuzzy, the glowing light continuing to block out Chicago if we were still there. I sniffed the air and couldn't detect any scents at all. Freaky, since I'd always had a heightened sense of smell and used it as much, if not more than my other senses to keep me safe.

Michael sat up, eyes widening when he looked at me. Not *at* me, behind me. His face tensed, not in fear but in mild alarm.

What would an archangel have to fear? His evil brother, perhaps?

I motioned Maddy out of the way and turned to face Lucifer. There was going to be one hell of an angelic showdown...

Except it wasn't the devil standing behind me.

Aphrodite and two other females stood hand-in-hand. Each was wrapped in a Greek toga.

"Di?"

Her eyes were weird...bleached out with a ring of fiery orange around them. "Leave her be," she said to Michael. "Depart this place before we do you irreparable harm."

The giant rose, cat-like, wings in disarray. "You would threaten *me*?"

"You are not a god."

But Di was. From the auras of the other two, I sensed they were equally goddess-y. Instinctively, I sniffed the air.

Nothing. No odor of any kind.

The female on Aphrodite's right was dark-skinned and pale-eyed. The rings around her irises were purple. She stepped forward. "This one is under our protection."

"Nemesis." Michael curled a lip and snarled. "You only protect the vengeance demon because she is one of yours."

Nemesis? The Greek goddess of divine retribution. *Sweeet.*

I'm not one to bow to anyone or anything, but my legs shook, and I was dizzy, my head still struggling to reclaim normalcy. I went down on one knee, facing her, and prayed I didn't fall on my face.

As a child, my mother had given me a statue of Nemesis and set it on a shelf overlooking my bed. Until Queen Maria took me from my parents, I'd fallen asleep every night staring at Nemesis' beautiful, stern face. Dreaming of what it would be like to be her—a goddess rather than a demon, exacting retribution.

Maddy kneeled next to me, her aura telling me she was scared but determined. She didn't understand what was happening, but she wasn't running away.

*So like me.*

Her hand crept into mine. She gave my fingers a squeeze. Volante, of her own volition, snaked down my arm and wrapped herself around our wrists, binding us together.

An electrical charge from the connection ran up my arm. Maddy felt it, too. We exchanged a *WTF* look, and her hand tightened even more. Whatever was holding my brain hostage snapped, a rubber band breaking. I drew a breath, wiping the blood from my chin, and the pressure between my ears lessened. I could hear better, and Maddy's features cleared.

But I still couldn't smell.

Michael's wings spread, fluttering. "I will not stand for your impertinence."

"And I won't stand for your hubris," Nemesis said.

"Disrespecting you is not hubris." Michael flared his wings to full length. The sight was hypnotic, causing my magic to cower from the force of it. Full angel-mode coming up. "You Fallen are no more gods than I am."

Wait. *Fallen?* I wiggled my ear, wondering if my hearing was going out on me as well.

"We're not angels, and although our kind has fallen out of

favor in modern times, we've been worshipped for thousands of years," the goddess on Di's left said. She held a spear in her free hand and wore a helmet with an olive branch emblazoned on it. Her irises had red rings...blood red. "Longer than your Father. We cared for the humans he abandoned until he saw their love for us and decided to declare himself the *only* god. Kali guards our Fallen brethren and we support them. She is one of us...*defensores contra malum.*"

While I did protect humans from supernaturals, I'd never been called a *protector from evil*. I was a demon. On the flip side, I was a demon protecting angels from Michael, who, if you asked me, was far from good. My head hurt trying to sort it all out. Good, evil, did it matter?

Michael's lips curved in another sneer. "Lucifer's whores. All of you."

"You know, I'm getting tired of that word," Maddy said. She let go of my hand, and Volante released her. She stood, brushing gunk off her pant legs. "No one calls my queen a whore."

I wasn't used to everyone defending me, protecting my good —*cough, cough*—name. I rose to my feet, searching for something to say. This standoff was getting us nowhere. "I'm not giving you the sword."

"In due time, Kali Sweet." The look he gave me said he knew something I didn't. "In due time."

With a flap of his wings, he disappeared, the curtain of light and fog disappearing with him. Suddenly, we were standing in the middle of the highway, cars honking and whizzing by. Instantly, Di threw up a bubble of magic, forcing the cars to flow effortlessly around us.

She and I stared at each other. With Maddy's help, I stood, wavering slightly. "Thanks for saving me from that heavenly asswipe."

The goddess with the bow smirked. "Rarely do we intervene

between supernaturals and Heaven. In this case, we made an exception. We both owed Aphrodite a favor."

"Kali," Di said, "meet my friends, Nemesis and Athena."

"It's an honor." I wanted to shake their hands, but that seemed...forward. I was a demon, they were goddesses. I wasn't sure what the rules were and I'd already bowed to Nemesis, and now felt awkward as I met her gaze. "I'm a...a big fan of your work."

Her lips twitched, forming a patient smile. "And I of yours."

She knew of me? I stuttered slightly before I could stop gawking. "I can't tell you how much I appreciate the intercession."

Maddy nudged me. "Hate to break up the fangirl moment, but, uh..."

She pointed behind us. I followed her finger, and the goddesses turned in unison. A huge semi was bearing down on us, its headlights glowing yellow. The truck itself was black, with a gaping mouth of shark teeth on the grill. And behind the wheel? A manic-looking guy with pale skin and a set of glowing wings.

"He is such a toddler," Athena said.

"Always throwing temper tantrums," Nemesis added.

The semi was almost on us, Michael grinning madly. Smoke billowed from the exhaust as he ground through the gears and the truck increased speed.

"Will your shield hold?" I asked Di, instinctively inching backward.

She met my eyes and winked. "It's time for us to move anyway."

The three goddesses clasped hands, forming a bond once more. Magic zipped between them, snaked from their hands down to the pavement, and out to Maddy and me. It flowed right through my protection magic and tickled the bottoms of my feet. We grabbed hold of each other as the magic climbed up our legs and hit our spines. She hissed, but in a good way, and my eyelids fluttered at the heady sensation. It was like none I'd ever felt...and it felt damn good.

The semi's motor roared, almost on top of us.

"Di, I need to go to —"

The three goddesses raised their arms and I was sucked into a black hole. The rest of my sentence, the semi, Michael, and the highway disappeared in a single beat of my heart.

"—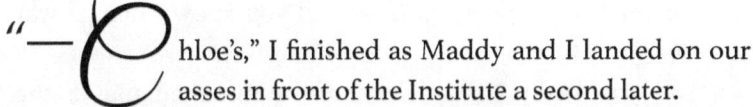hloe's," I finished as Maddy and I landed on our asses in front of the Institute a second later.

My car also appeared...at least what was left of it...punching through the security wards and setting off alarms. Di materialized in the next second *sans* her goddess counterparts. "What do you need at Chloe's?" she asked.

"Rad. He's after a perp that we need to stop."

Because of the alarms, Institute guards streamed from the buildings, their weapons and magics raised and ready. When they saw it was me and Maddy, they lowered their weapons and looked to Cole for guidance. He waved them off as Neve appeared and drove her wheelchair into the middle of our discussion. "What the hell is going on?" she demanded.

Cole stood over the wrecked car, eyeing the smashed and crumpled hood. He pointed at the two indentations. "Are those *footprints*?"

Di ignored both of them. "Rad has it handled."

"See?" Maddy said, standing up and giving me a hand.

"He needs backup." I brushed off my butt and cringed at the

sight of my car. "He needs me. Mo is nothing to mess with alone."

"Did Damon follow you into the field and back you up when you were the enforcer?" Di asked. Her eyes were normal again, the toga replaced with the sexy designer dress and shoes she'd had on at the Chicago House.

"This is different."

One corner of her mouth lifted. "Is it?" She closed her eyes for a second, then opened them. "Alexandru's vampire unit is there, helping him."

Maddy eyed her. "Do you have ESP?"

"No," Di said, then to me, "You're head of the Institute now. You need to learn to delegate and not micro-manage your people."

Everyone was an expert. "How did you know Michael was after me?"

"Did you really think Alexandru summoned me to the House to discuss the rebellious vampire from Europe?"

Yes. "He hired you to watch me?"

She smiled. Colgate models had nothing on her. "He asked me to keep a protective eye on you. You're facing some rather... overwhelming challenges right now."

What's new?

Neve rubbed her eyes. "Thank God. I was so worried. We'll all feel better, Di, knowing you're looking out for her."

Looking out for me. A strange concept to me.

After the trip through the beam-me-up Scottie transport, I still couldn't smell, and my balance was off. It beat being run over by an angel in a semi, but it made my arms and legs rubbery. The parking lot seemed to rise and dip in my peripheral vision. "I need to sit down."

I was hustled inside to my office, where I plopped on the couch. Maddy gave Cole and his head of security, a reedy-thin Mercenary demon named Gor, the whole story. Neve brought me a triple-shot espresso, and I almost cried because I couldn't smell the heavenly aroma.

Tipping the cup, I drank it straight down like whiskey. It heated my raw throat, but...*what the hell?* I tasted nothing.

Cole was watching me and saw my stunned reaction. "What?"

I looked at the empty cup. "Nothing."

"Your eyes are funny." He crouched in front of me, laying his hands on my thighs. "Look at me."

The magic and worry rolling off him made my skin itch. "I just had a run-in with an archangel who surfed my brain with his divine and very painful mojo. He probably screwed something up."

I almost told him I couldn't smell or taste, but something made me hold back. Cole trusted Gor, his security supervisor, and I should have too. But I didn't really trust anyone I hadn't walked through fire with, especially with my personal info. Appearing weak in front of Gor—not just recovering from the run-in with Michael, but *actually* having a disability from it— went against my survival instincts.

Cole turned to Maddy. "Go get Kirill."

My response was pure reflex. "I'm fine."

Both of them ignored me, Maddy giving me a *shut up* look as she hustled out. Neve was on her heels in her wheelchair. "I'll bring you something to eat," Neve called.

The thought of food made my stomach queasy. All I wanted was another triple shot espresso—except what good did it do if I couldn't taste or smell it?

Down to just the three of us, Cole made me tell him my version of the encounter, which was nearly exact to Maddy's. After I shared those facts, I asked Gor to leave us alone. The Merc demon nodded, his lips thin and taut like the rest of his body. His aura exuded protection and annoyance that Di and her friends' magic had busted Maddy and me through his security wards.

Cole walked him out the door, said something I couldn't hear once they were in the hallway, and came back in. He closed the office door, leaned against it. "You're not telling me everything."

"I told you everything that was important. And your head of security better figure out how to keep gods and goddesses out, or we're all going to die."

"It's not just your eyes, is it?"

So much for distracting him with the threat of imminent danger.

Pushing off the couch, I locked my knees and stood motionless for a second, making sure my legs would hold. Once I was sure I wouldn't belly-flop, I went to the mirror near the door. Sure enough, the pupil of my left eye was fully dilated, while the right was a pinpoint. A deep purple ring with a second white one circled both of my brown irises.

The effect was startling, making me draw back. Then, I couldn't help myself—I leaned in once more and studied my eyes. I scanned the rest of my face and neck. Bruises left from Michael's hand ringed my neck but had already faded to a pale yellow.

The rings around my eyes were probably a side effect of the goddesses' magic, not the angel's, but before I could tell Cole that, Kirill and Maddy burst in.

"Satan's balls. What did you get yourself into this time?" the archdemon and resident doctor demanded. Kirill grabbed my arm and hauled me to the desk. He made me sit while he examined me.

I reined in my instinct to push him away and sat like a good patient. "Michael went through my memories looking for something. I think he messed up some of my wiring. Then I got jacked by some goddess magic, which messed up my eyes, but I don't think that harmed me."

Kirill's eyes scanned mine, going back and forth between the pupils. "What's my name?"

"Kirill."

"What day is it? What year?"

"It's Monday, and I don't have a concussion, Kirill, I just can't..."

They were all staring at me, waiting for the big reveal. Lack of smell and taste seemed ridiculously anti-climatic.

"Can't *what?*" Cole insisted.

My sense of smell was important. Really important. It helped me recognize other supernaturals and helped me track my enemies. Told me as much, if not more, about those I dealt with on a daily basis than their body language and auras. If I wasn't firing on all cylinders, I was in danger and much less effective at everything. I had to see if there was a way to fix it. Plus, I wanted —needed—to be able to taste again. I like to eat. A lot.

*Please let this be temporary.* "I can't smell."

Cole's already worried features dipped. The worry was replaced with something stronger. "*Anything?*"

I hated to confirm his fear, but I did. "Not a damn thing since Michael choked me and dug around in my head." I looked at Kirill. "If he damaged something, why isn't it healing like my other injuries?"

Cole and Kirill exchanged a look, Cole's brows rising in question.

Kirill focused on my forehead as if the reason might flash across it in bold letters. "Recognition of smell is controlled by the frontal lobe. Goes hand-in-hand with taste. Can you taste anything?"

Reluctantly, I shook my head. "The thought of food nause-ates me. I couldn't smell or taste the espresso Neve gave me."

Silence. Kirill's face showed deep concentration. "My specialty is disease, not brains, but after you had that run-in with Maria's ghost and she knocked you silly last year, I ordered some equipment. Let's do some scans—CT, MRI—see what we find."

Brain scans. Dangerous territory. "You have an MRI machine?"

"In one of the outlying buildings. Haven't used it yet. I'll have it brought to the infirmary. You'll be my first."

*Oh, goodie.* Guinea pig, that's me. "You can't just lay your hand on my head and get a reading?"

"I'm not a witch doctor."

Too bad.

But I knew someone who knew someone who was. If worse came to worse, I'd call in a favor. My new friend Amy, known around here as the witch with the delicious ice cream, was not only Lucifer's pregnant girlfriend. She was best friends with a Vodun priestess. "Won't a giant magnet spinning around my head screw up my magic?"

"My guess is your magic is already screwed."

"Why?"

"What did your demon do when Michael played hopscotch inside your head?"

*Froze up.* "She was paralyzed."

"Exactly." He sounded smug. Then he reached out and punched Maddy in the arm hard enough to knock her to the floor.

"Hey," she yelled. "What was that for?"

"Retaliate," he said to me. "Seek vengeance for her."

"What?"

He stepped over to kick Maddy in the side. At least he tried. She moved fast, anticipating his attack this time, and grabbed his foot. Being a vampire, she was strong and a good fighter, but Kirill was an archdemon like Damon. He was stronger, faster, smarter. His foot broke through her hold, coming down hard on her chest and knocking the air out of her lungs. Rib bones cracked, her eyes bugged out, and she screamed, "Kali!"

"What the fuck are you doing?" I demanded.

"Retaliate," he repeated, pinning her down.

My vamp blood screamed. My demon danced. "Vengeance is mine," I said, touching my ring fingers and thumbs together.

Kirill hadn't raised any protective wall to keep me out. Magic bubbled up from under my feet, shot up my legs, and rocketed through the rest of my body. It hit my fingers and sent a wave of energy at him that should have knocked him on his ass.

Instead, tiny pink and purple fireworks exploded in the air around him, popping and fizzling out before they even touched his skin.

O-*kay*. That was new. "*Che cavolo!* I've turned into a fairy."

"See?" he responded gleefully. Removing his foot from Maddy, he helped her stand and laid a hand on her ribs, sending a dose of healing energy into them. Things mended and she took several deep breaths before she raised her leg and kicked him in the shin.

Kirill didn't even react. "You're compromised."

"This didn't happen when Lucifer prowled around in my head."

"Lucifer was looking for something specific. Some information. Michael wasn't."

"Yes, he was," I argued. "He needs to know where I'm hiding the sword."

"Does he?"

I looked at Cole, seeking confirmation. He was the best strategist I'd ever known. He folded his arms, scratched his jaw. "He knows the sword is here. He didn't need to paw through your memories for that."

"Then what was he doing?"

Cole sighed, a deep, *we are so screwed* sigh. "Fucking you up is my guess."

Good thing I was sitting on the desk or I would have fallen over. "That's it? He messed with my magic to *fuck me up*? Why not come after the sword?"

"Because this isn't about the sword," he said. "This is personal."

Maddy moved to my side, bug-eyed once more. "What will you do without your magic? You're a sitting duck."

"And it's duck season," Kirill added.

Always so helpful with the obvious. I puffed my lips and shrugged off Maddy's concern. "I'm sure it's only temporary. My blood and body are self-healing, and I have the added advantage of both demon and vampire blood circulating in my veins. That's a powerful cocktail. I'll be fine in a few hours, you'll see."

Boy, was I wrong.

## 13

*H*aving an enormous magnet whirling around your head is as bad as having an angel play pinball with your brain. Especially when you're told to lie motionless in nothing but your birthday suit.

Kirill had laid a white sheet over my body, but I still felt exposed. Not because I'm a prude about being naked in front of God and my fellow demons—I could care less. But because, once again, someone was digging around in my head.

Scary place.

The MRI thingie was loud and banged at random intervals. I couldn't smell it, which made the banging worse. With my nose out of commission, my hearing had become super acute. I'd heard of humans who'd lost their sight and found their hearing heightened, but I never realized it could happen to a demon who'd lost her sense of smell.

But then, I'd never heard of a demon losing their smell. Or taste. Being filled with the seven deadly sins, demons are a mass of the five senses. Pleasure, in whatever form we take it, relies heavily on the sensations we derive from hearing, tasting, touching, etc. All of our senses are amplified so we can extract the maximum enjoyment from the sins of gluttony, lust, greed, and sloth.

As I lay in the tunnel of the machine, my pulse raced, and my limbs flinched every time the thing did its bump-and-grind routine. When it finally stopped twenty minutes later, silence rained down on me, and I breathed a sigh of relief. Kirill's voice came through a speaker near my head. "Stay there while I have a look at the scans."

"I need to get back to work."

He didn't answer. I lay there for a minute, waiting for him to emerge with a prognosis. The tunnel wasn't bad once the noise stopped. Little by little, my muscles relaxed. My head felt lighter. Maybe the magnet had put things back in order.

I drew a deep breath through my nose, hoping I could now detect the machine's odor. Air filled my nostrils but no scent reached my brain.

I closed my eyes against the wave of disappointment. Why hadn't my blood restored my sense of smell by now?

Slowly, I felt myself drifting toward sleep. My body was exhausted, and maybe my brain was too. A short nap might do me good...just a few minutes while Kirill played doctor...

I dreamed in fits and starts. At one point I stood on the edge of a precipice looking down into a deep valley. I couldn't see the bottom but heard a multitude of voices calling my name.

Damon appeared on the other side of the crevice. He had the weird aura from my previous dream. "Jump."

I sniffed the air. His smoky wood scent trickled into my nose and I nearly sagged in relief. Other scents entered as well. Human smells from the pit at my feet, turning my relief to revulsion. "I don't want to."

"They're calling for you."

His aura was so evil I stepped back from the edge. "Why me?"

"You killed them. They seek your blood. Give it to them and silence their cries."

I swallowed hard. Even in my messed up dream state, I searched for the metaphor. Was this another choice he was demanding I make?

The humans continued to call my name. If I'd killed them, it had to have happened while I was under Maria's control in her court. Since that time, I'd saved humans...many, many more than I'd ever killed.

Didn't mean guilt over the pain I'd caused had disappeared, nor was I ready to jump into some pit with them so they could exact their revenge.

Hey, I'm a demon. Selfishness is organic. "I cannot save their souls by joining them."

"But you can save yours," Damon countered.

It was a lie. At least, I thought it was. "I don't possess a soul."

Which was definitely a lie. Sort of. Being one of the *vitiums*, there was some debate about whether or not I did, indeed, possess one.

"A soul is not a thing," Weird Damon said. "It cannot be taken from you or lost. You and your soul are one and the same. Save your soul, save yourself."

The evil Damon of my dreams sounded a lot like Salmad. "Next, you'll be telling me to meditate."

No reaction. Below, the voices dwindled down to one. "Kali?"

My heart stopped, my feet took me to the edge of the precipice again and I leaned forward trying to see more. A swirling mist rose from the pit and I heard my little sister's voice again. "Kalina, is that you?"

Inside my chest, my magic leaped alongside my heart. "Piper?"

"I can't find the light." Fear laced her voice. "I can't...I can't get out of here."

A trick. It had to be. My sister had died long ago, but she had been a vengeance demon like me, not human. I sniffed the air again, trying to pick up the coppery smell of revenge that should have emanated from her magic. The only odors coming from the pit were human.

"Jump," Damon repeated. "For her."

A flood of magic hit my back as though a dam broke, pushing me forward. My feet slipped on the rocky ledge, my arms cartwheeling in the air. Losing my balance, I tumbled forward, pitching into the mist and darkness.

Down, down, down I fell, my bones light as a bird's. My mind went blank and my emotions disappeared. There was no sound, no smell, no sensation except calm and peace. An absence of everything.

In some ways, it reminded me of floating on the air currents Rad had used to lift me off the ground. I didn't fight it, just let myself fall, wondering if I'd ever stop...and what I would find once I did.

A sharp pain in my arm woke me with a start. I blinked a few times, everything fuzzy...my vision, my hearing, my brain.

A set of lavender-colored eyes came into focus above me. "You said we need to talk." Tabriss's face was a thundercloud of determination. "I want to leave."

I sat up, the fog of the dream still lingering. The sound of Piper's voice echoed in my ears. A prickle of dread raised the hair on my arms, the evil in Damon's aura seeming to follow me into reality. My demon was vibrating inside my chest, itching to break free.

For some reason, I was in my Hello Kitty pajamas, and the sparkling purple bow on HK's headband snapped me out of my fog. I was in my own bed inside my apartment at the Institute. The lavender eyes in the pale face beside the bed belonged to Tabriss. When I looked at her, she edged away, her aura oozing fear and something akin to disgust.

Typical response from a Fallen. Angels don't like me in general, of course, especially when they see the demon inside shining through my eyes. *Heeeerrreee's Johnny!*

But if my demon was alive and well, maybe my mojo was back.

My apartment was off-limits to everyone except my inner circle of friends. "How did you get in here?" I asked, then looked around and muttered, "How did *I* get in here? I was in the infirmary a minute ago."

"Kirill brought you here in a wheelchair." Her eyes scanned my face and pajamas. "I thought you were sick, but he said you were simply worn out and to leave you alone, that you needed sleep. After ten hours, I was tired of waiting."

"I've been asleep *ten* hours?"

"Your eyes..." Tabriss pointed at my face. "They're all...black and shit."

Why hadn't someone woke me up? The nightmare continued to fade and I felt a burst of energy. I sniffed the air, hoping my blood had healed the damage Michael had done. I did smell something, but it wasn't Tabriss's Fallen scent or the normal smells of my room. I sniffed again struggling to place the odor. Burnt hair?

I swung my feet over the edge of the bed and closed my eyes, mentally soothing my demon. She was agitated enough these days without the aftereffects of the damn dreams. I couldn't promise to turn her loose, but I did promise her a session with Rad and his muscle-bound body.

Inside my chest, she quivered with anticipation and then settled down. After a couple of deep breaths, I opened my eyes.

They must have looked normal again because Tabriss relaxed.

She kept her distance, though. Outside, a spring storm raged, darkening the skies so much that I couldn't decide if it was night or day.

"What is this place?" She fingered one of my cherry wooden stakes lying on a bookshelf. "Are you a vampire hunter?"

"Yep, that's me. Buffy Sweet, vampire hunter." She didn't get the sarcasm. Where to start? "You know about vampires?"

"I know about everything. I've been around a long time."

I'd sensed that. No way was she as young as she looked. "How long?"

"I've lost count of the years." Her gaze stole to the window. Sadness flooded her aura. "Too long."

"So you know you're not human."

"Oh, I'm human, just not enough to die." She sat in a chair, sinking low and sticking her legs straight out. "I've tried every-thing—fire, beheading, fatal illnesses, war. I seem to have a knack for finding weirdos who want to kill me. They've all failed."

Insight trickled in. "You offered yourself to Mo?"

Her lavender eyes met mine. "He came the closest to finishing me off, I think, but then you rescued me." She shifted her gaze to the floor. "You fed me your blood, and now I feel... strange. Like a weirdo myself. I keep having odd cravings."

Talk about weird—I was having this discussion in my paja-mas. At least she was being honest and seeking answers instead of trying to run away. Guess it was time to lay it all out there. "You're an angel. One of Lucifer's Fallen. And the cravings are for more blood."

A slight lift of her brows. Not shock exactly. More like she thought my lunacy knew no bounds. "Lucifer? As in the devil?"

I nodded, let her digest it. We'd get to the blood slave part later.

"Right." She snorted, doubt lacing her tone. "He's real?"

She knew about vampires and monsters yet questioned the existence of the devil. "How about you head downstairs to my office? I'll throw on some proper clothes and meet you there in a minute."

Her eyes hardened. "I may be a freak, but I'm not an angel. I'm also not a baby. I don't need to be coddled."

When faced with the truth about their origins, most reincarnated Fallen initially reject the idea. Go fig. A few feel relief. They've lived their whole lives as outsiders, believing like Tabriss that they are freaks.

I understand how they feel since I'm a freak of epic proportions. I've tried to make the transition to knowing too much a little easier for them. "We have a lot to discuss. I'd prefer not to do it in my pjs."

She didn't care about my wishes. "I want the truth."

"And I'm going to give it to you." I rose and hustled into my walk-in closet. Inside, I switched out my HK attire for jeans and a black shirt. Reemerging, I grabbed Volante off the nightstand and she curled up around my arm. "The truth is ugly, Tabriss. I hope you're ready for it."

Her brows now rose in outright skepticism. "You haven't told me the truth about anything since you found me."

"I was trying to ease you into your new life."

"New life?"

She wanted the facts but didn't believe what I was telling her. *Nothing like a challenge.* "You want proof that you're a fallen angel and that Lucifer actually exists?"

Her chin rose a notch. "Yeah."

I could sense she wasn't kidding. If I didn't give her a hard and fast lesson about her magical powers tonight, she'd be gone by morning.

I grabbed her arm and hauled her out of the chair. "Follow me."

## 14

*I* led Tabriss to the training center. Neve's internal Kali radar alerted her to the fact I was up and on the move. She caught us in the elevator heading down.

"Where are you going?" she said, wheeling her chair in beside us.

Although the monster clock on the wall said it was three in the afternoon, there were plenty of supernaturals crawling around the Institute. "Tabriss is ready to find out more about her origins."

Neve cut her eyes to the Fallen, rubbing the Celtic pendant hanging at the base of her neck. "Can't Di handle that?"

Di had been handling a lot regarding the angels, and I appreciated how they took to her so easily. On some level, they recognized one of their own—angel, goddess, it didn't really matter. "I'm sure she can, but I have something I want to show Tabriss first." I petted Volante, and she pulsed on my arm in response. "What happened with Rad and Mo?"

"A big fight. Chloe's not happy since they messed up the front entrance to her blood bank."

"Smooth things over with her, will you?" I'd pay her a visit and bring her a gift later. When I had time. *Hahahaha.* "Did Rad apprehend Mo?"

"Yes. And then Alexandru and his crew showed up and took Mo with them. Radison is spitting bullets."

The elevator dinged, and I stepped off with Tabriss in tow. "I'll be done here in ten minutes. Send him to my office, will you?"

"He's not here. He's out working on that clown case." Her always somber eyes darkened. "Another child went missing after school yesterday. The same white van was seen canvassing the area a few hours earlier."

Damn. Neither the supernatural nor the human contingencies lacked for child predators. "Any leads on if the clown is supernatural or human?"

Neve shook her head.

Tabriss sighed. "You should go," she said to me. "Help him out."

A part of me wanted to. The vengeance demon that was so much a part of my makeup insisted I hunt the bastard clown down and exact revenge for the kids he'd hurt and killed. For their parents and the families who loved them. Some of which would never see their lost loved one again.

*Rad's handling it*, I reminded myself. He was the enforcer now, not me. As everyone kept telling me, I needed to let him do his job. "Until Rad has a stronger lead, I'd be in his way." I motioned to Tabriss. "Let's go."

Neve pressed a finger against the control panel to hold the doors open. "Do you want me to send up some breakfast for when you're done here?"

Supernaturals are nocturnal. We eat breakfast when the sun goes down and our last meal before it comes up. Either way, I was starving, but hesitated to say yes. Without the ability to taste anything, food had little appeal. I feared the earlier nausea might return.

I'd still need caffeine and energy. A demon without a substantial meal in her stomach was irritable and unfocused. By nature, I was irritable enough for three demons, even on a full stomach. "Eggs, toast, bacon, and coffee, please."

Neve loved feeding me. She gave me a big smile. "You got it."

As she disappeared behind the elevator doors, I led Tabriss into the gym. Cole was putting various vampire soldiers through their paces, and tight, tense magic swirled in the air. He hated vampires, and they weren't too happy taking training lessons from a demon. But I'd seen a marked improvement in our saving-humans column in the past few weeks, and I would need these soldiers to help me fight upcoming battles. Namely with Lucifer's big brother and quite possibly with Alexandru's older brothers as well. Not to mention his vampire fiancée.

Since the death of their father, Vlad, the royal vamp family had made grumblings about removing Dru from his Master vamp status in Chicago. Like most supernatural families, there was blood amongst the siblings. My guess was the only reason Dru hadn't already met with a disposal team was because of me. I'd saved his life by feeding him my blood, and he was a force to be reckoned with now in the vampire world. His brothers hated that he had the upper hand because of my demon blood coursing through his veins, but at least they respected it. They realized that if anything happened to Dru, they'd have me to deal with, and I wouldn't have even a single qualm about sending every one of them to Hell. After all, not only could my demon finish them, I had connections in the underworld and could make arrangements for them to have a one-way ticket to the lowest dimensions of Hell.

"What are we doing here?" Tabriss asked.

Cole spotted us and started walking over. He was dressed in sports pants and a wife beater. The tattoos on his arms looked particularly menacing today. Or maybe that was because of the snarl on his face and the pissed-off attitude he was radiating.

I smiled at him, loving the fact that the vampires were annoying the hell out of him. He'd feel better once I did my little pony show with Tabriss. "Cole and I are going to pick on you."

Her gaze ping-ponged from me to Cole and back to me again. "How will that prove I'm a fallen angel?"

Cole finally reached us. "What do you want?"

He was gritting his teeth so the words all ran together. *Whatdoyouwant?*

"I need your help." I winked at him. "Tabriss, here, needs to get a grasp on her magic."

Cole's expression softened ever so slightly. He knew my code and knew what I was asking him to help me do. He looked her gangly body over and lifted one brow at me as if asking if I was sure.

I nodded. "Ready?"

Tabriss took a step backward. "For what?"

Cole and I had worked together enough that our movements were synchronized. I went for her upper body, he took out her legs with a sweeping kick.

Tabriss landed with a hard thump on her back. I couldn't smell the fear coming off of her, but it was easy to see in her eyes and the sweat beading along her hairline.

There are human females who are tough mentally as well as physically. And there are females who think they're tough but fall to their attackers as easily as toy soldiers do when a child swipes a hand across them.

I fisted a handful of her hair in my palm and put a stranglehold on her neck. "Fight, Tabriss, or die."

Her eyes went wide, her hands flailing and striking at me. I released my grip on her hair and added my second hand to the vise grip I had on her throat. She gasped for air but none could get past my chokehold. Bucking underneath me, she lost that fight, Cole's body pinning her down.

Her eyes began to roll back in her head, and I swore under my breath. Where was that spark of magic I knew existed inside her? Why wasn't she fighting?

*Because she doesn't want to live.*

Duh. She'd tried unsuccessfully to kill herself for years, including, it seemed, by finding supernaturals who wanted to harm her. Yet she was still alive.

But I wasn't any old supernatural, and quite possibly, I *could* kill her.

I loosened my grip on her throat and let her gag and gasp to fill her lungs with oxygen. I waited until she'd heaved in several deep breaths...and then I hit her.

Right hook to the jaw. It was a beauty. Her head snapped sideways, then slowly came back so she was looking at me.

"You're sick," she muttered, her voice raw from the strangling.

An audience gathered around us, but I didn't take my eyes off her. "Defend yourself."

"Fuck you."

The nausea came back, but not because of Michael's rewiring of my brain bits. Cognitively, I knew this kid was an angel, but beating up someone so human made me sick to my stomach.

I hit her again, but this time, I saw a change in her aura. Thank the devil. *Thatta girl.* "If you don't fight back, I'm going to let all these vampires" –I waved at the circle of vamps now surrounding us – "have a turn at you."

Tears flooded her eyes, but there was steel behind those lavender orbs.

Good, I wanted her angry, angry enough to take a swing at me. Not with her fists but with her magic.

My demon watched the show with interest, refusing to join

the party until there was blood or magic or something worth getting excited about. I gave her a little goose, moving off Tabriss and promising my demon some blood. "Who's first?" I asked the vampires crowding around.

Cole looked disgusted as he released her and stood next to me. "What about me? I'll give her a go."

He cocked his head, his demon eyes black as sin, and gave her a grin that said he had a real treat in store for her. She jumped to her feet, recoiling. She bumped into soldiers who shoved her back into the center.

"I'll fight her," one of them said.

"Me, too," another offered. It was a female, and she reached out and felt Tabriss's bicep. "I haven't had angel blood before."

Tabriss jerked her arm away, her eyes now wild with fear as she swept her gaze around the crowd, landing on me. "What is *wrong* with you? Are you crazy? They'll kill me."

I shrugged nonchalantly as a vamp male reached out and touched her hair. "You're the one with the death wish," I countered.

She flinched away from one pursuer, only to find herself up against another.

Cole grabbed her by the neck and lifted her off the floor. Her back arched as he held her up for the vampires to admire. "To the winner belong the spoils," he said. "Palermo? I believe this one's yours."

The crowd parted; a beefy male stepped forward, eyeing Cole and Tabriss with wariness. Cole had told me about him. Big, tough, but a little slow on the uptake.

He seemed confused about what to do, so I drew out the dagger inside my right boot and quickly cut her wrist. She cried out, and blood, rich and warm, flowed down her fingers and dripped to the floor.

Fangs descended. Not just Palermo's but all of them. As their queen, I was connected to them, and I felt the rise in their blood lust and magic. My demon was on board now as well. She poked at my tenacious hold on her, aching to take the blood herself.

I didn't intend to let any of them actually have Tabriss, but I couldn't let her know that. As she squirmed, kicking out, I told her once more to defend herself. To call upon her magic.

My words seemed to land on deaf ears. She continued to fight against Cole's grip. Palermo might have been slow, but he was all male and his face morphed as he moved the rest of the way forward and grabbed her hand, her kicks bouncing off of him like a hummingbird's wings.

He forced her wrist to his mouth and lapped at the blood running from it. She screamed. A low moan went through the crowd, every vampire in there feeding off her fear as well as the scent of her blood.

Palermo didn't waste time. He sank his fangs into the cut I'd opened and began to drink.

"Stop," she begged, and I felt a pulse, a quake in the air around me.

"That's it," I told her. "Do you feel it?"

"My arm is on fire. That's what I feel!"

Another pulse, this one stronger, rippling out from her core. Cole glanced my way. I motioned for him to keep her where she was. "What else?"

"Hate. I fucking hate you!"

Ring finger and thumb touched instinctively, throwing up a weak shield around me just as magic exploded out of her. A blinding light and shockwave rippled through the gym. Even with my bubble of protection, I fell back, knocking into those behind me and landing on my ass.

It took a minute to right myself, my equilibrium see-sawing. As I untangled myself from the vampires who'd cushioned my fall, I saw a crater in the floor, a bright glow of light emanating from it. I staggered over, looking down and searching for her. "Tabriss?"

"What?"

The voice came from above me, not below. I glanced up, and there she was, sitting on a ceiling rafter, her face showing shock and the wound on her wrist no longer bleeding.

Vampires rousted themselves, brushing off their clothes and checking their weapons. I smiled up at her. "Welcome to your new powers."

She flipped me the bird.

## 15

*J* took Tabriss to the infirmary and bandaged her hand myself. "Aphrodite teaches a magic class to the Fallen every night at ten p.m. Make sure you attend."

She sniffed indignantly. "What happened back there doesn't prove Lucifer is real or that I'm an angel. You're not one, are you?"

Ha! I finished wrapping her hand and secured it. "The man who was here earlier? Who wanted to take you? He has a very specific job he does for Lucifer."

"What does he want with me?"

"Lucifer is rescuing the Fallen."

Nervous energy ate at her. "Rescuing us? Doesn't sound very evil. What does he plan to do with us...er...them?"

"Long story and not mine to tell."

She narrowed her eyes at me. "When you told that guy to take a hike and leave me alone, I thought you were nice."

"Nice, never. Protective, maybe."

"Why would you be protective of me?"

I made busy work of putting the scissors away and cleaning

up the bandage wrappers. "You remind me of my little sister, Piper."

She was quiet for so long, I turned around to make sure she was still there.

She was, holding her injured hand with the other. "When did she die?"

"How do you know she's dead?"

"The tone of your voice, and you got all stiff and weird when you said her name. I had a sister once, too. I know how it feels when they die."

A warm sensation wormed its way into my chest. My demon recoiled, but I rather liked it. I suddenly wanted to spill everything to Tabriss. Tell her about Piper and ask about her sister.

But I had a ton of work to do and Kirill wanted to go over my test results. "She died a long time ago, but I still miss her. A lot."

Tabriss jumped off the exam table with a rattle of paper. "I miss mine too, but she's better off dead than living my life."

Harsh, but probably true. "Get some breakfast and go wait for Di in your room. I'll see you later."

"That guy, the one who works for Lucifer? He's coming back to get me, isn't he?"

Straight backbone. Terse voice. Acting tough, but fear oozed from her aura.

"You don't have to be scared of Damon. He's gruff and annoying, but he won't hurt you. He works for Lucifer and has the best interests of the Fallen in mind."

"Why can't I stay here like the others?"

"I'm told you're special but that's all I know. I assume your powers are needed for some highly sensitive and important work."

She said nothing, just gave a quick nod and disappeared.

A half-hour later, I was sitting at Damon's desk, scarfing

down the breakfast Neve had left and cursing Michael for stealing my sense of taste along with my ability to smell. Bacon without the flavor or smell is like chewing odor-free leather.

The espresso I downed at least gave me a boost of energy. Kirill wanted to meet at sundown and go over my results, so I still had time to get some paperwork done. I just hoped my magic was back online. The weak protection bubbles weren't worth much, and I would now suck at smelling my enemies.

Testing it with some hesitancy, I reached deep, connecting with the floor and then pushing down, down, down, all the way to the earth. A tickle of return energy, like a greeting, danced across the bottoms of my feet.

I took that as a good sign. Gritting my teeth, I tugged at that energy, and sure enough, I felt a surge—small but oh, so good —circulating up through the floors that separated me from the ground and entering my legs.

The clock across the way dinged the hour. Pointing my fingers at the hands, I sent a jolt of energy at them.

No pink flowers exploded from my fingertips this time. *Bye-bye, fairy.* Instead good ol' earth energy came forth, hit the clock hands, and sent them spinning wildly.

*Yes!* Relief. I sent another flick of magic at the hands, returning them to their previous position.

The door to the office opened and Rad stood in the door-way, his golden eyes dark and dangerous. His magical energy swept into the room, raising the hairs on the back of my neck.

"You really should knock," I said, my clever wit always ready for a sparring match. "I might be fucking the boss or something."

"That's my job." He shut the door and flipped the lock, those eyes and his aura sending out a healthy dose of lust. "And I'm here to collect the bonus you owe me for saving Tabriss and snagging Mo."

Oh, goodie. I was feeling ready to celebrate since I seemed

to have at least regained my powers. "What do you want for your bonus?"

"You."

Ditto on the *goodie*. "Jesus said, 'Resist not temptation' so I guess I'm all yours."

"*Evil*." Rad snagged a slice of bacon and bit into it, talking around the mouthful. "He said, 'Resist not evil.'"

"Same thing."

He grinned. "You think I'm evil?"

Not as evil as some of the supernaturals I'd been dealing with. "In a good way."

He plopped down in the chair across from me. "How's the head? Maddy said you had a run-in with Michael and he did something to you."

Speaking of evil. "He messed with my brain and now I can't smell." I looked at the bacon Rad was happily munching on. "Or taste."

He stopped eating. "Is it permanent?"

"Don't know."

"What's Kirill say?"

"He ran some tests. The verdict is still out. I'm meeting with him in a few to see what he found."

His gaze dropped to the golden sword lying on the desk, the wings on the handle all black. "Will this thing kill him? Michael?"

"Wondered that myself, but hell if I know."

"You should carry it with you. Everywhere. He shows up again, see if you can kill him."

"He's an angel. Nothing can kill him, can it?"

"It might at least send him back to Heaven."

True. "Can we stop talking about angels and get to the evil part of this bonus stuff?"

He didn't bite. "I should probably go with you any time you leave the Institute from here on out."

"Because you're experienced in handling pissed-off archangels?"

"You need a bodyguard, Kali."

"What I need right now..." I got up and circled the desk to stand in front of him. My fingers undid a button on his shirt. "... is you."

He took me then, on the desk, shoving the sword aside. Our bodies met in a rough, driving desire, our magics flying around the room and clashing as violently as our bodies.

I gripped the edge of the desk as he slammed into me, nails digging into the polished wood. My demon rose with such force, my vision whited out. A second later, I heard the wood under me screeching, splitting...

The next thing I knew, we were falling, the desk blowing apart right where we were pummeling it.

As we hit the floor in a pile of splintered wood, Rad drove into me one last time and I cried out, my demon screaming for all she was worth.

# 16

"So, what's my prognosis?" I asked Kirill as I blew into the infirmary ten minutes late. It had taken some magic and good old-fashioned elbow grease to clean up the desk remnants and put them back together. As long as Damon didn't look too closely, he wouldn't see the one missing splinter still embedded in my ass. No need for him to realize his desk had, at one point, been kindling.

I'd already instructed Neve to order a new one, an exact replica, from the nearest furniture store.

Kirill looked up from a computer tablet across the room. "Finally. It's not like I have nothing else to do except wait on you."

*Wah-wah-wah.* "There was an issue in Damon's office." A very large issue with golden eyes and the power to bring me to a desk-exploding climax. "Sorry."

I was *so* not sorry.

"The good news is,"—I wiggled my fingers in the air—"my powers are back."

Kirill looked down at his tablet, unimpressed. "Your MRI is inconclusive."

"Inconclusive? What does that mean?"

"Don't be dense. What do you think it means? It means you were zapped by an angel, and the MRI shows nothing except this."

He flipped the tablet around so I could see the screen. I moved closer, but closing the distance between my eyes and the screen didn't help me decipher what I was seeing.

Oddball squiggles and what might have been runes dotted an ugly blob I assumed was my brain matter. "What the hell is that?"

"That's your brain," Kirill said. "It's been branded."

"Come again."

"Tattooed, inscribed, engraved, stamped, whatever you want to call it."

"With *what*?"

"Good question. Looks like some kind of ancient language."

Michael had inscribed something on my brain? "You're an expert at those. What does it say?"

"I'm not familiar with this one, believe it or not. Never seen it before."

We both stared at the screen.

"Is it Enochian?" Enochian was the language of angels, after all.

Kirill shook his head. "Nope."

"You're sure?"

"I've seen plenty of Enochian," he huffed. "This isn't even close."

He fidgeted, sliding a finger across the touchscreen and blanking it out.

My insides went cold. "What aren't you telling me, Kirill?"

He shook his head, started to get up.

I pushed him back down. "Tell me."

"Kali, this is out of my area of expertise. I don't know what it says."

Kirill hated not knowing everything. His ego is bigger than North America. He usually bluffs when he doesn't know something, so his reticence to tell me what he was thinking told me more than a bluff would have. "You have a theory. Spill."

He looked down at his hands.

Grabbing the arms of the chair, I scooted him around and got in his face. "Kirill, I've faced about everything Heaven and Hell can throw at me. It can't be that bad. Just tell me what it is."

Several seconds passed before he finally raised his gaze and met mine. "There are stories about the archangels. They have their own code, a separate language from the common angels. I thought it was a myth, but Salmad said..."

It was true. "Where do we find the decipher for it?"

"There is no deciphering legend. You need another archangel to read it."

I rocked back on my heels. There was only one archangel I was on speaking terms with, and I didn't particularly like him.

But I had to know what Michael had written on my brain. It might be the only way to reverse whatever he'd done to my senses.

I needed my sense of smell to alert me to supernaturals. I wanted to smell espresso again, to taste Rad's skin, and not lose my memories.

"Come on," I said to Kirill, grabbing him by the lab coat and pulling him out of the chair.

He blustered but came to his feet. "Where are we going?"

"Where do you think? To summon Lucifer."

$\mathcal{L}$ucifer Morningstar should be classified as one of the Seven Wonders of the World.

No lie, he is one picture-perfect angel. To call him beautiful is an understatement. The power oozing from his pores, his aura, is enough to knock me on my ass even if I turned my inner demon loose.

If you ask me, God didn't throw him out of Heaven because of his impertinence. He threw him out because Luc is the most perfect specimen ever created—too perfect even for Heaven to hold.

Of course, Lucifer and his female, Amy Atwood, tell a different story. She didn't like the way God did things, so she jumped from Heaven, and Lucifer supposedly followed suit.

I couldn't decide if they were exceptionally smart or complete idiots.

Jury was still out.

I may not be a fan of God, but I'm not one of Lucifer's either, even though I appreciate the gloriousness of his beauty and envy his power. He goes by many names in the Pit: Prince of

Hell, King of Hell, Number One Pain In the Ass. He is lovely to look at, but then he opens his mouth, and *bam*. Game over.

Take, for instance, when I called him to Damon's office using a magic spell his female had told me about.

His eyes sparked with anger as he materialized in front of me. "Why have you summoned me, demon?" he growled. "It better be to hand over Tabriss, or I will rip your intestines from your body and set them aflame."

See what I mean? The archangel has no manners. "Your brother attacked me earlier. He wrote something on my brain in some kind of secret angel language and screwed up my ability to smell and taste. I need you to read what he branded me with."

Lucifer's anger morphed into something else. Something I didn't understand. His eyes went flat, wary. "He wrote on your brain?"

Kirill handed him the tablet with the murky MRI photos. "I don't know how to decipher what it says. We thought you might."

Lucifer knocked the tablet away, stepped forward, and, before I could protest, put one of his large hands on my noggin.

The pressure was enough to make me want to scream, driving spikes of power that made my inner demon bounce and whirl like a beach ball caught in a hurricane. Whether he needed to do that in order to read Michael's message or he did it just for the fun of it, I wasn't sure.

Normally, I like pain. My demon loves it. Evil thrives on agony, after all. Physical, mental, and emotional. That's why humans are such appetizing guinea pigs for us. They're one big ball of nerves, inside and out. Often, their emotional nerve endings are far more sensitive than their physical ones. Demons thrive on that shit.

Which is why torture is akin to pleasure for us. We're not

wired the same as humans. Pain excites our powers, gives us a sick form of control and pleasure.

But what Lucifer's touch did to me wasn't pleasurable or satisfying. It brought me to my edge.

It wasn't the first time he'd gutted me. When we first met, he thought I was going to harm Amy. He gave me an instant dose of the plague, my internal organs revolting, blood running from my nose, my mouth, my very eyes.

Like I said, the angel has issues and absolutely no manners.

To say I wasn't excited about repeating that experience was an understatement.

An extremely cold sensation crisscrossed my brain, as if it were freezing each lobe as he probed it. My eyes rolled up in my head, and my body lost its ability to stand.

I didn't fall, though. That single hand had me in a lock, immobile and inert.

The probing seemed to last forever, and random memories flashed behind my eyelids: my mother's face, Damon's kiss, Rad's betrayal.

I tried to speak, but my mouth refused to work. My hearing became nothing but a droning buzz. I felt completely light-headed, my heartbeat slowing to a single, final, dull pulse.

When he turned loose, my bones were liquid. I slumped to the floor at his feet. I could smell it again, but I swear the only odor invading my nostrils was the fires of Hell.

I was dead.

Literally. Hell swam into my view, a desolate landscape of heat and atrocities that made my inner demon wail. Across the fiery planes, all manner of monsters came into view, circling, licking their lips.

And then...

Lucifer ripped me back to life and the earthly plane, and I drew breath.

A jolt of magic hit me. My senses came back online. Kirill's voice came to me, his face swam into view as I blinked my eyes open.

Lucifer towered over me, staring down at me with a look of seriousness that even for him was grave.

With Kirill's help, I sat up. My voice emerged ragged. "Did you have to...kill me...to read your brother's tattoo?"

If the devil could roll his eyes without actually doing so, that's what he did. "Take it as a warning to stay on my good side. And it's not a tattoo."

"So what is it?"

A muscle in his jaw jumped. He stared at me, but it seemed like he was staring through me, still reading my brain.

"Lucifer?"

His focus came back to me, his soul-black eyes meeting mine.

My brain, poor thing, shouted a warning. Automatically, I started scooting backward on my butt. "Just tell me what the fuck is going on."

"My brother used your brain for a specific purpose."

"Which is?"

"A message, Kali. He used your brain to send me a very unwelcome message."

# 18

"Okay, well, you got the message," I said to the king of Hell. "Now, how do I get rid of it?"

His lips firmed, and he looked out the office window, apparently wishing he was anywhere but here with me. "You can't get rid of it, and his message lays claim to an important pawn in the upcoming war."

"Can't you lay your hands on me and erase it somehow?"

His eyes met mine, their black depths filled with no.

"Who or what is the pawn?" I asked, feeling a new rush of exhaustion. Some part of me knew what he was going to say before he said it. I felt it in my bones.

Lucifer ground out her name. "Tabriss."

Yep, knew it. My teeth ground together. "He has no claim to her." He also had no right to write angelic bullshit messages on my brain, but that was a moot point at the moment since he'd already done so. "What kind of claim? Who is Tabriss, really? I know she's Fallen, but she's more than that, isn't she?"

"Tabriss has had many incarnations, each of them crucial in the history of angels and demons."

Which told me nothing. "Why does he believe he can lay claim to her?"

*And why do I feel such a goddamn pull to her?*

As if he read my mind, the corner of Lucifer's eyes narrowed. "The reason Michael picked you to be the deliverer of his message is significant. You are intricately linked to Tabriss."

"I sort of figured that out from the way my demon responded to her at Mo's."

Kirill shot me a raised eyebrow. I ignored him.

"Why do you think you feel a connection to the angel?" Lucifer asked in what I'd come to know from Damon was a patient schoolteacher voice.

Talk about annoying. He liked to play mind games instead of simply laying things out. "I have no idea," I said. "Enlighten me."

A twitch under his left eye let me know he found me dull, basic. I didn't want to play along, and he found that irritating. "Tabriss's human reincarnation before this happened during the time Jesus walked the earth."

A long time in between human embodiments. "She was one of the original followers?"

Lucifer nodded. "She was more than a believer. She was significant to Jesus."

A woman significant to the Son of God? "Oh, Christ, she was Mary? Jesus's mother?"

Lucifer looked at me as if I were an idiot. "Not *that* Mary."

I'm not usually slow to catch on, even when frustrated by the devil's unwillingness to come right out with the facts. This time, however, when understanding took hold of my branded brain, I had to lean back against the desk for support. "You've got to be kidding."

He shook his head, eyes flat. "Joking is not part of my nature."

For sure. "But..."

I fell silent, trying to piece together why Tabriss and her heritage could be important to Michael.

"Can someone fill me in?" Kirill asked, breaking the silence.

Lucifer spoke without taking his gaze from me. "The reason Kali feels a strong connection to Tabriss—and Michael has laid claim to her—is that she was once the epitome of sin."

Kirill, also staring at me, shrugged with confusion. "So?"

"She was Mary Magdalene," I told him. When Jesus cast out the seven deadly sins from her, he created the seven vices, which took the form of demons.

Kirill's face lit with comprehension. He snapped his fingers. "No wonder."

"Tabriss's power runs in your veins," Lucifer said. "The power of Jesus Christ is imprinted on your DNA as well."

But that would mean...

"No." My demon reared back. Tightness engulfed my chest. "That isn't possible."

Kirill's jaws jiggled as he nodded his head. "Anything's possible in the world of magic."

Anything *was* possible. "Not this," I insisted.

Lucifer cared little for my disbelief. "Tabriss is, in essence, your spiritual mother."

My head shook fervently. "My mother was Rachelle, a Sybill, who married John of Patmos, who changed his name to Goffredo Dulce when he and Rachelle left Greece and headed to Italy. He wrote the Book of Revelation based on my mother's prophesies. Prophesies the Catholic Church has held a tight rein on since the time of Christ."

"Rachelle gave you your physical incarnation on earth," Lucifer corrected. "Your true nature, the sinful side, comes from Tabriss."

I was afraid to ask, again feeling the knowingness of the answer deep inside my bones. "And my virtuous side?"

Lucifer nodded.

Kirill grinned. "Kali's dad is Jesus?"

Hearing it said out loud made me want to throw up.

"Tabriss's soul was always God's." Lucifer studied my face. "But yours, Kali..."

The weakness in my legs increased at his reluctance to finish his sentence. When did Lucifer ever feel reluctant about what he was about to say?

"What?" I said. "My soul, what?" And on the heels of that, another thought. "I have a soul? Like a human? There's been some disagreement about that."

He glanced at Kirill, back to me. "Your soul belongs to Jesus."

I took a long, deep breath as silence hung between us.

I'm physically quite fit and fast. My brain is also pretty impressive. Denial, though, even in the face of overwhelming facts, might be one of my downfalls. "Ridiculous." I waved a hand and laughed, the sound forced. "I'm a demon. While I may be one of the few with a soul, it belongs to you, the king of Hell."

I didn't wait for his reply or rebuttal. Pushing off the desk, I rounded the corner and plunked into the chair, ready to get back to business. "You still haven't explained why Michael has a hard-on for Tabriss. So what if she was Mary Magdalene? Why is that significant in your upcoming war?"

"Tabriss was one of the highest order of angels. Above Michael and I. He worshiped her in his own way, but she chose my side in the Great War of Heaven and was cast out. I think that her choosing me over him and our Father destroyed him. Later, in human form as Mary, she was tormented by Michael until Jesus found her and exorcised all her vices. Mary Magdalene fell in love with Jesus, and he with her. Another betrayal in Michael's eyes. Out of all of the Fallen, he hated her most, probably more than me, because she broke his heart. He vowed to never let her experience peace. Now, you and I have derailed his plans. We've taken his sword and found Tabriss."

I shrugged. "Boo-hoo for him. We aren't giving her back, nor are we returning the sword. What's he going to do about it?"

"What he's done to your brain will short-circuit your self-will bit by bit. First, your senses, then your memories. Eventually, it will poison your loyalties. He has the perfect way into your mind to control you. His message makes it clear that if I do not hand over Tabriss, he will use you against me."

"No one controls me."

"He will. Soon."

"How soon?" A brick of self-doubt landed in my stomach. "And how can he use me against you?"

"You are the most powerful supernatural on this planet, outside of me at this moment. It won't take long before his curse on your brain leaves you open to every suggestion he makes." His eyes met mine with gravity. "You're the only one who can kill my offspring."

The baby. He and Amy were going to have a child any day now. Prophecy said the child would reunite Heaven and Earth. The Fallen would be able to return to their paradise in the sky; humans would get their own version of it, as well.

Michael would hate that. His brother and the love of his angelic life returning to their heavenly home as if nothing had happened. "I will not kill your child, Lucifer. You know that."

"He'll be able to use you as a vessel and channel himself into you. You'll have no choice but to do his bidding."

*You have to choose.* Damon's voice from the dream echoed in my mind, setting off a spike of pain behind my temporal lobe. *He's coming.*

At least I could still remember the dream and the sound of Damon's voice. "We need a way to revert Michael's curse."

He punched the desk, making me jump and leaving behind

an imprint in the wood. "There is no way, aren't you listening? Since Tabriss is your spiritual birth mother, she is the one and only way to stop you from carrying out Michael's commands. She has the power to stop you, and he knows it. That's why he wants her. If he has her, he's unstoppable."

Kirill tapped a finger on his chin. "Why don't you just kill Kali?"

It was my turn to raise an eyebrow.

"What?" he said as if killing me were no big deal.

Probably wasn't to him.

"We're not turning Tabriss over." I leaned back and rocked the chair. "If it comes down to it, and I lose my ability to fight Michael's directives, she and Lucifer can take me out."

I turned to the devil. "Meantime, this supernatural is going to figure out how to stop your asshole brother once and for all."

"How?" both males asked in unison.

I had no fucking idea, but it would be a hot day in Paradise before I let an angel beat me.

## 19

The next evening, Tabriss sat across from me, a glass of my blood in her hands. She looked paler than normal and I could hear her stomach growling, but she refused to drink.

I laid out everything about Michael and his little head curse. "Could be days, could be hours. I need to know that if I go crazy, you'll stop me."

She stared at me with her mouth half open and a frightened look in her eyes. "You're already crazy."

"I thought we'd convinced you of your powers and you had accepted your role with us."

"I'm working on it, okay? Cut me some goddamn slack. Learning I'm an angel with powers is one thing. Telling me I may have to use those powers to kill the woman who saved my life and brought me here is another." She set the glass on the desk, her features suggesting she wanted to vomit. "Plus, Mary Magdalene? Jesus? I feel like this is the weirdest trip ever. Like heroin and every other hallucinogenic drug mixed in a cocktail and shot directly into my veins."

"I'm sorry I don't have time to coddle you and introduce all of this with a step-by-step beginner's guide on how the universe works." That was true. It seemed like one minute, I'd been protecting her from learning about her powers, and the next, I was dumping the Titanic of magic into her lap. "Are you up for the task or not, Tabriss? I need to know."

She liked to dish out sarcasm, but she didn't like having any sent her way. Her lips firmed, and her spine straightened. "I doubt I can do more than Lucifer."

"Lucifer is pretty damn powerful, but you have a direct connection to me. Blood and spiritual. He needs you and your power over me to shut me down when the time comes because Michael will be able to use me as the ultimate weapon against him. This is some heavy shit, I know that. But the future of the world, the Fallen, and humanity rests in your ability to do what has to be done. I know deep down you're a warrior. I need you to embrace that."

She gnawed her bottom lip, staring at the floor for a long moment. "I can do it."

"Are you sure?"

"No, but that doesn't matter, does it? I mean, do I even have a choice?"

"You always have a choice." At least now she was catching on. "My weaknesses are few, but I do have a couple. They may not matter when Michael takes over my mind and body, but they might. My magic derives from the earth. Break my connection with it and it might help you overpower me. Use Rad—he knows how to do that."

"You're in love with him."

What did that matter? "We share a complicated history. He knows my weaknesses."

"He *is* your weakness."

Her meaning wasn't lost on me. "Even if I'm under Michael's curse, it's not wise to threaten Rad's well-being in order to stop me."

"Sure," she said, rising from the chair. "Whatever."

But as she hurried out of the office, I knew she was making plans.

I CALLED the rest of the vices living at the Institute in for a meeting, gave them the lowdown on my upcoming Michael possession, and asked them to back up Tabriss in the event I went full-on assassin mode. They were full of questions I couldn't answer, most concerned about their own connections to Tabriss. Like me, they had been cast out of Mary Magdalene by Jesus, but none felt the pull to her I did. None had shared their blood with her either.

Salmad stayed after the others left and offered his assistance in finding any chink in Michael's armor we could use. While it seemed doubtful the priest could unearth anything more than Lucifer had already told me, I gave him the green light to do some digging. I'd learned over the past few months that his research abilities were quite impressive, and I knew he needed something to do, something to give him the illusion of control.

"We could always lock you in the dungeon with Maria and the others," he offered.

My ego took affront, but it was a legitimate option. "It may come to that. Be sure Cole is on standby."

He gave me a curt nod and left.

My brain felt fuzzy as I slumped back in Damon's chair. Was it because I'd slept and ate little in the past few days, or was Michael's poison already taking control?

Neve had left a pile of pink message slips on the desk, along with bills that required my signature and files I had to peruse. Decisions needed to be made, issues dealt with, and I had no desire or inclination to do any of them.

I buzzed her and requested she send in Maddy and

Brianna, too, if the vamp was around. I'd seen her earlier in the halls with Maddy, both disappointed over the lack of any demon hunting to be done. I had another job for the pair.

A little while later, a knock sounded. I digitally signed another form on my computer for Neve and closed out the file. "Come in."

"What's up, boss?" Maddy asked.

I needed a break – to sleep, to think, to prepare. "I need you two to take over for me for a while."

Brianna crossed her arms over her breasts, the leather of her new black jacket creaking softly. "Take over what?"

"The Institute."

They both gawked at me, then Maddy laughed. "Haha, good one."

I stood and grabbed my black jacket from the hook near the door. "Neve will walk you through the paperwork. Di is helping Dru with the renegade vampire from Europe. I'll handle Irina, our fake vampire princess, tomorrow. Mo is out of commission for the time being, and his gang is quiet for now. Unless it's a true emergency, don't call me."

"Wait!" Brianna looked panicky. "You can't be serious. We don't know anything about running the Institute."

"Kirill can help if you need it. Mostly, you need to keep the Fallen happy and decide who's up next on Rad's demon hit list. Oh, and the HVAC in the training room is on the fritz, so call the repairman. His number is listed in the blue file, bottom drawer."

I swung out the door, took a deep breath, and headed for the Institute's underground garage. Damon wouldn't mind me borrowing his Land Cruiser, right?

Before I made it to the elevator, footsteps sounded behind me. "What are you doing, my queen?"

Brianna hated using the queen moniker, even though it was accurate. For once, however, her tone was one of true concern.

I blew out a sigh. "I need to do research on Michael before he takes over my body." I gave her the Cliff Notes about what had happened and what was about to. As I spoke, Maddy joined us, her face contorting as every fact spilling from my mouth damned me more. "I know you guys can handle the day-to-day stuff here and give me time to get my shit together before it all goes down."

"I'm going with you," Maddy said. "I'll be more help to you wherever you're going than I will here."

"I'm going too," Brianna said.

The elevator dinged and the doors opened. "I appreciate your desire to help, but I need to do this alone."

"Why can't you do it here?" Maddy asked.

"Because there are too many distractions. I need to go somewhere I can be alone and think."

Maddy chewed her lip. Brianna wrinkled her brow.

"I need you two to handle this for me." The elevator doors started to close. I shot out a hand to hold them open. "As my vampires and as my friends. Please."

I didn't say that word too often. The two exchanged a worried look.

"Keep your cell on," Brianna said. "If you're not back in three hours, we're coming to get you."

That wasn't long, but it was better than nothing. "I'll see you soon."

Downstairs in the garage, I stopped as an idea hit me. I didn't like it being open season on Kali for Michael.

Heading to the dungeon, I considered my options to acquire the spell I sought.

Maria, an angry demon. Check.

Victoria, an even angrier vampire-witch. Check.

Parker, a human Noctifector. Check.

Parker couldn't help me unless I needed some of her blood for the spell. While I'd love to bleed her after all the problems she'd caused me, I knew her blood would be too weak for any spell of protection.

Queen Maria was powerful. She could cast the spell I wanted with no problem, except she hated my guts and would most likely do anything to hurt me rather than help me.

*The witch it is.*

When she was human, Victoria was a powerful witch and leader of the Satrina Arcanum. Thanks to a vampire king named Nudra, she ended up my blood slave. I disposed of him, making me queen in his place, but Victoria still managed to raise Lilith from Hell before I could stop her.

And then I'd used her to send Lilith back to Hell. Vicky was a vampire now but still a powerful source of dark magic. I needed some of that mojo.

Her cell was max security but not a horrible setup. She had a bed, a toilet, a sink. She got regular blood meals—although no longer my blood, thank the fires of Hell—and she had her books. My one and only concession. I allowed her to pour over her ancient witchy texts and write spells to her heart's content.

Not that she was ever going to use them unless they profited me.

I opened her cell door and stepped inside. "I have a job for you."

The vamp blood in her veins snapped to attention. Her kinky red hair hung in wild abandon over her shoulders and down her back as she sat cross-legged on the floor doing what looked like meditation. "I don't work for you," she said without opening her eyes.

Each of her hands formed a mudra on her knees. She appeared unconcerned that I was there, but her blood was running in fourth gear. Volante shuddered on my arm, feeling the pull of her magic.

"I need a protection spell. A strong one, and you're the strongest dark witch I know."

She'd made a tiny origami Buddha from a piece of paper. It sat facing her, mirroring her body position. "Fuck you."

"That's not very Zen, Vicky."

Her mudra fingers morphed, and she flipped me off in stereo.

"You may have noticed I have a lot of leverage here. Your fate is in my hands."

"My soul is infinite. Kill my body. My spirit will never die."

More Zen shit. Had my dark witch gone to the light side? "Come on, Vicky. Vampires don't possess souls, you know, and you don't want me to kill you. You've got big plans for breaking out of here and hooking up with Lilith again."

One eye peeked open. "I don't know what you're talking about."

"Of course you do. You've been trying to break the spells over the Institute and call her forth to save you."

The other eye came open. "I will never stop in my quest to join her."

*There's the witch I know and hate.* "Then why don't you kill yourself and head to Hell?"

Her chest rose and fell with a heavy sigh. "I will bring her back to rule Earth. You'll see."

"Not on my watch, but I am willing to make a deal if you help me with the protection spell."

She tilted her head slightly, itching to take the bait. "What kind of deal?"

My demon wanted to taste her, to feed on her magic. I held it in check, mentally stroking Volante to keep her calm as well. "I'm going up against the archangel, Michael. He's a fun guy. Thought you might want in on the action, and in return, I'll lighten your sentence. Make your stay here easier."

"I don't need *easier*. Lilith will reward my sacrifice when she returns."

"Hate to burst your bubble, but she's not coming."

That smug smile she loved to throw out made an appearance. "We'll see, won't we?"

"Well, while we're waiting for that monumental day, do you want in on screwing the archangel or not?"

She fiddled with another finger position and adjusted her seat. "Instead of protecting yourself from him, why don't you suck his power away?"

Nice thought. "A demon can't claim an angel's power."

She closed her eyes and resumed her meditative stance. "With the right spellwork, you could."

Was she yanking my chain? Having a good mental laugh at my expense? Misleading me so she had leverage?

Most likely all three.

"Really?" I said, heavy on the skepticism. Her ego was as big as Canada. "You're powerful, Vicky, but not that powerful."

Her closed eyes flipped open once more. "You doubt me?" Incredulous. "I called Lilith forth from Hell to walk the earth. You don't think I can trap an archangel and help you siphon off his powers?"

She had a point. I didn't trust her, but between her dark magic and the vamp blood, she might be my Loki. My enemy, but a powerful one, willing to help me if she could get what she wanted. "What do you want in return?"

That smug smile crept over her lips. "You must be desperate if you're bargaining with me."

"Not that desperate. If you don't want to help, no biggie." I turned to the door. "Maria will help. Have a nice life, Vicky."

I made it halfway through before she shouted, "Wait!"

Who was the desperate one now?

"No, no, it's okay," I said, backing out the rest of the way and starting to close the door. "We hate each other and you're not willing to put that aside to get out of this cell for a few hours. I get it. See ya."

A wave of magic flew at me, Vicky on its heels. Her vampire

speed was definitely up to par. She latched onto the door and I let her stop it, the two of us eyeing each other through metal bars. Volante coiled, ready to strike, and I commanded her to wait.

Vicky's vamp blood reached out and teased at mine. "Please don't go."

The supplication was fake, but what a turnaround. Gone was the ego—not gone, per se, but subdued. A rarity for sure.

I had no illusions that Vicky would refrain from trying to off me and escape if I let her out of her cage. I had a plan to keep her on my magical leash, and bottom line, I wanted to know if her spellwork, combined with my supernatural powers, might be strong enough to return Michael to Heaven permanently.

Lucifer's witch, Amy, had once sent Gabriel back home, but only temporarily. I knew Lucifer would never let me hook my power source up to hers in order to up the wattage of angel banishing. Vicky was the next best thing.

Forcing the vampire witch back with my magic, I opened the door all the way. I kept a wall of magic between us in case she tried to jump me. "To start with, you provide me with a protection spell that will hide me from Michael. If you can handle that, we'll take the next step to mess with his powers."

Her nostrils flared, and her throat worked. Wheels in her head turned as she tried to find a way to turn this situation to her advantage. Finally, she nodded. "One protection spell coming up."

# 20

*A* few minutes later in the underground garage, I opted for the shiny red Porsche rather than the subdued black Land Cruiser. Once outside the gates, I rolled down the windows and let the wind blow my hair as I took the machine to 100 plus on some back streets, weaving in and out of traffic with grace and skill. Horns blew and humans shook their fists at me.

Hey, what's the point of having superior reflexes if you never get to use them?

A few minutes later, my home came into view, and a surge of relief went through me.

Home. Once a church, the gothic, castle-like structure had withstood a lot of battles between good and evil. Most recently, my showdown with the Four Horsemen of the Apocalypse had nearly wrecked the place. Rad and Dru had spent long days and nights restoring the interior to a semblance of its former glory.

The night we took on the Horsemen, I lost Damon. The second worst night of my life. The first was the night I lost my mother, father, and sister.

Losing Damon created a similar feeling, one I hated all the more because Rad had caused it.

Hence, his desire to restore my home as best as he could. Truth be told, I think he felt as bad about what he'd done as I did.

Damon was a pain in my backside, but he was my pain. A long time ago, he'd saved my sorry ass and given me a reason to live. In the interim, he'd driven me crazy, making me the Bridge's enforcer but giving me little leeway. Damon liked being in control. Being a control freak myself, I understand his motivations even if I don't always agree with them.

The church seemed to glow in the twilight—at least, I hoped it was from the setting sun.

I parked the car out of sight on the side and walked slowly up to the doors. Ten feet away, I felt the pull of the graveyard behind the house and the evil buried there. Within that ground was a portal, a Hellmouth.

And I hadn't been diligent with my binding spells lately.

Wraiths and earthbound spirits called out to me. Volante slithered around my arm at the feel of it. A vibrational tug of dark, dark magic hung in the air.

I opened my supernatural self and felt around the perimeter. While my physical senses might be dead, thanks to Michael, my magical ones were back to almost normal.

Nothing had escaped from the portal. No ghosts hovered outside the boundaries of the cemetery. I'd deal with the binding spell upkeep later.

Right now, I needed peace and quiet. No Bridge Institute, no angels, no Rad, no responsibilities.

Laying a hand on the stone wall next to the door, I tuned my magical Spidey sense into the interior of my home.

Dark magic flooded my feet, wormed its way up my legs. I drew in the Earth's grounding energy and let it fill me. Every cell in my body tingled and my blood rushed faster. The demon inside arched and wiggled and finally sighed as the shot of energy gave her a high.

I didn't detect anything unusual. No uninvited guests, no malignant energies from the last battle.

Shifting my hand over to the lock, I sent the mental command to open, felt the wards lift, and heard the deadbolt flick back. Yes, I utilize magical and practical mundane means of security. You just never know who might show up on your doorstep and want in.

Inside, I closed the door behind me and leaned against it. *Home.*

I'd experienced many homes in my years walking the planet. Some places never left an impression on me, my wanderlust too needy, the energies of the different places too weak to entice me to stay. I've never been one for fancy digs or expensive furniture, but I do enjoy the baser creature comforts.

This abandoned church should have felt foreign and hostile to me. It did not. There was a darkness to it, a brokenness. Those who had sought religion, salvation, or sanctuary in this place had not found it, yet it had still served a purpose. It had provided someone somewhere along the way with hope.

Rad and Dru had mostly rectified the damage done by the battle with the Four Horsemen. It was odd for the two of them to find camaraderie in the rebuilding of my home, but they had called a temporary truce and worked as a team. Yes, they'd used magic, but also good ol' fashioned sweat and physical labor. A few days into their quest, I realized that it hadn't been undertaken for any purpose other than to make me happy.

As I surveyed their handiwork, it struck me all over again. My friends, Di and Neve, had often encouraged me to be happy, and had tried on occasion to infuse their own happiness into me. Similar to when a friend is in love and seeks to find you a companion, too. Or a new convert tries to bring you to Jesus.

It was different with Rad and Dru. They sought to make me

happy in this way to bring me peace, comfort, and to show their love and respect for me.

So, while my day-to-day interactions with them were contrary to this act of generosity, I carried their kindness, their altruism, in my heart.

In the kitchen, I fixed myself an espresso, even though it was somewhat pointless, just to feel normal. The simple act gave me more comfort and calmed my nerves. Digging around in the freezer, I found a steak. As it cooked, I boiled water and tossed in pasta. There were moments as I stood at the stove and cooked I could almost smell the seasonings I had put on the steak and the garlic I tossed in the skillet to make the sauce. I willed myself to remember the last time I had stood here and cooked a similar meal. Willed myself to remember different moments in my history inside this church. I would not lose my senses and eventually my memories without a fight.

Facts, ideas, and theories pounded against my skull. Tabriss, Mary Magdalene, Jesus. It was enough to make any demon howl with torment. I poured wine, loaded my plate, and climbed the stairs to the roof. There, I sat under the stars and ate, Volante resting by my side.

The food tasted like nothing, the texture in my mouth causing my jaws to tighten. I ate anyway. My body was lethargic from lack of food, and I needed the blood-red steak and starchy pasta to refuel, whether I enjoyed the smells and tastes or not.

Tabriss was my soul mother, and Jesus had saved both of our souls by casting me out of her.

What were the odds?

While Michael had singled me out because of my superior magic, the *vitiums* and I were all in this together. If he somehow failed with me, he would attack the next of the deadly sin vessels.

The night was cloudy, and I wondered as I chewed if Michael was somewhere above me, watching. I hoped so. Let him see that whatever he'd done to try and harm me wasn't working.

The graveyard stretched out before me, the spirits active. The moment I'd set foot on the rooftop, I'd flicked enough energy at them to make them stop calling to me so I would have some peace during my meal. They hovered like sick children along the edges of the cemetery's walls, watching and waiting, their magic bleeding into the air, the ground, the worlds beyond what the eye could see and the body could feel.

I had just finished my last bite of fettuccini when the spirits scattered, backing away from the northwest corner as if I'd lit a heavenly fire there. Volante vibrated with urgency and I allowed her to curl up and around my arm.

Automatically, I sniffed the air, then cursed. I channeled my annoyance into sending out magical tentacles to feel for approaching danger.

The supernaturals who appeared on the outskirts of my property line were a mixed lot, but the way my blood reacted, they were all vampires. At some point, they may have been witches, warlocks, or psychics, but all had been turned.

Some boasted old, old magic. Others were imbued with fledgling, immature power.

None were friendly.

The screeching started inside my blood and spread to my chest. An odd sensation I hadn't felt much in my three-hundred-plus years. The magic each entity had possessed prior to becoming a vampire was still inside them, crying to be released.

Humans had a saying about not being comfortable in their own skin. The same happens with supernaturals. When one type of magic is taken over by a stronger, darker magic, a similar disconnect happens, hence the screeching sensation I was experiencing.

For a heartbeat, I thought of Vicky. The two sides of her

supernatural nature—witch and vampire—didn't fight each other. Was it because of my blood running in her veins? Or was she equally at home in both embodiments? I believed she'd been such a powerful witch to begin with because she had latent demon blood. That could also be the reason she embraced all dark magics equally.

I set down my plate and picked up my wine glass. Was it too much to ask to have a few minutes alone? "Show yourselves, creatures of the night, or go back to the gutters you came from."

My eyes were well adjusted to the dark. I had no trouble spotting the male who slid up to a tree that lined my property off to the right. "You hold no command over us, demon."

I didn't bother looking at him full-on, sipping my wine and continuing to watch the graveyard. "Do you not recognize the pull in your blood?"

A female shot forward to stand a few feet in front of him, her magic slamming out at me. "You are no queen to us, you whore of Lucifer."

There was the witch. Emboldened by her aggression, more of the vampires stepped from the shadows. Four more sets of eyes gleamed at me, even in the darkness. Teeth descended in full-mouth smiles.

Six vampires. All powerful creatures. Their magics tightened in a swirling chaos of potent fury trying to wrap itself around me like a python squeezing its prey. They were eager to fight, to shed blood, to prove themselves.

*Outcasts.*

Vampires lived by stringent codes and rules. Those who refused to follow them were kicked out of their House or ripped to shreds by their fellow vamps.

This group had left on their own. I could sense it in the suppressed magics, crying for release. Because their underlying magics were so strong, they had never felt as though they fit in among their Chicago House blood-sucking contemporaries.

They couldn't help but break the rules because their magics would not let them rest or be comfortable in their vampire skins.

Outcasts roamed the city and suburbs, creating havoc and destruction. As the bridge enforcer, I'd handled my fair share of renegade vamps. Most cases ended in me staking the blood-suckers.

The demon inside me tickled my chest, eager to do the same tonight.

Demons don't generally wrestle with conflicting magics. We are what we are.

As a *vitium*, however, I had some idea of the renegades' struggles with finding their rightful place on the supernatural totem pole. I'm still not sure about mine, and I don't expect I ever will be.

Unfortunately, a group hug wasn't going to happen. Kindred spirits or not, they meant to do me harm. Vicky's protection spell had been for Michael only, but I didn't need protection from the outcasts.

"Why are you here?" I demanded, though I already knew. "Do you seek the portal? You know you can't handle that kind of power."

The male spoke again, linking his fingers with his female companion. "This land is ours now. Leave or be destroyed."

"Are you threatening your queen?"

"As Hecate said, you are not our queen."

The female, Hecate, spit on the ground as if to emphasis his point.

Threats bore me. As the other four stepped forward to form a line with their alpha and his partner, I flipped a wave of magic at them. Nothing extreme, just a taste of my power.

The entire line wavered, the female using her previous witchy skills to throw up an invisible wall of protection in front of them. It slowed my magic, but didn't stop it.

Still, she smirked, believing that was the strongest my power could get and obviously feeling proud that she had deflected it.

*Vicky would like and hate her at the same time.*

I raised my glass to her in a mock salute. She had no idea I could blast through her wall with nothing more than my pinkie finger if I so desired.

The spirits inside the cemetery continued to cower in silence. So strange. They feared this group, but why?

"You've been feeding off the energies here, haven't you?" I asked, mostly out of curiosity. "Torturing the already tortured souls in order to get high."

A slender, lanky male snorted with disgust. "You think that's our only lot in life? To get high?"

Pretty much. "You aspire to loftier goals?"

His face hardened, pissed at my tone. "We work for the true master."

The female rammed an elbow into him, shushing him. "You will join the souls in the cemetery, whore of Lucifer."

Man, I was sick of that label.

"I'm sorry to dispose you of that moniker, but Lucifer sleeps with only one female, his beloved witch. He barely tolerates me. You really should come up with a more accurate nickname."

My joking had the desired effect. The witchy vamp bared her teeth and snarled.

The magic she hurled at me was venomous and fiery, fueled by raging emotions. Snatching it from the air was child's play; sending it back to her with a little kick of my own magic was fun.

The energy hit the full line of them, knocking all six onto their asses.

And I'd barely moved a muscle to do it.

Yep, my magic was back on and fully functioning, and damn, if it didn't feel good.

"Consider your next move carefully," I told them, all teasing gone. The game had grown old. I didn't take to anyone defiling the church and cemetery that I called home. "Stay down and pledge your allegiance, or you will never get up again."

The words were barely out of my mouth when the witch catapulted herself through the air and suddenly stood in front of me. The vampire in her was on full display, but it was the witch that burned with rage.

Her magic hit with some force, but what should have angered me made me laugh. I shook my head as she reached out a hand to grab me, and I sent a bitter wave of magic at her throat.

She gasped, hand stopping in midair. The other flew to her throat, where I choked her without laying a hand on her.

I set down my glass and stood. I could have snapped her neck or tossed her from the rooftop, but my demon was hungry for blood.

So I forced her to her knees and stood over her, forcing her head back from the squeezing pressure around her neck. "How dare you come here and feed off my pets," I snarled. "How dare you threaten your queen. Know your place, witch."

I placed my hand on her forehead, and the shock of my power made her eyes roll up in her head. Leaning down, I put my face in front of hers and soaked up the fear radiating off of her body. The buzz it gave me was heady. The blood in her cold, night creature body sang to mine.

As I sucked up her magic, my physical connection to her acting like a straw, the surge of energy tingled my nerves and fluttered in my chest. Just think if I could do this to an angel...

"Know your true master," I whispered.

And then I crushed her skull.

Blood and bone exploded from the spaces between my

fingers. The worry and anxiety I had been feeling for the past few days blew to bits along with it. The evil in me flooded my system with a sweet relief I savored, my demon clawing and biting and eating away at the fresh rush.

The high didn't last long enough, and disappointed, I flung her body from the roof to the cemetery. "Eat, my pets," I called to the ghosts.

With only a moment of shocked hesitation, the rest of the renegade vampires ran off.

"Show your face again," I yelled after them, "and your fate will be a hundred times worse!"

A soft clapping came from the driveway, growing louder as Dru emerged from one corner of the church. "There's the demon we all love and fear."

He was splendid in the slice of moonlight that broke through the clouds at that moment. As if God wanted me to see him in his full, evil glory.

I wasn't even breathing hard from the confrontation, but my breath caught in my chest at the power glowing around him. The night was his element, his home. Silver danced in his eyes as he drew closer, lust and depravity singing in my freshly drugged veins.

I could barely find my voice. "What are you doing here, Dru?"

"Looking for you, my queen."

There was always this push-pull of magnetic electricity between us because we'd shared each other's blood. Always this dangerous desire. A heady pulse throbbed between my legs, my head swam with need. "I'm taking the night off," I muttered, knowing he could hear me with his heightened vampire senses.

His gaze dropped to my bloodied hand, and he licked his lips, his fangs on clear display. I'd felt the tips of those fangs buried deep in my neck. I longed to again.

A grin crooked one side of his mouth, my desire evident, no doubt. "I went to the Institute but no one knew where you were. I was concerned about your welfare. I had a bit of a challenge, but my blood tracked you."

The protection spell had perhaps dimmed our connection. "You know I can take care of myself."

In the graveyard, the spirits gorged on the female vampire. Dru lifted one brow. "I can see that."

If he stayed or got closer, I'd be in trouble. The high might not have lasted long, but my blood lust had been switched on. There had been a time in my life when I'd have gladly lost control and let it run its course.

But that time was long gone. Control was my guiding force these days. Damon depended on me. As did Lucifer and his angels. Humanity. "You should leave."

"I need you to see something."

*I'm sure you do.* "Not tonight."

"You'll want to see this without delay," he insisted. The silver in his eyes was still there, but his tone had darkened. Become more serious. "I, personally, am at a loss as to how to deal with it, Kali."

There were few things that could cause Alexandru, Master Vamp, to be at a loss.

Against my better judgment, I took my dirty dish and empty wine glass downstairs and followed him to the Chicago House of Vampires.

Because, really, what else did I have on my plate?

## 21

"*W*hat's wrong with him?" I asked.

Dru and I were in the House's lowest dungeon, several levels below ground, staring at Mo, the Dread demon, through thick steel bars.

Mo was chained to the far wall by his ankles and wrists. Blood streamed down his arms from where he'd pulled so hard on the shackles the metal had cut his skin. The same at his feet. Meanwhile, his back flexed and released, his neck arching wildly. His eyes had gone a pale blue, the pupils completely gone.

"Tell me what you see," Dru said.

Mo had been gnashing his teeth, foam running from one corner of his mouth until I'd stepped into his line of sight. He'd cocked his head and his pupil-less eyes had seemed to lock onto me. As the latest body spasm passed, his head came back to center, and his focus landed on me once more. His chest heaved, his body trembled. He strained toward me, the chains on his wrists and ankles clanking.

"A rabid half-vampire, half-Dread demon," I said. "What did you do to him?"

Dru gave me a chiding look. "The cause of this is not due to his incarceration, I assure you. When Rad turned him over to us and we put him down here, he was pissed but healthy. Has been for the past several days. I was hoping you might have an idea as to what caused this or even what exactly *it* is."

Mo leaned as far as the chains allowed, twisting his arms into an unnatural state. His nose sniffed the air near my hands. Volante tightened her grip on my arm.

I'd washed the witch-vampire's blood from my hands while cleaning up my kitchen before we'd left. As Mo's tongue came out to lick at the air, I wondered if I should scrub them again.

"I have no idea. It's like he's..."

"Possessed?" Dru finished for me.

"That's not possible." But I felt the tug in my gut that said it was indeed so. "Demons possess humans, not other demons."

"Nor vampires," Dru added.

Mo's jaw clamped and unclamped. He raised his head, his eyes staring at my face. "My deemonn,"—his voice croaked and snagged on the vowels—"fresh from the feeeeast. Whom did you kill? Did you taaaste her blood?"

"Who are you?" I asked the entity inside him. "How are you possessing a demon?"

A raw laugh issued from Mo's mouth. "Do you not knooow me?"

I exchanged a look with Dru. Clearly, we were both out of our element. "No, but your imitation of a grade-B horror flick is spot on."

Maybe if I pissed the thing off, it would show its true colors.

"Maria wants to fuuuck you," the thing stated. "Just like the old days. The threeee of us, what fun we could have, eh? You, me, and the queeen?"

Dru sent me another inquiring glance, which I ignored. Maria had forced me to do many things at her feet during my bondage to her. Her orgies had been legendary, even in supernatural circles. My body, as well as my magic, had been used many times. Even though demons normally take pleasure from such maleficence, it was not a time I enjoyed ruminating about.

"Tell me your name," I commanded, zapping Mo's body with a finger of magic. "I grow bored with your antics."

The thing spit out a series of grunts and words I couldn't decipher, perhaps a forgotten language. The thought gave me pause. The entity might be older and more cunning than a simple demon using Mo's body.

"What did he say?" Dru asked.

I shook my head. "Speak in a tongue we understand, you weak-ass supe. If the best you can do is possess a lowly demon and talk in riddles, we have no time for you."

Even that did not anger the thing. He smiled at me through Mo's face, a blood-red tongue darting out to lick the Dread demon's lips. "You are almoost ready. So close. I shall enjoy using you as I once did so long ago. Your body, so ripe, so delicious."

Mo sniffed the air again as if he smelled a feast. His eyelids fluttered closed and he sagged to his knees. His body swayed for a moment, then fell to the ground, face-first.

Dru put out an arm, pushing me back as if he expected the thing to jump from Mo to me. Without a word, he placed his body in front of me and backed me toward the door.

"Guard him," he said to the vampire standing near the arched doorway leading to this block of cells. "Keep me posted of any changes. Even the slightest adjustment in his countenance or voice, you understand?"

"Yes, Master," the vampire replied, bowing to me and to Dru as we passed by.

I accepted Dru's hand on my elbow as we ascended the stairs. His Master vampire blood was heated to boiling with his concern for my safety. I patted his hand. "You should ward him, his cell, and the House."

"I already have. Who is possessing him?"

"I have no idea."

"The spirit knows you."

An accusation. We passed the next layer of guards, them bowing, us nodding at their allegiance as we took the last flight of steps to the ground floor. "Dru, you know of my history at Maria's court. There were many supernaturals who enjoyed her favors."

His hand slid to my lower back as he escorted me through the final door from the basement into the main living area. His jealousy now mixed with his protective energy, wrapping around me and causing my pulse to speed up. "And yours?"

Explaining my past would not solve our current problem, but he wasn't going to let it rest until I gave him something.

"My Master," a young vamp said as she passed. She bowed low to both of us, a group following her, echoing her words and her bow. "My queen."

"Rise," Dru said with slight exasperation.

I took his hand and drew him toward the stairs leading to his office. "I request privacy for this discussion."

He followed on my heels, his hand once again resting on my lower back in a possessive gesture. We passed more vampires who lived at the House, and Dru told one to bring us every chocolate dessert available from the kitchen.

It was a nice gesture since he didn't know I couldn't taste anything. I have a thing for chocolate. The House employed a cook and a baker, both of whom whipped up plenty of food to go along with the vamps' blood-filled dietary needs. If there's one thing vamps enjoy besides blood and sex, it's decadence.

Inside his workspace, it was dark. A flick of his fingers brought the wall sconces to life. I took a seat on the black leather couch facing the fireplace. After pouring dark-colored liquor from a cut-class decanter, he handed me one of the squat glasses and took a hearty swig from his own. Then, he stood next to the mantel, staring at me and waiting for an answer to his earlier question.

"The torturing I did for Maria is on me," I told him, hoping to keep the discussion short and sweet. "My vengeance demon loved every moment of it. The rest, however... I did not willingly take part in. Rad was the only demon I slept with by choice."

If there was anything I could say to ease his mind and upset him at the same time, that apparently was it. He paced away from the fireplace, hovering by his desk. "Do you have any idea what the spirit means by you're almost ready for him to possess you?"

"I don't recognize the spirit but understand the rest. Michael attacked me yesterday and branded a message to Lucifer on my brain. The attack left me unable to smell or taste, and eventually, it will rob me of my memories and make me unable to resist Michael's efforts to use me to kill Lucifer's child."

Dru's countenance went a paler shade of vampire porcelain. He dropped into his desk chair. "When were you going to tell me?"

"I'm telling you now."

"What are we going to do?"

I liked the way he said 'we.' "We're going to exorcise that bastard inside Mo back to Hell and I'm going to figure out how to use Michael's sword against him."

"Is that all?" Smart-assy.

I smiled. "Sounds fun, right?"

"Not particularly. You know how to perform an exorcism?"

"Sort of, and I happen to know a priest who can back me up."

"And Michael's sword? How are you going to use it against him?"

"I have a plan." *A loose one anyway.*

"Care to share?"

Hard to share the details when I didn't have them entirely figured out yet. "Not yet, but I promise I won't leave you out of the loop."

Not seeming appeased in the least, he downed his liquor.

## 22

*V*icky's protection spell held until I was back at the Institute. Neve, Maddy, and Brianna yelled at me for not answering my phone—they'd apparently been texting and calling, but I'd turned off the thing while at the church and had conveniently forgotten to turn it back on, missing my three-hour deadline by a good forty-five minutes.

As I walked through the halls, they reeled off a litany of issues they'd had to deal with while I was gone: the copy machine had broken down yet again, the dual hot water heaters couldn't keep up with the amount of showering the angels were doing, and a fight had broken out between Tabriss and Hilary, one of the angels who'd arrived over a month ago.

I'd really wanted to spend the full night at the church and watch the sunrise, but the sun was coming up, and I was back at work. My demon was hyper from having dealt with Michael, the goddesses, Vicky, the rogue vampires, and a possessed Mo. As the Three Stooges followed on my heels, complaining about my absence and reeling off their problems, my demon scratched inside my chest, her sharp claws ripping through my lungs as if she were peeling wallpaper off her cage. I needed another go with the vampires at the cemetery. Fresh blood and a little violence always hit the spot.

"Enough." I whirled on the three females. I had more things to worry about than copy machines and hot showers. "Call the office supply place and order a new copier," I said to Neve. All three took a step back, no doubt seeing the demon in my eyes. "Maddy, have Di place a supernatural timer on the showers. She can also assign the angels bathroom shifts. Brianna, talk to Tabriss and Hilary. Put the fear of God—or Lucifer, I don't really care which—into both of them. If they get into it again, put them in the torture chamber."

"Um," Neve said with reluctance. "The torture chamber is now the chapel, remember?"

A rogue grin twisted my lips. "Then I'll turn Damon's office into a torture chamber, and believe me, I will bloody well enjoy inflicting maltreatment on anyone who complains about their accommodations that, oh, by the way, I don't have to grant."

I turned and headed for the stairs. Neve called after me. "But you said there was no money for a new copier."

"Tell Lucifer to pony up," I said. "He's got plenty of coin."

"But...but..."

I hit the door to the stairwell. "And tell the priest I need to see him."

She would never talk to Lucifer. He scared the shit out of her. But I figured if she wanted that new copy machine bad enough, she'd either overcome her fear or find an alternate source of funding.

A small cluster of angels stood grouped in the stairwell near the second floor. They went wide-eyed when they saw me and immediately stopped talking. I paid them little heed. "Shouldn't you be in the training center?" I said as I passed them.

The two female angels fled toward the door. The bolder male, an arrogant prick named Yael who was always stirring things up, said to my back, "Cole isn't there. What's the point?"

I stopped mid-step and turned to face him. Even though he was a step below me, I barely had to look down to meet his eyes. "What's the *point*? Did you not just spend an eternity buried in the Lost City Angels? Are you not preparing to join with Lucifer to take back Heaven?"

He shrugged, his obsidian eyes looking more demonic than angelic. I couldn't smell his magic, but it still tingled my other senses. From what I remembered, he had a spicy, bitter edge. "I know how to fight other angels. What I need is a demon."

There was challenge in those midnight black eyes. An invitation. One I had no time or inclination to oblige.

A caustic reply teased the tip of my tongue. I bit it back. The angels were like spoiled children. Some of them had evolved after going through the Great War of Heaven. Others had turned bitter and martyr-ish. The only way this angel would learn not to bother me in the future was for me to put him in his place now.

Balling both hands into fists, I gave him a patronizing smile as if I might seriously be entertaining his childish provocation. Then I loosed my hands, flinging out a punch of magic at him with all ten fingers.

The magic hit him as I intended, smacking into his angelic aura like a sonic boom. He hadn't even considered I might lash out at him, so he had no shields up.

He flew across the stairwell, hitting the concrete wall so hard the blocks broke. His body dropped to the landing, where he went fetal.

"You bitch," he bit out, grimacing with pain as he slowly uncurled. His companions—eavesdropping below—ran back up the steps to bend over him and try to help him up. "What the hell is your problem?"

"My problem is you, Yael. Get back to the training center and figure out how to defend yourself from me. Once you can do that, then you can ask me what the *point* of training is."

I left him with his friends and continued to my office.

Rad was squatted on the floor by the door. Cole leaned against the wall across from it, one knee bent, his booted foot leaving marks on the paint. They were talking in low tones and Cole actually had a grin on his face. It was so rare to see them together and not at each other's throats, I paused.

But, of course, they felt my magic and heard the fire door shut behind me. The two fell silent. The grin slid off Cole's face.

"Where the hell have you been?" he asked, glaring at me.

Rad gave me the same question silently with his eyes.

"I had business at the vamp House." It was partially true. I unlocked the office door and shrugged off my coat.

They followed me inside, Rad flopping down on the sofa as I hung my coat on a hook. "That's not what Brianna said."

"Mo is possessed," was all I offered, flopping into my desk chair.

The two men exchanged a look—one that said there was something they weren't telling me.

Rad sat forward, elbows on knees. "I caught our clown. He's downstairs in a cell next to Maria. You were right, he's not just an urban legend. He's real, and he's a sklero demon."

"Sklero?" That made sense. The Greeks had based their *sklêro-paiktês* theatre clowns on actual demons who played like children. The demons also played *with* children, only their version of playing included sexual molestation and cannibalism. "Did you find any of the missing kids?"

Rad shook his head. "That's why I didn't off him. Figured you might want to interrogate him and see if you could find out where his hideout is."

"Good plan." I pushed myself back out of the chair, feeling

older than my three hundred and some years. "Let's go ream this guy."

"One problem," Cole said, standing in front of the door with his feet planted and his burly arms crossed over his chest.

"What's that?" I asked.

"He's possessed."

"You're kidding."

Rad put his palms up. "We weren't sure what it was, and then you said Mo was possessed. That's the only term that comes close to the way this demon is acting. Like he's possessed. How is that possible?"

Before I could explain, Cole jumped in. "How exactly did you figure out Mo's possessed? How can a demon be possessed by another demon?"

"Not a demon." As I glanced down at Michael's sword lying on the desk still, it seemed to glow. "Michael."

"Fuck," Rad said.

I plopped back down in the leather chair. "I don't know how it works exactly, but the demon possessing Mo made reference to my time at the Court with Maria, only it wouldn't state specifically who it was, and I have the distinct impression it was goading me and Dru. For what purpose, I'm not sure, but after thinking about it, I believe it was trying to get me to lash out at it. Either that or perhaps get Dru angry at me. I had a group of rogue vampires assault me during the night, as well as a run-in with an angel right before I got up here. It's got to be Michael. He's infected me by suppressing my senses, and while he's waiting for me to become vulnerable, he's turning other supernaturals against me to weaken me further."

"Distraction, diversion, and division," Cole said, nodding. "Classic three-prong technique to weaken your enemy."

A knock on the door sounded. Cole opened it to Salmad. "Kali? Neve said you needed to see me."

I motioned him in. "Is it possible for Michael to possess

supernaturals but make it look like it's demon possession? We believe he can possess me because of my spiritual lineage, but what about other entities?"

Salmad's bushy brows squeezed together. "Why would an angel such as Michael have want to possess other entities?"

"A Dread demon, who's part vamp, as well as another demon downstairs are showing signs of demon possession. The Dread spoke of me being *almost ready* for Michael to take control of me. The archangel is coming at me from multiple sides. I need to know how to protect my flanks, so regardless of whether he has the motivation, can he do it?"

Salmad sat and rubbed his hands together. His eyes twinkled a bit, as if sharing his knowledge made him happy. Probably did. "Michael is an interesting character, and definitely the most famous of all the angels, outside of Lucifer. He's only mentioned three times in the Hebrew Bible, but he took on enormous importance to the Jews who see him as their personal protector."

"The *Hebrew* Bible?" Cole asked.

"Old Testament," I supplied. "Which doesn't tell me if he's actually capable of possessing other entities, including me."

Salmad didn't acknowledge my impatience. "In the New Testament, he's seen as Heaven's protector: '...*there was war in heaven. Michael and his angels fought against the dragon, and the dragon and his angels fought back. But he was not strong enough, and they lost their place in heaven.*' Revelation 12. Most people consider him a protector of humans as well, not only spiritually but physically. He's been sainted and had churches named after him."

"I'm aware he's famous." I tried not to gag. "That doesn't answer my question."

"Of course." Salmad sat straighter. "There are religions and scholars who believe Michael is a reference to Jesus Christ himself, in heaven, both in his pre-human state as well as his post-resurrection state."

Great. "He's not Jesus. He is, however, a pain in the ass."

"He's often depicted pinning down a demon with his sword, which I believe symbolizes slaying the ego."

"Or slaying a demon." At his raised brow, I added, "Sometimes an angel slaying a demon is just an angel slaying a demon. There's nothing symbolic about it."

"Can he possess her?" Rad asked, growing impatient. "And could that actually open the door to exorcising him back to Heaven?"

Good thought.

Salmad stood. "I'll have to do some research, but since he's the angel who brought a legion of fellow angels against Lucifer in Heaven, I'd say he can do pretty much anything he pleases. However, I doubt any demon can handle Michael, or any archangel for that matter, possessing them. The angelic energy would be far too intense."

And yet, the nudge in my gut was there. Maybe he had ways to tone down the angel mojo. "The war against Lucifer was in Heaven where Michael was most powerful." My gaze dropped to the sword on my desk. "What's his power source when he's on earth?"

All eyes followed my gaze. With all of our energies directed at it, the golden sword glowed, shimmering with power.

"He's a heavenly being," Salmad said. "His energy source is internal from God Himself."

I pointed at the sword. "But he channels it through this, doesn't he? That's how he conquers evil, demons, whatever. He needs his sword to connect him with Heaven's power just like I need the earth to connect me with mine."

Salmad looked perplexed. "I suppose that is a possibility, but I doubt..."

I was already up and moving, snagging the sword. "Cole,

call Dru and tell him to bring Mo and meet us downstairs in the dungeon. Rad, you and Sal, come with me."

"What are you doing?" Sal asked as Rad followed me out the door.

The sword felt heavy and light at the same time in my hand. "Testing a theory."

## 23

*T*he sklero demon was as ugly as any clown, tiny compared to Mo, and full of a pixie or imp type of energy. Big eyes, big mouth, spiky hair, a childish, grating laugh. That laugh echoed down the hall of cells, raising the hair on my arms, as I peered in at him through the six-inch slit of his cell.

It's no surprise to me that so many humans have nightmares about clowns. There is nothing remotely cute or funny about them, or the demons that originally inspired them, in my opinion.

*Those poor kids.* I wondered if any of the missing children were still alive. Fat chance this demon would tell me.

But I had Michael's sword on my side, and I know a thing or two about getting entities to talk.

The sklero acted much like Mo had. It chattered unintelligently, giggled, locked pupil-less eyes on me as I watched it through the door. I had the feeling it was telling me something, but I didn't understand its language of choice.

"What do you think?" Rad asked. "Possession?"

"Foaming at the mouth, seizures, those eyes..." I nodded. "Same as Mo, only more *Chuckie* and less *Evil Dead*."

"Have you been Netflixing without me again?"

"When do I have time to Netflix?"

Sal stood on my other side. "I don't believe I've ever seen a demon possess another demon."

"Exactly." The sword pulsed in my hand. Volante had moved to my other arm, not liking the angelic juice coming off of it. "Which is why I think Michael is possessing both this one and Mo somehow. Which means he's found a way into the Institute."

A heavy silence fell as my entourage absorbed that.

"Even if he is inside this demon," I said, "he can't seem to do anything of importance yet, and that's how I intend to keep it. He's stirring up the Fallen too. I don't know how, but he is. Anything he can do to cause me trouble and keep me distracted from protecting myself from him."

"Smart." Rad acknowledged Cole who came down the dank hallway and joined us. "The more he keeps you off your game, the more vulnerable you are."

"The vamps are on their way," Cole said. "What are you planning?"

"I haven't decided." I shrugged. "A little torture, a bit of bloodletting, maybe some killing."

"Kali," Sal warned.

"As the enforcer, you know I put an end to many demons in order to save humans, right?" I asked the priest.

He let go of a tight sigh. "I'm aware."

Rad bristled slightly at the condemnation in Sal's voice. "This bastard hurt and killed six children in the past couple of weeks. He deserves to die."

Sal nodded, his Adam's apple bobbing. "You're right. He's probably unrepentant and unredeemable."

Redemption. What an interesting and truly human concept. I swept my hand over the physical and magical locks. "Let's get the show on the road."

Inside, the demon lunged at me. I smacked him with the flat side of the blade and sent him flying back against the stones. He hissed, his cheek sizzling from the burn clearly outlined on his pasty skin.

"Who's possessing you?" I demanded.

The others followed me in, filling the cell with protective energy. These chivalrous males, feeling the need to safeguard my well-being, made me smile.

It also made me itchy because, seriously, I am more powerful than all of them put together, even on a bad day.

The sklero bared his teeth in what was supposed to be a grin, leaning forward and licking his lips. "The Master wants you. He can already taste your obedience. Submit to him."

"I doubt he tastes anything other than my insolence." I leveraged the point of the sword at his face, and he backed up. "I'm not really the obedient type."

"Whoa." Maddy appeared in the doorway, Brianna looking over her shoulder. "What the hell?"

"Do you work for Michael," I asked the demon. "Is he possessing you?"

A cackle. A twist on his chains. "I am your downfall."

"Many others have thought the same, and yet, here I am." I poked him in the chest, drawing another hiss as steam rose from his dirty skin. "Is your master the archangel Michael?"

A string of that other language exploded from his mouth, along with spit. Drool ran down the side of his big mouth.

Yummy.

Maddy stepped into the already crowded cell. "Why would Michael want to possess *that*?"

"The Lord moves in mysterious ways," I said.

Sal coughed at the snide comment.

Poking the demon lower, I pressed the sword tip to his nether region. "Where are the human children you kidnapped?"

The sizzling sound was bad enough, and apparently, the smell of his burning privates must have been atrocious since all around me, my fellow supes began gagging and covering their noses. For once, the inability to smell held an advantage.

The demon screamed, cursed, and slammed himself as far back against the stones as he could. A rush of sweet power skipped through me.

Ah, yes. I do love the power of inflicting pain. It is dangerous and intoxicating.

This was what the demon in me was born to do...torture and kill for vengeance. While I'd suppressed my baser needs many times over the last few centuries, the craving was still there, always waiting, always at the ready.

Power, for me, is as exhilarating as sex or dark magic. Not power like being in charge of the Institute—that was about control and order. Managing people and things. The type I craved was about dominance, potency, and having a being at my mercy.

I breathed deeply, enjoying the heady sensation of it tingling my blood.

Though an angel rather than a demon, I suspected Michael felt the same way. He was used to getting his way, having humans worship him almost as much as, if not more than, God.

The sklero breathed in gasps, his back flat against the wall, blood and pus dripping down his legs. He chuckled, but the sound was strained. His blue eyeballs whirled in their sockets. "Children. So...delicious. Cleaned their bones, I did. Their souls are his."

The power lighting up my cells cooled, my stomach churning. "Whose? Your master's?"

"He told me they were mine for the taking. All mine."

"In exchange for what?"

The demon banged his head back on the stones hard enough that I heard a crunch. "Mine, mine, mine."

I sliced the blade across his chest, getting his attention. "In exchange for what?"

He leered at me, body twitching as a black substance oozed from the wound. "Blood for blood. Bone for bone. Soul for soul."

Cole huffed. "This is a waste of time."

I sensed Brianna go on alert, and at the same time, a new sensation entered my bloodstream. "They're here."

Dru and his vamps had arrived with Mo. I motioned for Cole to meet and escort them downstairs. He left the cell, and I felt Brianna leave to follow as well.

"Are any of the children still alive?" I asked the demon.

His drooling lips turned up in another macabre grin. "They dance in my blood."

"I'll take that as a no." Stepping forward, I pressed the tip of the blade to the base of his throat. He froze, but the grin didn't fade. "Tell me Michael didn't give you those children in exchange for you allowing him to possess you."

"You're next, you know." A swipe of his tongue along his upper teeth. "The master has promised me the most delicious feast."

I heard Cole, Dru, and the others coming down the stairs. Felt the tug of Dru and his vampires on my blood.

"Sorry to ruin your party," I said to the sklero, "but I'm not dancing to you or your master's tune."

With that, I ran him through with the sword.

It flashed a bright yellow, and the demon chained to the wall exploded, sending body parts and black goo everywhere. The explosion of magic knocked me backward, where I bounced into Rad, feeling like I'd just been zapped by a giant lightning bolt.

Rad and I hit the far wall with enough impact, even my superior reflexes couldn't keep me from rebounding so hard I ended up on my knees.

Once the room stopped glowing, I picked a blue eyeball from my hair and shucked it to the ground as I regained my footing and stood. I offered Rad a hand and pulled him to his feet as well.

Sal was also on his ass, wiping black stuff from his face. "Was that necessary?"

*Hell, yeah.* "Suck it up, priest."

Rad helped him up as I wiped the blade off and went to meet Dru.

Mo was covered in what appeared to be plastic wrap, but I felt the invisible magical filaments buried in the clear restraint. They had a quality that created a tough binding with the Dread demon's own magic, making it nearly impossible, possessed or not, for him to break.

Cole led the group into a cell next to the dismembered sklero, and I waited until Mo's head was freed from its binding. The two vampires who'd carried him in moved aside, and Dru stepped closer to me. Another layer of protective magic joined that of Rad, Cole, and Sal's. Even Maddy, Brianna, and the vampire guards teemed with it.

Which gave me a moment of pause.

As supernaturals, we faced danger on a daily basis in order to survive. While some of it put us on edge, there were few things any of us truly feared.

Yes, I was the leader of the Institute, Rad's lover, and the queen of the Chicago Nation of the Undead – all reasons to protect me – but I sensed the rise in magic in the cell had more to it than that.

They were scared.

More scared than any of them had been when we faced the Four Horsemen and the impending apocalypse.

This wasn't just about me. If Michael could take over demons at will, if he could possess me and force me to kill Lucifer's child, anyone could become a pawn in his game.

To those of us in that dungeon cell, being an archangel's bitch is worse than Armageddon any day.

I pointed the tip of Michael's sword at Mo's throat. "I killed your friend, the sklero. You're next unless you answer my questions. I know Michael is possessing you. That he offered you something in exchange for your meat suit. What?"

Mo's head rolled from one side to the other. His eyeballs were now a shade of greenish-yellow. His tongue lolled out of his mouth, but he didn't respond verbally.

"Answer me."

The Dread screamed, his head going back, neck muscles straining. The next second, the sword flashed, and smoke shot out of Mo's mouth, heading for the ceiling.

"Oh, no, you don't." I cursed, jabbing the sword at the smoke, the essence of whatever possessed the Dread trying to escape.

After the mess with the sklero demon, I'd mentally upped my own protective shield so I didn't get knocked off my feet again. Good thing I did. The sword clanged against the vapor, instead of passing through it, hitting a shield of protection and rebounding on me.

I held firm and felt Rad's hands land on my arm holding the sword. Volante shivered. Next came Dru's hands, then others. Their magics coursed through me, and I stabbed at the vapor again.

With another burst of energy, it exploded. Hot, jagged particles, like embers of a fire, rained down on us, singeing our clothes, burning our skin.

While the others made haste to knock the embers away and put out their smoking clothes, I hacked at the smoke some more. It evaporated in a poof of light that blinded me momentarily.

Hands patted my hair, my shirt. Sure enough, a section of my hair was smoking, and I had a significant burn hole in my shirt, which Rad and Maddy worked to put out. The top of one boot was still on fire, the heat working through the leather. For a second, I flashed back to my bedroom when Tabriss had woken me, and I'd thought I'd smelled burning hair. A harbinger of what was to come?

Mo was no longer with us, his body a lump of smoking carcass on the floor. I pressed my boot against his leg, snuffing out the tiny fire.

"So much for that." I did a quick inventory of my group. All seemed well, although a bit worse for wear. "I didn't even get to draw blood."

Vexed and exasperated gazes returned mine.

"Sal," I motioned at the priest with the sword. "That smoke that left Mo's body – angel or demon?"

He shrugged. "I couldn't say."

"That flash of light?" Maddy said. "That was no demon."

"But it was a pretty small flash for an angel," Rad added.

I waved my entourage out of the cell. They formed a circle around me in the hall. "But the smoke definitely appeared demon-like, right?"

Everyone nodded.

So, were we dealing with good or evil? I still wasn't sure.

"Ooh, I know." Maddy snapped her fingers. "Maybe Michael's like Voldemort. He's divided up his soul into seven Horcruxes, and each one can possess a demon and make it do his bidding."

Rad and Cole both rolled their eyes. Sal looked confused, not understanding the Harry Potter reference. Dru and Brianna had curious expressions as if they were conducting their own mental conversation—probably because they were. One I had no interest in eavesdropping on.

At first thought, I blew it off like Rad and Cole. Then Dru's eyes caught mine, I could see the internal debate going on in his head. *Is it possible?* he mentally asked, drawing me into the vampire conversation.

*I'm sure I wouldn't know.*

"Sal, you might be right." I crossed my arms, the sword dangling from my right hand. "Michael is exceptionally powerful and a demon body would be an impossible vessel for him to fully possess because his angelic energy would destroy it. Maddy may be right, too. Michael may not be dividing up his soul, but perhaps he's dividing up his powers."

Dru nodded. "Even a little bit of angel juice could eventually turn a demon mad, but before it does, Michael uses the demon to taunt and threaten you."

"Like a terrorist," Cole said, leaning against the wall. "He gets under your skin, makes you fear him, and drives you crazy not knowing when or where he might strike."

I felt the air change, stiffen, and my pulse did a hard bang at the base of my throat. Michael's sword buzzed in my hand, almost painfully, as the king of Hell's magic swirled in, dark and seductive. Lucifer materialized a few feet away in the shadows.

His eyes glowed as they locked on me right before he stepped out of the shadows. Everyone backed away, gazes downcast, magics jumping. "I felt a tremor in the shield over the Institute. What have you done?"

A tremor, huh? Michael was in for a lot more than that if I figured out how to kick him and his wings back to Heaven.

"What if his target isn't me?" I asked the group, ignoring Lucifer's question.

Which was dangerous, yes, but I had the uncanny feeling

Michael's sword itched to take a swing at Lucifer and would protect me if the devil tried to hit me with any magic.

Which was pretty damn cool if you asked me, and I wasn't above provoking Lucifer to find out. I tightened my grip on the sword, now enjoying the reckless buzz vibrating my palm.

Sal glanced at Lucifer, back to me. "What do you mean?"

I addressed the devil this round. "Michael used me to send you a message, saying he would possess me and kill your child. Why didn't he just do it? Why send you a message first? Why give you time to raise your defenses and prepare for his attack?"

Lucifer gave me an impatient glare. "Is that a rhetorical question?"

"Is your brother a bully? Does he want to make you squirm?"

"Of course, he's a bully, and yes, he would love to put me on the torture racks and have a go at me."

"Under this roof, he has the original Mary Magdalene and the seven vices, as well as the Fallen in great numbers. You visit on a regular basis. If I were him, I would figure out a way to smash through our wards, powerful as they are, and wipe us all off the face of the planet."

One long finger that had no doubt wielded a lot of destruction through the millennia pointed at the sword. "He cannot destroy me and the Fallen without using that."

"It's like the elder wand." Maddy snapped her fingers again. "And Kali?"

"Yeah?"

"You took the elder wand from Michael, so it belongs to you now. That's why he has to possess you in order to use it!"

Lucifer frowned in confusion. Apparently, he wasn't a Potter fan either. "That's not how it works."

"How *does* it work, then?" I asked. "I know the wand—I mean, the *sword*—is how Michael channels his power, and it belongs to him, but I did just use it to de-possess a couple of demons and send them back to Hell."

"You?" Lucifer's dark brows went skyward. "You used the sword?"

"I did. On a dread and a sklero."

"They had no souls," Sal put in. "Perhaps that's why it destroyed them via Kali. It might be different if she were to turn the sword on you or your child."

Those dark brows lowered like a heavy fog settling over us. "Perhaps."

The weapon in question seemed to be coming down from its high over killing the demons, the buzz tapering down to a soft hum.

"At this point, that's a technicality we can't count on." I motioned at Cole and the others. "I want the Institute put on high alert. That smoke that came out of Mo, whatever it was, disappeared in a flash of light, but that doesn't mean it's not still here somewhere. Maddy, get Di and a couple of her favorite angels to scan the entire place and everyone in it, from top to bottom. Make sure there is no unwanted entity hanging around. I don't want anyone else falling prey to Michael's little game."

Turning back to Lucifer, I found the king of Hell had disapparated. *Figures.* He wasn't one for long, meaningful conversations, and I'm sure he feared the Institute had been compromised. Either that, or he might have wondered if Michael was distracting him in order to go after his female and child.

Which, I had to admit, wasn't a bad tactic. Michael seemed to be quite the strategist.

I gathered the vampire guards who had brought Mo in and two of my dungeon guards Cole had trained. "Go over the remains of the demon bodies and check for any kind of mark, like a tattoo or any sort of talisman—a necklace, keychain, coin, you get the idea. Michael may have used something like that as a possession tool or magical conduit for his power. If you find anything, quarantine it and bring it to me."

I left them to clean up the messes and led my ragtag group of supernaturals back upstairs to my office.

While Lucifer and some of the others may have doubted my intuition, I knew I was right—Michael was throwing up smoke-screens. We didn't yet truly know his endgame.

# 24

*T*he private Gulfstream on the runway oozed magic from each and every window, door, and metal seam. Dru and I stood at the front of the vampire contingent, ready to greet his princess, rain falling softly on the umbrellas that Brianna and Cole held over our heads.

A dozen vampires formed a V behind us, their heightened, nervous energy making my own hop and fizz as if it were lava exposed to the rain. Six black Escalades waited for us and our guest.

But I had a plan, and it felt good to feel some control in my current out-of-control world. The Institute had been given the all-clear trom Di, and nothing on the bodies of the demons I'd sent to Hell suggested Michael had used any kind of special portal to possess them. "You're sure Princess Irina left her daddy-o at home?" I asked Dru.

"I confirmed it with the pilot." His blood fizzed along with mine—more so, even. He had a lot riding on my plan—his whole future, in fact. Plus, he didn't know the details since I hadn't shared them. He wasn't the queasy type, but he was a bit on the stuffy side when it came to vampire rules and decorum. "Why is that so important?"

"Trust me."

The Gulfstream's ramp descended and a tidal wave of magic rolled down the steps and out to us. I sensed it flirting with my magic, taking a sniff to see what I was.

Beside me, Dru clenched his fists.

I'm far from a gracious host. Without moving a muscle, I smacked Irina's shadowy, nightmare magic away and sent a follow-up shot of demon/vampire *try that again and I will stomp all over you* magic back to her.

A second later, she appeared at the top of the stairs, glaring.

With everything else going on, I hadn't had the chance to stalk her Instagram page, but Maddy's description summed up Irina nicely. The nightmare was decked out in a Paris runway outfit, with enough emeralds and rubies on her body to sink a ship. Amazing the private jet could get off the ground.

A small woman hustled out of the plane and skirted around Irina, carrying a roll of what appeared to be carpeting.

The woman, gray-haired and permanently bent at the waist, gave a snap of her wrists and the carpet unrolled and floated down perfectly, hugging the steps like it was made for them.

*For fuck's sake.*

Dru's nails would soon draw blood if he kept clenching them. Reaching over, I played the part of his lover and queen, taking one of his balled hands and stroking it. The clenched fist relaxed, and I slipped my fingers between his. He shot me a look. I smiled at him as if he were the most amazing supernatural on the planet.

*Don't worry*, I told him. *I've got your back.*

He checked himself. A return smile told me he trusted me. He was in for the ride and would support whatever I did.

Power. I love it.

Around us, our vampire clan released a collective mental

breath. As their Master relaxed and shifted into his normal, dominant role once more, they were reassured. Together, he and I would face this problem and send it—her—packing.

For half a second, I felt for all of them. It wasn't bad enough that they had to fear Michael's wrath and childish vengeance on all of us, they also had to deal with a vampire princess who wasn't even a vampire, threatening to take over Chicago. The irony was, they had to place their faith in me – the demon they called queen. Talk about damned if you do, damned if you don't.

It was driving them mad with worry.

Which made me smile even wider as I flashed my pearlies at Irina.

Once the older woman disappeared, two males took her place, flanking the nightmare. Dark suits, sunglasses, and a pissed-off attitude. Bodyguards.

I couldn't smell them, but from the way Volante chafed against my arm, I sensed they were properly attired with weapons.

*Merc demons?* I mentally asked Cole.

*Nope,* he responded. *Not demons, per se. More like...*

He stopped as both of the bodyguards pointedly looked at him as if hearing him speak of them aloud.

*Wards,* I mentally demanded of everyone in our group. *Raise them, now!*

Mine had been in place since the moment we arrived. For me, it was habit. I didn't go many places, especially to meet someone new, without a tight cloak over my thoughts and emotions.

Dru's were also carefully hidden, but most of the others hadn't bothered, not realizing our visitors would be able to listen in on our telepathy.

The snap of personal protection magic hit so hard in our

group of supes, it felt like a shockwave. Irina and her guards felt it too, bringing a snide smile to her ruby-red lips.

A nightmare who could pick up on vampire/demon thoughts? That was a new one for me.

My instincts told me to move carefully. Like Michael and his hidden agenda, I suddenly had the sense Irina was more than her designer dress and high heels.

I hate introductions, especially when I have to play a role I don't fully embrace, but I did so, allowing Dru to go through formalities. Irina's magic was slippery, smoke-like, as it danced around me while she was informed of my place in Chicago House.

One of her skinny brows arched at the same time her lips turned down. "But Alexandru," she said as the rain began in earnest, "I'm to be your queen."

"Too late," I said, enjoying this little power play. I knew she wouldn't give up easily, and I was looking forward to the challenge. "However, with some negotiation, I'm sure we can all come to a new agreement that gives you my position while benefitting me as well."

"Negotiation?" Her dark eyes studied me with faint curiosity. Her pert pink tongue darted out, licking her bottom lip, and then her teeth chewed on it, sex kitten-style. "I'm afraid you don't understand the situation, Ms. Sweet. I have no need to negotiate for a title that already belongs to me."

I suppose that little display was supposed to confuse the stupid vengeance demon rather than make her message clear.

As Dru had warned, she was coming for me and looking forward to eating me up.

*Basic bitch move there, sweetheart.*

Princess Irina still didn't understand who she was dealing with, although the rubies in her earrings and necklace darkened at my energy, suddenly a threat.

They do that, you know. Queen Maria wore a giant one

around her neck at all times, relying on it to warn her of imminent danger. Maria's often turned nearly black when I was around – one of the reasons the Queen kept me at her mercy.

Too bad Irina relied more on her bodyguards than her ostentatious jewelry.

I, on the other hand, didn't need rubies or anything else to warn me of threats. If any other supernatural had graced me with such a blatant warning, I would have set Volante on them in a heartbeat. As it was, Dru's hand, still entangled with mine, gave a sharp squeeze. "This is America, not Romania," he told Irina. "The politics are complicated."

"Let's get out of this rain." My voice actually came out good-natured. I motioned Irina and her guards toward the SUVs waiting for us beyond the gate. "We wouldn't want to be accused of bad manners, would we, Master Dru?"

That earned me a look. When did I ever refer to him as my Master? The flood of heat that engulfed my blood told me he liked it. A lot.

I would need to remind him this was just a game.

Moments later, everyone was in an Escalade and winging away from the airport. Only we weren't heading to the House as Irina expected.

The nightmare was about to become a prisoner, along with the others in my dungeon. From the lead vehicle, I dialed Neve. "Arrival time fifteen minutes, depending on traffic. You and Salmad better have my torture chamber ready."

# 25

*ou can't do this,"* the princess raged at me from behind the bars of her new cage.

Her bodyguards had been dead before we hit the Institute's gates. Cole and one of Dru's security men had knocked Irina out, dragged her down to the dungeon, and shoved her into a cell.

It was too easy, I tell you. Too damn easy.

The wards down here were enough to suppress her magic, even when she came to and realized she was my prisoner.

I was on a roll, interrogating and exacting vengeance, and I was eager to play with Michael's sword again.

For now, I stroked Volante, who hung around my neck. "I don't like having you here anymore than you like being here. Call off the wedding, leave Dru and the Chicago House alone, and you can be on your way."

"I will never bow to you."

"I'm not asking for your subjugation, although I would enjoy that." I ran a finger along the metal bars, close to her increasingly panicked face. "I'm protecting the Chicago House, as is my duty as vamp queen. You are not a vampire princess, and although you and your family claim that there is an engagement in place, no one here in America cares one wit about that, and the vampire king who arranged it is long dead, making the engagement null and void."

"We are bound by a *constringo*," she yelled as if I were deaf. Her voice echoed off the dungeon's walls. "That contract can never be broken!"

Spit landed on a rust-coated bar, and I backed up. "Never say never, Irina. My friend, Sal, looked it up and told me right before we got here that there is a clause that applies in this situation. Both parties agree to annul the agreement and exchange a new blood oath that it is so, and the salt bond will dissolve."

"Bullshit. There is no such clause."

"I'm afraid there is, and either way, the *constringo* will end here tonight. See, I have friends in very low places. Friends with angel magic."

"Angels? What does that have to do with this?"

Michael's sword was in the corner. Every time I glanced at it, it glowed, letting me know it was ready to do my bidding. All I had to do was ask.

Boy, did I want to ask.

"Angels, *vitiums*, Mary Magdalene, even Lucifer." I flicked some magic at her. "Some pretty damn powerful entities live and work here at the Institute. The place I am in charge of. We all believe it's in our best interest to remove the *constringo* – at whatever cost that entails to you – in order to keep the House out of your control."

I hadn't discussed this with anyone, not even Dru, but I thought it was a nice touch to make it sound like I had.

"Lucifer?" Irina spit again, this time on purpose and directed right at me. "You don't have the power to break the *constringo*. No one does. Alexandru is mine, which makes me queen of the Undead here, and there's nothing you can do about it. Not even if you throw the name of the Prince of Hell around. As *if*!"

She thought I was bluffing. In her shoes, I would have thought the same.

I picked up the sword, the black hilt warming instantly in my palm. Raising the blade, I turned it back and forth in front of the bars. The meager light of the cell was replaced with the sword's angelic illumination, making Irina gasp and step backward.

"Do you know whose sword this is?" I asked.

Her gaze locked on the blade, the white light morphing to an icy blue shade that reminded me of Michael's eyes.

When she didn't answer, I continued. "Archangel Michael's. Ever heard of him? I used this sword yesterday to send two demons back to Hell, but not until after I tortured them a little just for fun. I'm curious how much good I can get out of this thing. I bet it can break your salt blood bond to Dru. Shall we try it?"

Her gaze turned wary. Obviously, this was new territory for her, but she was smart enough not to spit on me this time or rush to false bravado. That pink tongue of hers snuck out again and licked her bottom lip, the wheels in her head spinning.

She didn't want to believe she'd been had and searched for a way to disregard the possibility. "Why would you be in possession of Michael's holy sword? A demon cannot wield such a thing. You lie."

I shrugged. "Touch it. See what happens."

Self-preservation is one of the strongest motivators around. She took another step back, her inner dark magic warning her in a way her rubies couldn't. "You've cursed it, this imposter sword. I would not be so gullible."

I had to admit, that was smart.

"I do have some powerful witches down here in these cells," I told her, motioning behind me. "But no one needs to curse the sword, and I would never believe you to be gullible. I'm telling the truth – this can cut the evil right out of you and leave you a vegetable, never able to invade someone's dreams again, much less take over the Undead House. If you don't believe me, I'm happy to prove it to you."

Near-silent footsteps came up behind me. "Show her this."

Maddy held out her phone. She'd pulled up a video of me using the sword on Mo earlier.

"You recorded the exorcism?"

A smack of her gum and a nod. Her eyes were solemn, almost pleading with me to get rid of the nightmare once and for all. "Insurance for something like this," she said.

I motioned for her to hold it up, then shifted out of the way so she had better access to the peephole of bars and the pale face of our prisoner on the other side.

As the video played and Irina blanched a shade of angelic white, I set the sword's blade on my shoulder. "Looks fun, right?"

Irina turned her back on us and paced away. Maddy replayed the video, turning up the volume so Mo's cries rang amongst the dungeon stones. A row away, I sensed Maria's demon and Vicky's vamp blood rising to taste the fear and pain that hovered in the air.

"Stop it," Irina yelled a moment later as the sound of Mo's sizzling skin echoed off the stones. "Shut it off!"

I nodded at Maddy to pause the video. "Ready to agree to my terms?"

She hadn't even heard all of them yet, but it didn't hurt to push. She was, after all, facing a painful death by a holy sword.

She whirled, pinning me with her sharp gaze. "I want to speak to Alexandru."

Dru had observed the whole thing from a shadowy corner a few feet away. He stepped forward before I could wave him off. "You've yoked me to this agreement my whole life, Irina. It's time to let it go. You'll be fairly compensated, but I will not marry you."

Compensated?! *Pul-lease.* "I think it best if I do the negotiating, Dru."

He rolled his eyes, and Irina grabbed the bars from the inside, giving him a look that reminded me of the old damsel-in-distress routine. "Please, Alexandru. There is no compensation for what your family took from me. My mother! I can never get her back! But being with you – I've dreamed of being your bride since I was a girl. I've been schooled and brought up as royalty to be your queen! You cannot want this...this demon freak...instead of me."

Her voice rose on those last three words, making it sound like a question. I snorted, the label *demon freak* swimming around my brain. She had that right.

Volante snaked down and tightened on my left arm, and the sword's glow went a dark red that was deeper than Irina's rubies, as if the blade were mirroring the blood lust I felt for the bitch.

At the blood-red glow, Maddy, Dru, and Irina all fell back in unison.

*Shazam!* I was really starting to like this thing.

"Last chance, Irina." I spun the sword and pointed the tip at her. It felt so natural, so right, in my hand. "Agree to end the contract, by which you can take your nightmarish ass back to Europe and go on with your life, or I'll end said life here and now."

"Alexandru!" she squeaked. "Help me!"

The vamp Master crossed his arms over his chest and sent her a flat, uncaring stare.

"Can I have her earrings?" Maddy asked, peering at Irina's jewelry. She moved closer and acted like she was trying to see the nightmare's feet. "What's your shoe size? Those are Louboutins, aren't they?"

Irina made a growling noise and her magic surged, even though the wards in the dungeon suppressed the worst of it. She hit the bars, and with my extraordinary speed, I deftly grabbed Maddy and hauled her back. I had the sense that Irina's spit might hold some kind of poison, and hell, if any of us needed yet another contagion to deal with.

At the same time, I stuck the sword through the metal and nicked the vampire wanna-be princess on her bottom lip, burning a jagged line across it.

She screamed and fell back, grabbing at her lip as she hit the far wall. As the echo faded, Maria and Vicky's magics hummed again. Even Dru's magic *thudthud-ed* against mine.

Maybe that damsel-in-distress thing works for some people.

I laughed. Out loud. Rather than feeling sorry for her, or getting high on her pain, I thought it was humorous.

Could have been the surge of Michael's power in my veins, too.

"Dru's going to call your father and you will speak to him," I told Irina, who now crouched on the floor, back against the wall. "You're going to tell him the deal is off. You don't want to marry Dru or stay in Chicago. The nightmares are to leave the Undead Nation alone from here on out. If he does not agree to that, or you go back on your word, I will hunt you down and kill you. Are we clear?"

I saw her jaw work. It worked some more. The gears in her head turned, but once again, self-preservation kicked in. Finally, she nodded, one sharp dip of her head.

I waited, expecting a comeback, another threat, some type of retort. None came.

Dragging Maddy behind me, I nodded at Dru to make the call and work out the arrangements for his former fiancée to return home with a new contract in hand. I didn't want to leave the area until I was sure everything went through without a hitch, so I led Maddy to the other row of cells and leaned my back against the stones. The hum of wards and magic melted against my skin.

"Thanks for the help," I said softly, listening to Dru discuss the return of Irina with her father. He was his usual cocky and competent self again, and I let go a tiny sigh of relief.

"Can I keep the ring?" She held up her hand and flashed it at me. "You know, since you're so grateful?"

Smart kid. A little manipulative, but I relented. "Yes, you can keep it. For now."

She did a fist pump in the air. "You're welcome, btw, and now will you admit that I'm the most efficient of all of your vamps and demons alike and give me a promotion?"

"Promotion?" When had she become so ambitious? "To what, Mouse?"

She shot me a narrowed-eyed look at the nickname she no longer embraced. "Liaison between the House and Institute. You need a personal assistant who understands both and can streamline your responsibilities so each receives equal attention. Right now, you're forced to deal with a lot of shit that isn't important, and it's taking time away from what is. Need I remind you that an archangel did crosswords on your brain and you're in danger of becoming his minion? You need to figure out once and for all how you're going to deal with Michael and his threat to all of us. You can't do that when Neve's bombarding you with complaints about copiers and hot water issues, and Dru's hiding in his office doing doom-and-gloom Eeyore impressions over his responsibilities."

"Hey." The Master vamp emerged beside me. "I take umbrage at that."

"Take whatever you want," Maddy said, not understanding the definition of umbrage. "Kali has more important things to do than" —she waved her arm toward Irina's cell—"worry about shit like your love life. Which, I might add, Master, you should be very grateful for. Not only did she save your ass, she saved the House as well."

Dru looked affronted at her forwardness, but after a second, he snapped his heels together and offered me a low bow. "My queen, your sycophant here is correct. You have my undying gratitude."

"I'm not a psycho," Maddy said, again misunderstanding the reference.

"Some days, you remind me of Damon," I said, pulling on a strand of her hair. "Only in reverse."

Dru straightened, and Maddy looked confused. "Whatever, dude. Do I get the job or not?"

I wasn't in the habit of handing out job descriptions. "Put something in writing for Neve and I'll sign it, but don't think you're going to spend all of your time in the media center watching movies. If you want a real job, you've got it, but I expect you to work as many hours as I do."

Her lips spread in a grin. "I need a new wardrobe. I bet you have the perfect stuff at your place." She blew me an air kiss and marched off with vampire speed. Her voice echoed down the stairs and through the halls. "I'll be back in a little while!"

"You just created a new monster," Dru said.

"Everything *capisce* with your ex-fiancée?"

He took Maddy's spot across from me and leaned on the wall. "On the surface, yes."

"Let me guess: You don't trust her or her father to prevent this from turning into World War III?"

"I've insisted on her agreement in blood before she leaves, but that doesn't mean she and her kind will not try to drive the Undead mad again."

I shrugged, Maddy's words echoing in my brain. "It's a mad world."

"I mean it when I say you have my gratitude. Whatever I can do for you in exchange, I shall."

"Anything?"

A fission of lust trickled through the air, tickling at the base of my throat. He stepped forward so he was right in front of me. His fingers stroked my jaw and chin. "All you have to do is ask."

"Don't go after Di."

Those Undead fingers dropped to his side. "What are you talking about?"

"She's my best friend, Dru. I saw the way you looked at her like she was a beautiful conquest. I get it; she is beautiful and way out of your league, but she might be curious and take the plunge. You'll both regret it if that happens, and I'll be caught in the middle."

He snickered and stroked my neck this time. "My ruse worked, but not the way I had intended."

"Your ruse?"

Magic rose. The fission of lust grew and swirled. "I wanted to make you jealous. I misled you into thinking I wanted to bed your friend in an effort to see your reaction. I was hoping you might be jealous and see yourself coming to my bed instead."

We'd been through this a dozen times. With his blood running in my veins, it was hard to deny the chemistry. But the point was moot. My heart belonged to a demon.

A half-demon, anyway. "You know I'm in love with Rad, and besides, I hate vampires, remember?"

He smiled at the joke and I expected him to walk away and finish his business getting his new blood contract with Irina in place. Instead, he lowered his face an inch from mine. "The offer stands."

He dropped a kiss on my lips, startling me, his fingers holding my chin in place.

"What the fuck?"

I jumped back, Rad's voice sending alarm bells screaming in my head. Next thing I knew, my demon lover took a swing at the Master, and caught unaware, Dru went down.

He didn't stay down, however, his strength and speed bouncing him back up just as fast. A full-on fight was about to break out until another entity arrived out of thin air. With the wrinkle of his angelic nose, he swept both males aside and pinned them to the wall.

Lucifer then glared at me. "How very disappointing to see your abuse of power, but then you are a demon."

My ire surged instantly. "Turn them loose, and for your information, this was nothing but a simple misunderstanding. I'm not using my power to turn the vamp Master and my boyfriend into alpha dogs fighting over me."

Lucifer looked pained. "I wasn't referring to the dogs." He released them, and both males slid down the wall to the floor, their magics and egos deflated. "I was referring to what you've been doing with Michael's sword."

"Oh." I felt slightly abashed, but it didn't last long. "Why wouldn't I use it if it gives me an advantage?"

"You are such a demon."

"You've mentioned that. I happen to be a damn good one, for your information, so watch the derogatory tone."

I'm sure no one had ever spoken to him like that. Honestly, I don't know where it came from.

Maybe I had a death wish. Or maybe the sword was making my usual overconfidence even more authoritative.

"Kali," Rad warned.

Lucifer drew to his full height. Dark magic ripped down my spine like a hot knife cutting me open. "Watch your own tone, or I will filet you right here."

Right. "It's the sword." Whether it was or not, I set the thing against the wall and stepped away from it, acting properly admonished. "It's very...intoxicating. And powerful, and—"

"Enough," Lucifer interrupted. You cannot use my brother's sword for miscellaneous phenomena to make your life simpler."

"He's using pieces of his magical mojo to possess demons and turn your Fallen against me, remember? The more I use the sword, the more I understand what makes Michael tick, so if you want me to avoid being used by your brother to go after your female and offspring, it's in all of our best interests for me to use the sword for anything I deem appropriate."

"I'm not referring to the demons Michael apparently possessed. I felt a ripple in the cosmos again a few minutes ago. You were using the sword, and from the looks of it, this situation had nothing to do with the Fallen or Michael."

"I didn't actually have to use the sword. I simply made the threat and resolved an issue that needed resolving for the safety of everyone under this roof."

He didn't believe me. I wasn't sure *I* believed me. But it was a good bluff and I wasn't backing down. Lucifer needed to get on board with how I handled things, or he would be on the losing end of the stick in the long run. The king of Hell was used to being as omniscient and all-powerful as his Father, so I wasn't sure he understood or could wrap his mind around that fact yet.

"Be careful, demon." His voice was even lower and more ominous than usual. "You walk a thin line. Perhaps the sword is Michael's way into your vessel. The more attached you become to its power, the less of your own willpower you possess."

He disappeared in the blink of an eye, and I released the breath I'd been holding.

Ignoring the nudge of my intuition that he was accurate in his suspicion, I helped Dru and Rad to their feet. "If you two want to waste time fighting, have at it. Dru, you owe me an apology for stepping over the line, not only with that kiss, but trying to manipulate me by using my best friend. And Rad, you know I love you, so stop letting your sensitive male ego get in the way. When you two are done with the fisticuffs, you can find me upstairs. I have work to do."

"Kali." Rad stopped me with a hand. "Wait."

Dru, his mouth a tight line, headed away from us. "I will make all of this up to you, my Queen, as soon as I'm done handling House business."

As the vamp Master disappeared up the steps and Irina cried softly in her cell on the other side of the dungeon, Rad drew me deeper into the shadows. "I'm sorry," he said, stroking my hair out of the way. "Are you okay?"

The shadows felt good, away from Michael's sword, away from the night's events. I leaned against Rad and let him rub my back as I brought him up to speed on Dru and Irina.

"Do you think he's right?" I whispered. The sword still stood several feet away and glowed as my gaze lighted on it. "Lucifer, I mean. Do you think the sword is luring me under some kind of power-trip spell because it damn sure feels good."

Rad caressed my hair. "Maybe we should put it in Damon's safe for now."

Damon's safe held an assortment of magical weapons and other things I couldn't imagine. "I don't have the combination."

"Get it."

The demon inside me was strong, and she had fed on the torture I had inflicted that day, now craving more. That's what sin and power do to you, demon, human, or angel.

A shudder ran through me. I raised my head and kissed him, needing to feel his strength and humanness. His desire immediately matched mine.

The kissing turned to other things. He hiked up my skirt and lifted me from the floor. My legs went around his waist and I let him enter me.

As Rad took me against the stone wall, the prisoners around us moaned, their magics, suppressed though they were, blending with our hedonistic appetites. We both cried out our pleasure a few minutes later, Rad banging me into the wall a few more times before we sunk to the floor, exhausted and quivering.

When the last of our pleasure subsided, leaving a lovely hum under my skin, he helped me up, righted my clothes, and stroked my hair back into place.

Even Volante had succumbed to the passion Rad and I had been surfing. I found her coiled around the blade of Michael's sword like a Kundalini serpent rising.

Great. Even my whip had fallen under the sword's power. Or maybe she had decided to embrace it since I had.

Reluctantly, I grabbed the angelic weapon with Volante still attached and followed Rad upstairs.

# 26

 *F*un isn't part of my vocabulary these days. As Rad pulled me quickly along the first-floor hallway to the kitchen, our fingers intertwined, I laughed for the hell of it, and it felt good. The sun was just beginning to rise, which meant most of the demons, vampires, and angels were bedding down, and outside of the security details changing guard, the place was eerily quiet.

Exhausted but starving, I was as ready for a snack as Rad seemed to be. From one of the walk-in coolers, he emerged with cheese and a bottle of champagne. "Grab some glasses," he told me.

A loaf of French bread, a couple of turnovers, some crackers and jam joined the champagne and cheese, all going into a basket. Then Rad grabbed my hand again and started jogging through the empty halls and up the silent stairwells to the rooftop. At one point, we passed Cole, who yelled something about Dru and his princess leaving the premises, but I was laughing too hard to care

The previous night's storm had cleared, but dark, angry clouds hung off to the northeast, blocking the sun. Golden rays shot through the clouds here and there, mixing with shadowy amethyst.

Watching the sunrise is still one of my favorite things to do. As Rad popped the champagne and filled the glasses, I fed him a grape and tore the bread into chunks.

"Remember that time we ate on top of Castle Sant'Angelo?" Rad asked, handing me a glass.

Castle of the Holy Angel. Interesting topic of conversation with Michael's sword lying nearby. "That was a long time ago."

"What a view." He sat next to me, staring out at Lake Michigan, and I wondered if he was referring to the past or our current view. "We were both so young then, facing insurmountable odds at having a life together."

I clinked my glass with his. Insurmountable odds then meant Queen Maria. "And here we are, three centuries later, in a different country, completely free from Maria's influences, and yet, facing similar doom."

"Lucifer will come through. He has his angels now. His army. I'm not worried."

Such a liar.

The castle in Rome he'd referenced had originally been built by Roman emperor Hadrian as a mausoleum for himself and his family. Through the years, it served many other purposes, such as a prison, papal fortress, and more recently, a museum. The name became *Castel Sant'Angelo* after Michael apparently appeared on the roof of the mausoleum, sheathing his sword to signify the end of the plague of 590.

It was rare Queen Maria ever let me out of her sight, but when Rad and I first fell in love, we often took stupid risks. I'd told him of my desire to stand where the famous military angel had supposedly stood so long ago, and Rad—always wanting to make me happy—had snuck us out so we could view the sunrise from that very same roof.

A quick coupling on that roof had flipped the bird at

Heaven while giving us both pleasure. Upon our return to Maria's court, we didn't escape discovery, but the punishment she doled out was worth every minute of our irreverent and unsanctioned tryst.

As I scarfed down a cherry turnover that I couldn't actually taste, I studied Rad's profile. A ray of peach-colored light crept toward him as if trying to sneak up on him. "Are you testing me to see if I'm already losing my memories?"

He shot me an incredulous glance. "Of course not. I just was thinking about that sunrise so long ago. It's one of my favorite memories."

Like the others, I sensed his fear and trepidation about the future. He was scared he was going to lose me, one way or another. I'd lose all memory of him and become Michael's killing machine unless Tabriss stuck to her word. Even if she didn't destroy me, Michael or Lucifer would.

"You think Michael's going to win this fight, don't you?" I was only half accusing him, half teasing.

He glanced down at the champagne in his glass. "Is it that obvious?"

"You're not the only one." I finished my pastry and took a long sip of my bubbly. At least I could feel the tiny explosions going down my throat. "Everyone is worried."

"We've never faced this kind of threat before."

This might be my last rooftop sunrise. I didn't want to talk about Michael and the dread that had rooted itself in my chest. There was no way this was going to be easy—that was a given —but spending time worrying about it wouldn't help.

"No matter what, I will not go after Lucifer's child."

He sighed heavily. "If you don't, someone else will."

The thought struck me dumb for a moment. I hadn't considered that Michael would keep going after the child, even if I foiled his plan to use me. "Be careful of your words, Beaumont." I pointed upward and then down. "There is always *someone* listening."

Meaning Lucifer. He would consider Rad's logic blasphemy, the words of his enemy.

"You know it's true. And this prophecy about the child...as demons, why do we care if Heaven and earth are reunited and the Fallen are allowed to return to their home?"

I glanced around, ready for the devil to appear at any moment and strike us down. Then, sending Rad a stern look, I raised my voice slightly and put some lighthearted joking into it. "Well, I, for one, would be thrilled to see them gone. No more whining about hot showers. And those feathers! They're everywhere. Yeesh. With them gone, the Institute could get back to normal, and that's all I want."

Rad rolled his eyes but took the hint. "I suppose."

I softly punched him on the arm and handed him a chunk of bread with jam on it. "No more talk of Michael or angels. Let's enjoy our breakfast."

Half an hour later, our hunger satiated in more ways than one, we packed up our rooftop picnic and adjourned to my shower to remove the last of the sticky jam from various parts of our body. We tumbled into my bed and fell into a deep, peaceful sleep.

I WOKE SOMETIME LATER, in the dark, and peered at the dark surroundings. *Where am I?*

The place seemed utterly unfamiliar.

It was certainly not my normal chambers in the castle where I served at the whim of the supernatural queen, Maria.

Rolling over, I found a tasty-looking male next to me, naked and snoring softly in his sleep.

*Il sangue*, my demon whined, and I licked my lips.

Blood. He had it, and she wanted it.

Hmm...

What's a demon to do when temptation lies sleeping next to her?

I sniffed the air and detected a scent that reminded me of the Mediterranean. My blood stirred, and the demon inside my chest reached for him. *Blood*, she demanded again.

Laced with the ocean smell, I caught the hint of something else – *human*.

So the male was a mix-blood. A half-breed.

*Not my usual type.* Humans disgusted me.

A memory awakened, fuzzy and dull. Along with it, the inside of my wrist throbbed. Brushing at the skin, my fingers touched a raised welt of flesh above the pulse point. Even in the dark, I could see the teeth marks, not fully healed yet.

*Mon dieu!* The half-breed had drunk from me!

He was my blood slave.

My palm slammed against my forehead. *What have I done?*

Slipping from the bed, I used my night vision to find my discarded clothes, quickly pulling them on. Maria would have my head for such an indiscretion. She would kill the male as well. Or have me do it, constraining him to the rack where I would be forced to torture him to death.

*Kill him now*, my inner voice demanded.

Quick. Painless. It would be a charity, a mercy to him.

To me.

Volante swayed nearby, coiled on a hook. Below her, a sword glowed softly, beckoning to me.

A sword? Mine or the male's?

I didn't remember any such sword ever gracing my palm, but at the moment, I could remember naught but my demon status and my place in Maria's court. Why was my head so foggy?

Gingerly, I touched the sword, then recoiled, my demon hissing.

But then the sword glowed brighter. Enchanting me. Drawing me closer...

*Kill him.*

*Blood.*

*Mercy.*

I could not resist its seductive and entrancing pull. I hefted the sword and felt its weight. The power thrumming through it pulsed and ran up my arm, filling me with strength and clarity.

*Kill the half-blood.*

Which was too bad. He was a delectable little thing...

Carrying the sword to the bed, I lifted it in the air over the male's throat, studying for a moment.

And then, with regret, I plunged the powerful sword down.

## 27

"*K* 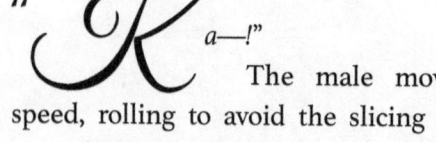 *a—!*" The male moved with swift, accurate speed, rolling to avoid the slicing blade at the last possible second. One muscled shoulder took the brunt of the sword's gleaming silver, a gash appearing where the tip made its mark.

His ocean scent exploded into the air, chaotic fury lifting the ends of my hair and sending my blood pumping hard again. He jumped from the linens, the bed now between us. Even in the bedchamber's shadows, I saw his chest heave.

It was a nice chest from my viewpoint, thick and muscled over tight abdominals and a very large—

"What the fuck are you doing?"

His words cut through my ogling. Steam rose from his wound as if the blade had branded him rather than laying open his skin.

"Identify yourself. Who are you?" For some reason, the language that rolled off my tongue was the Queen's English rather than my native *Italiano*. "What is this place?"

"Kali?" The male's expression went from coiled fury to fear. "It's me, Rad. We're in the Institute."

"My name is Calina."

"You shortened it to Kali, with a K."

Never. "You took of my blood."

He nodded, his body growing more controlled while the scent rolling off him rose like a turbulent ocean wave.

*Have a care, Kalina. This one is dangerous.*

He held up a hand as if to calm me. "I'm your blood slave. Your lover. This is your apartment inside the Bridge Institute. Remember?"

What madness was this? "Are you a trickster demon? You smell human and...something I can't place."

"Shit." He rubbed a hand over his face and lit the lamp on the nightstand. The lamp was magical, seeming to have neither oil nor wick. Then, the male who called himself Rad began a story that involved Lucifer, fallen angels, and me as the leader of a group of supernaturals. As he spoke, I heard the faintest accent in his deep voice. Parisian? "You don't hurt humans anymore," he said, sliding on a pair of trousers. "You save them."

At this, I laughed. Hell most certainly had frozen over. "How much wine did you partake of tonight before you seduced me into your bed, half-breed? Your human half has made you drunk. Either that or my powerful blood has short-circuited your mind. My allegiance is to Queen Maria. I'm under her bondage. I know nothing of this Bridge Institute you speak of, and I'm quite sure I've never encountered Satan in the flesh. I would not forget such a thing."

"But you forgot me," he said – his face was a mask of what? Pain? Sadness? "The only male you've ever loved."

"L...loved?" I choked. Before I could argue, I saw the look in his eyes. The longing.

The half-breed cared for me. No one had cared for me outside my parents and little sister.

I have not ever known myself to be speechless. At that moment, I was.

The male pointed at the sword. "That belongs to Michael, the archangel. Michael fucked with your brain, Kali. He took away your ability to smell, knowing it would screw up your demon and eventually cause you to lose your memories. That's what's happening right now. I thought it would be more gradual, but this is you we're talking about. You never do anything half-assed. It's not the 17th century, and this is not Rome. You haven't worked for Maria in over three hundred years. We're in America now. Maria is chained in the dungeon downstairs."

Archangels and the Colonies? My eyes nearly bugged out of my head. "Madness! My sense of smell is as accurate as always; demons cannot touch Heavenly steel, and there are no chains that could ever hold the queen."

"You can smell?"

"Of course. Are you daft? Why do you mislead me with such lies?"

He held out a hand again, seeking to placate me. His lovely eyes were still filled with sadness—so much so that I felt a tug inside my chest. "Put down the sword, and I'll prove it to you. Right outside the door, you'll find vampires, angels, and other demons who live here at the Institute. They answer to you."

"Vampires?" I laughed again, but a tight pit of anxiety took root in my diaphragm. "*Basta*. Enough. If there are Undead anywhere in this place, I will drive stakes through their hearts."

Gripping the sword tighter, I snatched Volante from the hook and motioned at the chamber's door. "You'll meet the same fate if you try anything."

A controlled sigh left his lips, and he suddenly chuckled, shaking his head. "I can't believe you remember Maria and not me."

Thinking about his body and the bed we had obviously shared, I was sure my lack of memory was a travesty for me as well. But I never was one for jesters and I had no patience for this one. "*Andiamo.*"

Let's go.

With another shake of his head, he opened the door and led me into a world I did not know.

THE SUN SAT low in the sky, sending streaks of pale yellow over the body of water I gazed at from inside a modest chamber the half-breed referred to as my office.

We were not alone. A group of beings crowded in with us, each discussing my situation as they dissected me with their eyes and prodded me with their magic. From the human in the wheeled chair who had no use of her legs to the silent but worried demon leaning against the wall watching my every move, all of them seemed quite concerned.

The tangle of magics combined with their thick, suffocating worry made me itch. If I had not been a touch worried about the soundness of my own mind, I might have lashed out at them.

Not only could I not understand half of what they said – not because I had gone completely mad, which was a possibility – but the language they spoke was English, yet it wasn't.

"I reached out to Lucifer," a male demon who seemed to have placed himself in charge said. Kirill? I'd been hit with so many names and faces they were beginning to run together. "So far, no response."

A demon dressed in priest's robes rubbed a hand through his hair. I had no trouble remembering his name was Salmad, since a demon in priest's garb was hard to forget. I steered clear of him, wondering what his affliction was if he risked such sacrilege. No respecting demon would ever be caught such. "This is bad. This is really bad. What are we going to do?"

A cocky male – this one more pleasing to the eye, but unfortunately a member of the Undead – hovered near me. "We will figure it out. Kali is not a danger to anyone."

"Yet," the reserved demon on the wall added. Rad had referred to this one earlier as Cole.

Cole's gaze disturbed me. I sensed his keen desire to protect me but also a sense of duty to stop me if the group decided I was a danger to them.

Radison had shown me various contraptions, some as small as my hand and others as large as one of my torture racks, with moving pictures and sound. Cell phones, TVs, cameras, something called YouTube, and the Internet.

Powerful magic, these things.

As I stood now in the office, my mind continued to try to work out this puzzle as my blood rose and fell strongly with the handsome vampire so close. Rad had introduced him as the Undead Master of Chicago House when he'd arrived during my tour of the building. Chicago—the name felt strange on my tongue.

When the vampire had opened his mouth to expand on the discussion, Rad had cut him off. I was curious since my blood had such a strong reaction to him, and my demon did not seek to kill him. If anything, I had the horrible desire to kiss him.

*Cazzo! What is wrong with me?* I hated vampires with a passion.

It was terribly confusing.

There were several more demons standing behind the priest, all with gazes glued to me. Something in my blood responded to them as well, but I had concluded the vital fluid pumping through my heart was an unreliable instrument of measure since it seemed to react to everyone present. Surely, I had not shared my blood with all of them.

"I wish to see the queen," I said, whirling from the window to face Rad. "You said she was in the dungeon downstairs."

"That's a terrible idea," the priest said. "We don't know how it might set her off."

Her, meaning me, or the queen?

The vamp Master, Dru, already on edge, stepped in front of me. "Brianna and I will protect Kali at all costs."

How...sweet. I could not stop the wrinkling of my nose.

Cole pushed off the wall, glaring at the Undead. "She's my charge. I will keep her safe."

*Santa Cielo!* The testosterone flew in the air. I was going to kill them all, just to stop this...this...overbearance of something close to *famiglia*.

Family. Where were my parents and sister? I had asked Rad about it during all the back and forth, but he had waved off the inquiry. At one point, while I asked about them, Salmad had dragged Rad to the side. "Just how much has she forgotten?" he'd asked.

Rad had replied, "She's only sixteen or seventeen in her mind. She has forgotten nearly three centuries."

I gripped the windowsill so hard, my knuckles turned snow white. My seventeenth birthday was a few short days away...

At least, I thought it to be so.

"Stop it." The vamp called Brianna stepped from the corner of the room. "We have to work together. All Kali wants is to see Maria, and we won't let the succubus out of her cage. Kali can peer through the slit in the door."

"Take me to the dungeon," I insisted to Rad.

On our way downstairs, we passed packs of angels. Each time, my demon hissed, and I drew back. The sparkling magic in their auras made fire boil in my stomach. The sword, still in my hand, trembled every time one drew near. I was sure I had never been in the presence of such power before, but I knew it for what it was unerringly.

Was it possible Radison spoke the truth? Was the steel in my hand of Heavenly ancestry?

*Merde.* It could not be. I glanced at the sword swinging at my side. Michael's sword. How could a lowly demon like myself touch, much less carry, such a thing?

On the main floor, a woman burst through the front door, bringing in a wave of fresh air redolent with the smell of strawberries. "Kali!"

She was stunning. A goddess.

Literally.

I had never met one of these in person before either, but that didn't mean my magic didn't know the very real presence of a being on par with the angels. She glowed nearly as much as the sword in my hand, and her very presence stopped me in my tracks.

Before I could shake myself from the cloud swirling around me, the goddess enveloped me in a hug. The strawberry scent assailed my nose, heady and enchanting.

However, my demon rebelled from her touch. This was the opposite of my magic. A being like this could twitch her nose and destroy me where I stood.

I touched my thumbs and ring fingers together, raising my protective shields. They snapped into place with such force that the goddess flew back and hit the wall.

Everyone gasped. Being immortal, she was unharmed and landed on her feet with a perplexed look. "What the hell?"

"I told you, she doesn't remember anyone," Rad told her. "You can't expect her to accept you with open arms, Di."

Her perfect porcelain face was a wonder. "I'm her best friend. She wouldn't forget me."

"My what?" I blinked. How was it possible this day could get any stranger?

She smiled as if I were a child who needed a gentle, simple explanation. "I'm your best friend, Kali."

Right. Of course, my insanity would extend to such a thing. "And who are you exactly?"

Frustration morphed her perfect features for a split second and the smile faded. "It's me. Di."

"Di?" What goddess did I know from the Queen's history books named Di? "As in Dianna?"

"Gods, no! I'm no Roman warrior goddess! It's me, Aphrodite!"

Aphrodite? Now, my mother's teachings issued forth. "The Greek goddess of love and beauty?"

"Yes." She nodded heartily. "Ring any bells?"

A few angels and more demons had gathered around the group, gawking. The human in the wheeled chair cut through the crowd. "I thought *I* was your best friend, Kali."

I wondered if I had been the cause of the woman's disabled legs. "Rest assured, human, I have no friends, goddess or otherwise."

Aphrodite exchanged a troubled look with Radison. "Maybe seeing Maria will jog something in her memories."

The priest worried his hands inside the sleeves of his robe. "Where is Tabriss? She should stay close, just in case."

A murmur ran through the angels. "In case what?" I queried.

Salmad shifted his weight, looking uncomfortable. "Lucifer put her in charge of—"

"We don't need Tabriss," Rad interrupted. Dru, Rad, Cole, and Di formed an instant circle around me. "Everyone stand down."

Stand down, *si*. I tired of this frustrating game. Annoyance burned in my veins. "*Basta e basta!* Take me to the dungeon."

Mayhap, they would leave me there. The thought held mercy. At least I might find peace if left in a cell alone.

I wanted desperately to believe they were as insane as they made me feel, but the moment I stepped down into the building's underground prison, I felt her presence.

Maria.

The succubus queen who'd taken me from my parents and sister and raised me to be an instrument of brutal torture.

My feet stopped midway down the stone steps, the earth magic heavy and binding. Whoever—whatever—existed in these warded prison cells, they were good and truly trapped.

Throat closing, my demon rebelling, I fought a wave of dizziness. Immediately, Rad's hands were on me.

The vampires' blood called to mine, stroking, soothing.

All around me, I felt the waves of energy wrapping me in a bubble of strength, pushing me forward.

No demon of right mind would descend farther.

I took another step down.

*Breathe, demon. Breathe.*

One more.

My foot landed on the dusty floor. The scent of blood was strong here. Magic hung from the rafters as if in waves, layer upon layer, in every direction. Even if a prisoner broke through one layer, he or she would meet with hundreds more, each like a barrier of forged steel. Hard, impenetrable. For those of us not prevailed to remain here, the dungeon seemed to want to force us out.

The sensation made me gag slightly. I coughed to cover my weakness as Rad led me down a long, dark hallway. The stones oozed with moisture from the cold-warded magic, and I pressed a hand to my throat to control my gag reflex.

At the far end of one corridor, we stopped in front of a door sealed with an extra dose of warding and another layer of what felt like bewitching. I sensed the presence of at least one witch nearby and she was a powerful one. Had she been forced, as part of her sentence, to contribute her skills to keep the most powerful succubus I had ever encountered contained?

If so, bravo to her.

As I stood side-by-side in front of the cell Maria occupied, Rad took my empty hand, twining his fingers with mine.

I glanced at him and, for a quick heartbeat, everything else fell away. A snippet of a memory—of him singing—floated across the hazy landscape of my brain. I felt a tug of something warm and dare I say...joyful, low in my belly. "Rad?"

He saw the flicker of recollection in my gaze, for he gripped my hand tighter. "Yes, Kali. Go with it. Remember. Come back to us. Come back to *me*."

And then something hit the door so hard I jumped.

Truly, the impact was so forceful that I would not have been surprised to see an outline of Maria's body on our side of the door.

Rad did not jump or even flinch. His gaze stayed solidly on mine. "What did you remember?"

Already, the sound of his voice in melody receded to a whisper. A dream.

I shook my head. "Nothing. It's gone."

Disappointment flashed across his shadowed face. He gave my hand another squeeze. "Ready?"

Was I? Something told me that everything he and the others had told me was true. If Maria were truly in this cell, my fears would be confirmed. Then what? What would I do?

Rad's hand was suddenly an anchor for the chaos inside my head. The Master vampire stepped up to my other side. I drew a deep breath and nodded.

With a flick of his hand, Rad unlocked and opened the window slit by magic, a set of tightly spaced metal bars criss-crossing the actual opening. Dark magic, familiar and rank, poured out. I met the crazed eyes of the succubus who had enslaved me in her court.

"You," the demon—no longer in human form, but a slithering, blistered mess that appeared more sea creature than anything else —hissed. The lump that was her nose wrinkled, and I felt her inhale, sucking at my magic. My body seemed to move forward on its own accord, drawn to her like a magnet. "You are mine. You will always be..."

The sword flashed bright enough to blind me. At the same time, Brianna yelled, "Close it!"

Half-shielding my eyes, I glanced over and saw that the vampire was struggling against the magic as much as I was.

How was that possible? Was the Undead bodyguard connected to me in the same way as her Master?

Rad slammed the portal shut, a wave of his hand sealing it once more and breaking the connection she had drawn between us. Everyone, the vamps, demons, and even Aphrodite breathed a giant sigh.

All manner of colorful curses flew from my mouth, some directed at Eve, God, pigs, prostitutes, demons, and even Lucifer himself. I stumbled backward, both Rad and Dru catching me by the arms and keeping me upright.

I was no longer under Maria's bond.

And if I were to believe those surrounding me, she was now under *mine*.

Funny, it hadn't felt that way.

Silence hung as heavy as the wards. Those in attendance seemed to be waiting for me to say something.

What could I say?

"How is this all possible?" My voice came out strong while my insides quaked. I was not known for weakness, but having my world turned upside down in such a fashion felt like drowning. Part of me wanted to return to the warm bed upstairs and let sleep take me, hoping I might wake up in my normal state. Part of me feared this was the new normal.

The Master brushed a strand of hair from my cheek and caressed my jawline with an intimacy that made me draw back and want to kiss him at the same time. "Because, my dear Kali, you are one of the most powerful supernatural creatures on the planet at this time. You run this Institute, you are the queen of the Chicago Undead, and Lucifer is relying on you to house his Fallen."

I turned from him, his words like explosions in my brain. Queen of the Undead? I seriously thought nothing more could rip away the tiny thread I still had on reality, but that seemed to do it.

Worse, the sting of truth in my blood assured me it was undeniable.

I sought refuge in Rad's arms. I'm not sure why, but it felt as if it was the most natural thing to do in this most unnatural, topsy-turvy new world.

"Is there wine?" I choked out as Rad pulled me close to his chest and rubbed my back. The solid beat of his heart calmed me; the salty scent of him filled my nose, and I breathed deep, grasping at his shirt. "I'm in need of large quantities."

A collective chuckle passed among those with us. Wrung out, I allowed Rad to lead me away from the cell. Alexandru again took up residence on my other side, the rest of the group following down the desolate hall.

Before we could ascend to the main floor, a young male rushed down the steps. "There you are!"

He flew to me, and I was once more engulfed in the arms of a stranger. Unlike the goddess who claimed to be my best friend, this one smelled of feline.

A shifter.

Shoving him away, I held my breath and noticed his eyes were red. The all-too-familiar siren song in my blood howled, and exasperated, I glanced around at my companions. "Is there anyone here I have *not* provided my blood to?"

A few actually raised their hands, and I felt slightly mollified, but the shifter ignored them. "Kali, it's Maddy. She's missing. I think she's been kidnapped."

He held up a gadget similar to the one Radison had shown me earlier and referred to as a cell phone. A strange girl in a moving picture struggled against rough hands, screaming with fangs bared as she was dragged away. I had no idea who she was, but I clearly recognized the ring on her right hand.

"They took her," the shifter said. "They're going to kill her."

# 28

"*W*ho is this female?" Along with the ring on her finger, I recognized the strange pull in my gut. The pull that said I was indeed the Queen of the Chicago Undead.

And someone was threatening one of my vampires.

It was at that moment that I decided to embrace the madness. Whatever dream or alternate reality this was—purgatory, no doubt—I might as well accept it. Raise a little hell. I had never been one to back down from a challenge, and my father and mother had raised me to embrace my role as a vengeance demon. I would do so no matter the time or place.

"It's Maddy," the shifter insisted again, his heavy brows furrowed.

Another sniff of the air and I realized he was a were-cheetah. Very controlled, but still a cat.

He went on. "She was at your place, looking for clothes or something. She texted me, asked me to come over. I was on a date, you know, with my new girlfriend, so I blew her off. The next thing I know, I get another text with a video. I figured she was flipping me off, so I ignored it at first. When I finally checked it, I found this. They must have jumped her and filmed this bit to use as blackmail. They didn't know who to send it to, so they sent it to the last person she texted – me."

Rad took the device and watched the moving picture – video – once more. "This is Arman, by the way," he said, introducing me formally to the were-cheetah. "He's your blood slave."

I eyed the vagrant-looking young man. "Exactly how many do I have?"

"A few," Rad answered, handing off the phone to Dru. "Plus, you saved Dru's life by giving him blood."

"We are forever bonded," Dru added with a lustful grin.

No wonder I wanted to kill and kiss him at the same time.

"Lucky you." My rude tone belied my words. "And I am somehow queen of your Undead? Please tell me we are not bound by the marriage ceremony."

Once more, I was enveloped in heated male testosterone. "You aren't," Rad replied.

Arman bounced on the balls of his feet. "Can we get back to Maddy?"

"You care for the vamp?" I asked him. "And she for you?"

"I... I love her."

"You said you were with your girlfriend and ignored Maddy when she...tested you."

"Texted." He glanced at Rad and Dru. "What's wrong with Kali? She's acting weird."

"We'll explain on the way," Dru said. Then, to his bodyguard, he said, "Bri, bring the car around. We must head for Kali's house."

Brianna grabbed the shifter's hand, and they sprinted up the stairs ahead of us. "I thought I lived here," I said to Rad as we followed.

"You do, but before you took over the Institute, you lived at your own place, an abandoned church."

We hit the landing of the first floor. "Consecrated ground? You jest."

"'Fraid not."

The goddess was on our heels. "Kali, you shouldn't leave here. Remember what happened last time?"

The group stopped, gazes dancing between themselves.

"What happened last time?" I queried.

"Michael attacked," Rad explained. "That's when he messed up the wiring in your brain. Here, you're under heavy wards, but when you leave, your protection is apparently not adequate."

"Except yesterday, you were at the church," Dru said. "No one disturbed you until some outcast vampires showed up. They attacked you, but you scattered them with ease."

"That's right," Cole added. "You left Maddy and Bri in charge of the Institute. Why didn't Michael come after you then? Or at the airport?"

Rad gave me a hard stare. "You didn't tell me you went to your place."

I had no recollection of these adventures or what an airport was. "Must I seek permission for every move I make?"

"Of course not." Rad shot daggers at Dru, a wave of jealousy filling the air. "Why were you with her?"

Dru waggled his brows and ran the tips of his fingers down my arm.

My stomach rebelled at the intimate gesture. "Was I having a tryst with you?" I asked the vampire Master.

For a second, I saw the lie cross his features. He wanted to say yes, to mislead me or to rile Rad more. Instead, he shook his head. "I wanted her to see Mo's angelic possession."

"Sorry?" Who was Mo, and why would an angel possess him? "Why would I care about such a thing?"

"I'll tell you about it later," Rad said. "It has to do with Michael."

"Does the archangel seek revenge for some slight?" I had no idea why such a being would otherwise come after me. "Does he see me as a threat? No one has explained why Michael dislikes me so and has taken umbrage with me."

"I'll stay here with her," Salmad said. "Bring her up to speed. The rest of you find Maddy."

Cole checked his weapon, seeming quite at home handling a gun. "We have no idea who took her or why."

"It seems obvious." Dru glanced around. "They are either simple vandals—which we know could never break through Kali's locks and wards—or they were looking for Kali and must have convinced Maddy they were her friends. She let them in, and they kidnapped her."

Arman rushed in from outside, nearly crawling out of his skin. Truly, he had deep feelings for this vampire, which I found most ironic. The girl, who appeared to be in her teens when she was turned, held some significance to me. I would not have offered her the emerald ring otherwise. "Cole's question remains," I said. "Why? Of what significance is her kidnapping to *me*?"

Arman looked completely incensed. "Don't you know?"

"Since I have no memory of this Undead female or of the place she was taken from, I'm afraid not. But she is my charge, so I shall accompany you. Perhaps if I go to this place, I'll recall something of significance."

"No," Aphrodite and Salmad said. At the same time, Dru and Rad nodded yes, and Cole motioned me forward as though I were his equal in the soldier department.

Which made me feel even more confident.

Taking action felt good. Against their continued arguments, I left the goddess and priest behind and went with the males who had sworn allegiance to me. We would find the teen vampire.

It had been a hell of a few hours, and my brain was still a

mess, but my normal confidence had returned. In the back of my warped mind, I held out hope that this Maddy and I were friends.

Because I definitely needed a confidant right now who was neither human nor goddess but a lowly supernatural like myself.

## 29

The church left much to be desired, a castle some might call it, but quite small by those standards. Half of the bottom floor appeared to have been rebuilt, and the rest of the structure appeared slightly unstable.

It seethed with evil, however, and I immediately felt more at home here than I had in the building called the Bridge Institute.

Cole and I circled the outside, Brianna and Dru in front of us, Rad and Arman behind. "What is your allegiance to me exactly, soldier?" I asked the brooding demon. "My blood is not in your system and you are not of the Undead Nation, yet you seem diligent and rigorous about protecting me."

Cole avoided eye contact and scanned the mostly wooded area, the evening's shadows thick and delicious. "I'm your Warrior demon, your former bodyguard. You appointed me head of security, and since you don't work as enforcer anymore, you rarely leave the Institute and refuse to have a bodyguard."

Head of security had to be a significant job, no doubt, since I seemed to attract trouble simply by breathing. "There is something more. We are friends, *si*?"

A faint scent of magic left behind by the vampire named Maddy hung in the air. I breathed deeper, trying to catch where it came from. I could not sense any magic but that of more Undead. Could she have been kidnapped by her own kind?

"We're friends."

The response lacked particulars. I wasn't surprised. War demons were rarely comfortable with such discussions.

His silence, however, told me much. "You are hesitant to trust me in this state."

More silence.

*That would be a yes.*

"But you did prior."

His diligent gaze continued to scan the area. "You were a seasoned warrior before. A soldier who'd been through battle with me on more than one occasion."

"Me, a warrior?" Stroking Volante, I smiled. "I welcome that news. I will try not to let you down, but I must warn you—my victims are usually already bound. I am proficient with a whip and other torture devices once the prey is in hand, but hunting has never been my forte."

He gave a small nod. His magic was running high like the others, but he seemed more controlled. He was at ease with the idea of battle, much like I was with torture for revenge.

With the sword, I motioned at Brianna's backside. "What is between you and the vampire bodyguard?"

Cole stiffened, shooting a quick glare in my direction. "Nothing."

Brianna, with her vampire hearing, looked back at me, her face alarmed.

Their actions confirmed my suspicions of an affair. Not that I'd witness anything pass between them that suggested such. There was, however, a very distinctive vibration coming off the demon that was centered on the vampire, suggesting he wanted to have sex with her.

Perhaps the Master didn't know about their attraction. "My mistake," I said, winking at Brianna, who, despite her pale skin, seemed to blush.

At the back of the property, there was a gated cemetery. The moment I stepped around the side of the castle, a sensation that only demented spirits embody hit me full force. Rich, very dark magic seeped through the iron pickets whose tops speared toward the night sky.

What I could do to an enemy with one of those brutal spears...

"Kali?"

I had stopped in my tracks when the magic hit and now faced several concerned countenances.

"A portal!" Instantly, I was drawn to it, sensing the spirits felt some relief at my presence. "I live next to a Hell portal?"

"You keep it sealed," Cole said.

I laughed. "Why would I do that?"

No one seemed amused.

Trying to appear chastised, I lowered my head. "Right, because I care for humans now."

"You always did," Rad claimed. "Maria sucked it out of you for a while. She brainwashed you into believing you were truly evil. You're not."

Said the half-human who feared I might put him on my rack.

The air was redolent with woodsy smells, as well as that of old blood, rotting flesh, and skeletons. Looking off to the right, I saw a visible layer of energy where Maddy's assailants had dragged her into the woods.

I'd always been able to sense magic and smell the different odors produced by supernaturals, but I had never visibly seen energy trails before. Much like in the dungeon when I had picked up on the layers of warding, I now saw much more of the spirit world than I cared to.

"They took her that way." I pointed to where the tiny flickers of the vampires' magics still glowed. "All Undead."

"How do you know?" Brianna asked, looking in the direction I pointed. "Is your Spidey sense tingling?"

"I don't understand," I whispered to Rad. "What is a Spidey sense?"

He grabbed my hand. "Cole and Brianna, see if you can pick up the trail. I'll take Kali inside."

"The outcasts," Dru said, glancing up at the castle's rooftop. "They came back for revenge."

I stood my ground as Rad tried to pull me toward the castle. I wanted to go inside and examine the place that was supposedly mine but I had joined this party to find the girl and find her I would. "I can see the magic left behind by Maddy and her kidnappers. I can lead you to her."

Dru's face scrunched. He looked toward the woods and back. "You can see it?"

"It's faint, but yes."

There was a worried but hopeful exchange of glances between all of them.

"Who are these outcasts?" Cole demanded.

Dru motioned at the roofline. "When I arrived, Kali was up there, and they were challenging her. She disposed of a female who got in her face. The rest ran away."

I smirked. Dispose was such a tame word. "How exactly did I end the vamp?"

The Master gave me a quizzical look. "It was messy." He glanced at the others. "I'm guessing they gathered reinforcements and came back. When they found Maddy instead, they decided to kidnap her to get back at Kali."

"Well, what are we waiting for?" Arman strode for the woods. "We have to save her."

Rad sighed but allowed me to follow, him on my right, Cole securing my left.

As we walked through a copse of trees and undergrowth, I peppered Rad with questions. "How is it I turned the tables on Queen Maria?" "How have I survived for over three centuries?" "Do I still love espresso and pasta?" and on and on it went. Some of his answers were satisfying and others left much to the imagination.

The trail of magic led through the woods and into an area of abandoned buildings and large spaces Rad referred to as parking lots upon which horseless carriages apparently were known to rest. Those currently in view did not look like anything I would wish to travel in.

Here and there, nature was winning the battle of taking back the landscape, weeds and small trees pushing up from cracks and through fences.

"The path leads there." I pointed to the back of a dilapidated building.

"I can feel her," Dru said.

The itch under my skin indicated I could as well. "There appear to be four plus her. Very chaotic energy. Undead yet..." I tilted my head, trying to untangle the odd energy. "Something more."

"More?" Cole squinted toward the back door. "Explain."

"I wish I could. I know not what lies underneath the vampire magic."

"The vampire you dispatched was a former witch," Dru offered. "Could it be witch magic you sense?"

The shifter sniffed and twitched, ready to take animal form. "I'll find out and come back with more info."

Dru held up a hand. "Not necessary. They are definitely the outcast vampires from earlier, and regardless of what else inhabits their blood, they are dangerous."

"Except to me," I said with glee. Then to the Master, "You allow outcasts in your region?"

His dark eyes fired with annoyance that I would question

his rule. "They stay out of my way, and I have better things to do with my time than hunt harmless pond suckers."

I shrugged. "Seems like they are no longer harmless."

A muscle twitched in his cheek. "We cannot surprise them. They will kill Maddy before we can get inside."

Cole crossed his arms over his broad chest. "If they wanted to kill her, they would have done it already. They kidnapped her to get Kali to show up here."

Clever, but why? "Then I shall go in and kill them all," I said even more gleefully.

For some reason, the tone in my voice seemed to disturb my companions.

"It's a trap," Cole said.

Rad agreed with a nod. "How do we save Maddy, then?"

"Negotiate," Brianna offered. "They want Kali. Give her to them in exchange for Maddy."

"Are you nuts?" Rad asked.

I thought it was a perfectly brilliant idea. "I can take them," I assured him.

Dru seemed to find that humorous. "You don't even know who you are, Kali. The power you possess. On a normal day, you could probably kill them from here without even seeing them, but right now? None of us are really sure what you can and can't do."

"You think my magic is compromised?"

Their silent looks told me *si*.

I snapped my fingers with a new idea. "Pretend you've brought me as a prisoner to exchange for Maddy. I'll appear knocked out. Once she is free, I'll break whatever binds you put on me and kill them all. Slowly."

Another grin that no one returned.

These supernaturals were absolutely no fun.

Rad shook his head. "They won't believe for a second we're handing you over for Maddy. You're the queen of the Undead and the leader of the Bridge Institute. On top of that, you're the most badass supernatural in America."

It was nice to be so valued. "Then I say we go back to our original plan."

"We had a plan?" Arman asked.

"Storm the castle," I said. "Maddy will have to keep herself alive while we dispose of her captors."

# 30

ole and Dru supported my plan, while Rad and Brianna opposed it. Arman shifted into his cat state and snarled. Not being fluent in cheetah, I had no idea if he was for or against me.

"My blood is obviously the strongest and easiest to detect," I told the others, leading the pack past a sad-looking iron carriage. Where exactly did they hitch the horses to it? "It will disguise all of yours, especially if I give my magic a boost and flood them with it. I'll go in first, you'll sneak in behind me. On my signal, should I need assistance, you may join the fight. Brianna and Arman will secure Maddy, and the rest of us shall eliminate the kidnappers."

I glanced at Cole to see if my plan met his expectations. The tight grin of anticipation on his face told me he did. "There's no guard posted on the lookout. They're expecting you."

"You're sure there are no more than four of them, right?" Rad asked.

"I'm sure." Volante thrummed with the same anticipation I saw on Cole's face. The sword glowed with excitement. Both were as hungry for blood as I was. "Now, scatter, all of you.

Once inside, if I need your help, I'll raise the sword and call out..." I had to think of an appropriate word. "*Dio cano!*"

God is a dog. It is my favorite curse.

I didn't wait for anyone's approval, feeling the spark of power they claimed was mine rising to the occasion as I strutted confidently forward. Just how dangerous was I? I couldn't wait to find out.

Arman loped into the shadows. Brianna also disappeared.

Rad and Dru fell into step beside me.

"What are you doing?" I hissed, stopping before the entrance. "You cannot go in by my side."

The Master waved a hand and became invisible. I sensed his magic moving away, but not far.

Only my lover remained. "We do this together," he said. "You may be head of the Institute, and a badass demon, but I'm your enforcer. We work as a team."

Teamwork was unfamiliar to me. I did my work alone. But as I stared into his beautiful gold eyes and felt the chaos magic pouring off him, I did not doubt we were an effective pair in and out of the bedchambers. "Are you the reason I have survived all these years?"

"No," he said. "You did that on your own. I was kidnapped and incarcerated on the day I was supposed to marry you, and I did not see you again for three hundred years. Now, at this moment, no matter what you say or do, I will not leave your side. So suck it up, Kali. We do this together, or we don't do it at all."

No wonder I kept this one around. He was so sincere, so earnest.

So very human.

That's when it hit me—the reason I had stopped brutalizing humans. I'd fallen in love with one.

Granted, he was only half human, but that side of him was utterly irresistible. "Let's be done with this then," I said to him.

"So we may get back to the Institute and that comfortable bed of mine."

The look that came over him was enchanting, and I'm never one for such sentiment. In one quick motion, he jerked me to him and kissed me hard.

Tragedy that I felt compelled to kiss him back.

When he let loose of me, I was breathing hard. I may have been an exceptional supernatural in this alternate reality, but I was still female. Very much so, apparently, from the way my nipples were taught and my demon howled for more.

I was about to sneak one more kiss when a shrill scream split the night, and the vampire blood inside me lit as if on fire.

## 31

*Gli sciocchi si precipitano.* Fools rush in. Queen Maria had admonished me with the saying more than once. But angels be damned, I feared little, and cared not if I was foolish.

Angels are sissies anyway.

Maddy's screams rent the night as I flung the steel door open and charged inside. Was it a trap, as my compatriots feared? *Si, certo.* But the one thing intellect can't give you in a fight is courage, and of that, I lacked none.

Radison was by my side, both of us moving with our demon speed, mine highlighted with vampire blood and all the other magics flowing in my system. Along with my superior senses, reflexes, and the power of the sword in my hand, I practically flew through the abandoned rooms until I came upon my prey.

One of the Undead stood over Maddy, who was strapped to a roughly made torture chair. She lay prone, a mess of blood, bruises, and burns. Her abuser stood over her, painstakingly slicing fine cuts into the pale skin of her abdomen before peeling the strips away with slow, agonizing movements. Blood covered his hands, an evil smile on his ugly countenance.

He looked up as I burst into the room and the smile broadened. He raised a strip of Maddy's flesh, blood covering his hands and running down his forearm, and started to speak.

I had no interest in what he had to say, so I sprung forward and swung the sword.

One clean slice and the outcast's head left his body and sailed through the air, landing amongst a pile of wood and garbage in the far corner. His body dropped where it stood.

I kicked it away and put a hand on the girl. Sweat and tears covered her face and I wiped at her cheeks. "Fear not. He will not hurt you again."

"Ka...li." Her voice was raw from the screaming. "It's a..."

"Trap," I finished for her, grinning. "*Si*, I know."

The other outcasts emerged from their hiding places and were advancing on us. Rad, as bold as I, charged forward to engage a lanky male. As he dispatched that one, another opened his mouth and yelled crude names at me. Before he could finish, or a third could jump me, I had decapitated both of them. I don't believe either saw me coming, I moved with such speed.

The rush was pure ecstasy. I laughed with abandon. Truly, I had never felt such power in my veins.

The others in my team emerged, ready for a fight that was no longer imminent. Arman shifted to his human state and hurried to remove the leather restraints from Maddy. She was weak from loss of blood and fear, but her vampire nature would kick in shortly and assist her recovery.

Cole stood, guns in both hands, turning in a circle. "That was too easy," I heard him murmur.

"You may thank my wondrous powers," I told him, preening a bit as I casually wiped Undead blood off the blade. On my arm, Volante squeezed my bicep, letting me know she was quite disappointed she'd played no part in the destruction. I stroked her. "Next time, my pet."

"Kali..." Maddy was sitting up in the chair, feet on the floor, and Arman keeping her upright. Her pupils filled her irises, and she gasped, although I was quite sure vampires did not need to breathe. They kept saying they served...the true master. Someone...bigger."

*True master.* A sudden flashback hit. I saw a female vampire kneeling at my feet, heard my own voice saying, "*...know your true master.*"

I sucked in a breath, and Rad touched my shoulder. "Kali? Did you remember something again?"

Was I the outcasts' master? My gaze went to Dru. I started to explain the vision I had seen when a high-pitched screech reverberated inside the building. Everyone looked up, crouching and covering their ears. In the next instant, my vision went white. A burst of energy so powerful I felt my insides compressing hit us all.

My body, and Rad's, careened across the open space, and without the ability to see or hear, I lost all sense of direction. We struck the far wall with enough force to break bones and crack heads, then slid to the floor.

Something of substantial weight landed nearby, making the earth move. I felt the floor underneath my ass begin to cave in, and I flailed my arms, seeking purchase. At one point, my fingers found Rad – an arm or a leg, I could not be sure – before I was sucked into the light and sound.

The flashbacks began in earnest now, my body spinning in a whirlpool as my brain seemed to do the same. I was assaulted from all sides, mentally and physically, everything coming to me with sharp, jarring strikes. At once, I was seventeen years old...then one-hundred-sixty-five...two-hundred. Flashes of people, places, situations came at me with such momentum I could not breathe. The piercing wail rose, and the light turned a shade of red.

Blood. There was blood everywhere.

And the wail was my own.

My physical body vibrated with it all, shaking so hard my teeth chattered. My magic felt as if it were being ripped in two. As the pressure escalated, I believe it actually did because the last sensation I remember was my body exploding into a million pieces.

## 32

*M*agic is truly a wonder, regardless of its origin or the entity wielding it. Sometime later, I awoke in a fog, but back in the human form I'd been given centuries ago, and seemingly with all my memories. Every one of my senses was once again in working order, although there was such a haze of angelic magic hanging in the air, I couldn't be sure where I was.

"Rad?" I called. "Cole?"

My memories included the most recent ones, where my friends and fellow supernaturals had eased my way through Michael's curse to help me know myself again after I'd forgotten all of them.

*Thank the fires of Hell, I'm back.*

For some reason, Rad's words rang over and over like a mission bell in my head. *"I can't believe you remember her and not me."*

No doubt Michael had done that intentionally to inflict pain on those who cared the most for me.

"Maddy?" I coughed as the hazy magic tickled my throat.

Where was the sword? I patted the ground around me. "Dru? *Anybody?*"

"Ah, finally," a female said, but it wasn't Maddy or Bri's voice. "You're awake."

I recognized it, nevertheless, and the set of violet eyes that emerged from the fog on my right. "Tabriss?"

"Getting you here took more imagination than I anticipated." She wore all black, from her boots to the various weapons on her body.

If I didn't know better, I would have thought every item of her wardrobe was actually mine.

"Are you wearing my clothes?" I rose to my feet, my ears still ringing and my balance off. "Are those my boots?"

"Really?" She snickered and circled me, but her movements were deliberate, slow, as if she were very, very tired. Her lips sported blood-red lipstick, and she'd gone heavy on the eyeliner. "That's your most pressing question? Did I raid your wardrobe?"

"Maddy got hold of you, didn't she? This"—I waved a hand at her outfit and makeup—"is her work."

"I rather like it. It suits me better than all that angelic white shit, don't you think?"

Warning bells clattered inside my head. I stretched and cracked my back, sure I had a fractured rib or two. The back of my head stung, and for half a second, I wondered if the fog I saw came from a concussion rather than whatever Tabriss was doing. Covertly, I touched my thumbs and fingers together, strengthening my protective shield. "I assume you're going to tell me what you're doing here and what the hell is going on?"

"The outcasts were supposed to grab you at the cemetery, but they were a poor choice for that ambush, I suppose. You know what they say about don't give a vampire a demon's job."

"I have no flippin' idea what you're talking about, but I assume you're the *true master* they kept referring to?"

"I hear disappointment in your voice."

"That would be wrath, not disappointment. It's a deadly sin. Surely you've heard of it."

She smirked. "You had no trouble disposing of my team."

What exactly was her team supposed to do? Grab me for what purpose? "Did you think I would?"

A shrug. "I guess they did succeed in getting you here. All because of your love for a worthless little vampire."

The fog receded enough to catch sight of said 'worthless' vampire, and I checked myself. Maddy and Arman lay on the floor a dozen feet away, heads cocked at odd angles and eyes gazing sightlessly into space.

Dead. I knew it from those lifeless stares and unmoving bodies, but I still reached for them with my mind, my blood, my magic.

I got nothing in return.

I swung my head around, looking for the others. "What have you done, Tabriss?"

"Made a point."

I choked back the fear and rage in the pit of my stomach. Whatever had happened here, I would not let her get the best of me. "Your point is lost on me. Why don't you clarify?"

"You may be a powerful supernatural here on earth, but you've overstepped your boundaries again and again. You are not superior to angels. You are not a god."

"Never claimed to be." Cole's words rang in my head. *Distraction, diversion, division.* Was Tabriss another of Michael's weapons to keep me off guard? "But I'm guessing you believe someone— namely you—needs to take me down a notch."

She paced a few feet away. "I'm taking over the Institute. Consider this as your pink slip. Your services are no longer needed."

At this ludicrous announcement, I burst out laughing. "Is that so?"

"Michael wants you fully engaged on your new assignment."

"So you're working with him now?"

She stopped and faced me, chest out, head high. "He explained everything to me. You know, all those things you and Lucifer left out about who I am and what I meant to Michael."

I sighed. "He's playing you."

The air suddenly vibrated with a new energy. The fog lit with that all-too-familiar intense bright light, and the hair on the back of my neck rose like I'd been shocked.

Michael became visible as though he'd been standing beside me the whole time. I jumped back, starting to raise the sword before I remembered I no longer possessed it.

He was not the giant I'd encountered on the freeway, but he still towered over me, topping out at seven feet, if I had to guess. He smiled, his eyes colder than any iceberg. "Hello, vengeance demon. Welcome to your new assignment."

I swallowed down the innate fear and hatred his presence brought and hoped my guardian goddesses might be nearby. Hell, I hoped Rad and Cole might suddenly surface. Anyone— anything—that might help me keep my wits about me when facing off against such enormous power.

Because you know I can't keep my mouth shut. Not when Arman and Maddy lay dead a few feet away. I was going to say something that would get my intestines eviscerated. Or worse.

*Damon*, I mentally called. *Di!*

Hell, I even went all the way. *Lucifer! Could use some help here...*

"Sorry, big guy." I tried to sound casual as I stroked Volante. My attempt at confidence fell flat, but fortunately, I had been Maria's pet long enough to know how to disguise and control my innermost emotions.

*Do not show fear. Do not appear weak.*

*Don't take it personally.*

The last one, one of my credos, was the hardest to get around at the moment with Arman and Maddy lying dead a few feet away, but as always, it was still true. This wasn't about me. This was about two brothers who couldn't get along, and one wanted to make the other one's life, well, hell.

As if Lucifer hadn't been through enough already.

*Look at me, standing up for Lucifer of all beings.* "I can't work for you," I told Michael. "I *won't*."

My response didn't faze him. He seemed to expect resistance. "I bet I can change your mind."

Did I dare bet against an archangel? "What have you done with the rest of my friends?"

"Look around, demon." He motioned with a hand, and the fog receded inch by inch. "They're all here."

My stomach roiled. Rad, Cole, Dru, and Brianna were strewn around the ground, just like Maddy and Arman.

Every one of them dead.

I seethed, no longer able to stay detached. "You angelic piece of shit."

With a cry of rage, I lashed out, throwing my magic at both angels, *bambambam.* I hit them with everything I had, hatred pouring through me and fueling my powers.

They expected my tantrum, and at first, neither ducked, but the sheer force of my rage juiced my magic from super powerful to downright nuclear. Tabriss's hair lit on fire. Michael's chest showed a burn hole as if I'd laid a smoking cigar on it. Another sprouted on his chin.

*Bambambam.* I kept throwing everything I had at them.

Both of them had up shields, mind you. My magic tore right through them.

And then Michael flicked his fingers and I went sailing across the room, once again hitting the brick wall so hard I saw stars for a moment and nearly passed out from the sheer pain of the bone-shattering smack.

"Calm down, demon." He brushed at his burn wounds and they immediately healed. "I'll bring your friends back. All you have to do is complete your assignment."

I could barely breathe with my ruptured rib cage and the turmoil of magic spinning like a tornado inside my chest. "Fuck you."

He *tsked*. "Resorting to gutter talk. I expected better from you, but then, you are, at your essence, nothing but a lowly demon."

If only my outrage could mend my body faster so I could attack him again.

Luckily, my demon, always ready for a fight, came howling to the surface for revenge.

She hadn't been completely loose in a very long time. The dark force was so strong it lifted my body from the ground as my mouth opened, and I bellowed at the top of my lungs. My hands rose, my fingers pointing at the angels as evil broke the restraints I had placed on it so long ago.

The building could not contain it. Walls of brick and glass blew out from my fury, ripped from the foundation. The ground quaked, and my voice continued to shred the air. Bricks smacked into the angels. Their hair blew back, the clothes on Tabriss's body tearing apart and being sucked into the whirling chaos my demon created. They both shielded their faces with their hands. Michael's feet left the ground, and he had to smack at a roof trust that tried to spear him to bat it away.

No more roof, no more walls. Clouds skittered across the sky now visible above us. With my powers, I uprooted a dead tree from nearby and sent it at them.

Michael fought back now, taking control of the tree skeleton and whirling it back at me.

Which only served to piss me off even more.

The surrounding buildings fell, and the concrete parking lot buckled and groaned. The run-down fence surrounding the property ripped from its constraints and flew through the melee, wrapping around an unsuspecting Tabriss before she could react.

My demon could wipe out the entire South Side if I let her. All of Chicago, too. I desperately wanted to give her her head. Destruction felt good – better than good. It was like a shot of my favorite drug, the one I hadn't had in centuries.

Tabriss screamed curses at me – very un-angel-like – and the rusty metal fence disintegrated into a thousand tiny pieces. Every piece hovered in the air, and then they all turned toward me.

Death by metal projectiles. It would hurt, but I doubted it would kill me.

I narrowed my eyes at her and waggled my fingers. *Bring it.*

For half a second, I saw her flinch at the sight of my eyes. My demon was definitely making an appearance in more ways than one.

*Oh yeah. I'm one evil bitch.*

*And you're my blood slave, so give it a shot. Let's see what happens.*

My challenge was accepted. She straightened and raised her hands, sending the rusty metal bullets at me.

*Pingpingping*, I deflected them with ease, knocking them away. Volante swept through the air to knock more down.

Tabriss stumbled, grabbing at her abdomen. She bent in half, moaning.

My blood in her system wasn't strong enough to keep her from turning on me, but it was enough to give her a wicked bitch slap for doing so.

I started to breathe another tornado of magic into the air, knowing it would take out blocks and blocks and give me another surge of power, but doing so would not destroy the angels, only the innocent humans and supernaturals living in the area.

*Be smart.* Damon's voice echoed in my ears suddenly as if he were there. I glanced around, looking for him. Was I delusional, wishing so hard for him and his guidance that I was hearing things?

Most likely.

*Damon?* I called anyway. *Where the fuck have you been?*

At first, nothing, and then... *Be smart, Kali.*

*Thanks. Real helpful.*

But I repeated the words to myself. How did a demon outsmart an angel?

Michael raised his hands and clapped. Just once, but it was enough. My demon seized up, the chaos stopped, and the sun came back out.

"Quite a show," he said, clapping again, this time in mock applause. "I see why my brother keeps you leashed."

He placed a hand on Tabriss's back. "Are you all right?"

His touch seemed to restore her. "Just hungry," she said, straightening and licking her lips.

Without my demon's tempest, my physical body could not hold me up. I was still a broken mess. I slumped to the ground, once more defeated. Not even Michael's words were enough to keep me on my feet.

A part of me grieved for my friends. A part of me imagined driving Michael's sword into his cold heart over and over again.

Neither of those would bring Rad and the others back to life.

In the frozen landscape of my heart, my mind did as Damon commanded. My intellect kicked in.

I could not out-power an archangel, no matter the depths of my anger and grief. The only way to beat Michael was to outsmart him.

If I played my cards right, I could get him to undo the damage he'd done.

How?

He needed me. I would use that to my advantage.

I thought of Rad lifting me from the ground and incapacitating me. How I'd outsmarted him by pretending to give in.

Would a similar technique work on Michael?

What did I have to lose? My life meant nothing if I lost Rand and my friends.

But I couldn't have a change of heart too quickly. Michael was too smart for that.

"This demon will be your undoing," I muttered, barely able to get words out, thanks to my broken ribs.

"Tough talk from someone who can barely breathe," Tabriss said. She closed the distance to tower over me. "I heard you were uncompromising, but you really should take the assignment."

I coughed up blood, wiped my lips with the back of my hand. Her gaze zeroed in on it, and then she whipped around and paced a few feet away. I could hear her stomach growling.

I met Michael's gaze. "I won't kill Lucifer's child, no matter what the offer. If you're going to possess me, then do it and get it over with, but I will not go against the king of Hell on my own."

"Possess you?" He faked a shudder. "Why in Hades would I do that?"

"Wasn't that your plan all along? To weaken me so you could take over my body and kill Lucifer's offspring?"

"I do seek vengeance," Michael said, watching Tabriss as she kept her back to me. "But the situation has changed rather abruptly. The child is a sensitive matter I have already taken care of."

What? "Then why mess with my senses in order to wipe my memories?"

"A mere consequence of using your cerebral cortex to send my brother a message before the latest turn of events. Rather clever, wasn't it? That's why I'm Father's favorite."

I was going to kill him. One way or another.

"What *do* you want?"

He smiled. "I need vengeance on someone."

The sword hung at his hip, so I was no longer standing in his way in that department. And if he already had a plan for disposing of Lucifer's child, then whom did he want me to go after?

"I'm waiting with...bated breath," I said, with as much snark as I could force into my tone. "Spit it out."

"I've given you back your memories so you know his weaknesses. Do this job for me, and we'll discuss bringing back your closest *friends*."

At that, he kicked one of Rad's feet, making the lifeless leg bob. If I could have moved, I would have clawed Michael's eyes out and shoved his eyeballs down his throat.

I bit off a curse and forced myself not to react. "I'm listening."

Michael clapped his hands together as if delighted. "Awesome."

Awesome? This guy was spending too much time on Earth. "Just tell me who you seek vengeance on."

This seemed to surprise him. "Haven't you guessed?"

The niggle in my brain made me give him a quizzical look. *Surely not.* I prayed I was wrong. "You can't be serious."

His smile grew, and he glanced at Tabriss, who was now looking over her shoulder at us. "I told you she was sharp for a demon. Uncooperative but perceptive."

"Just say it," I spat, holding onto my aching ribs.

Michael crouched in front of me, his blond hair falling over his shoulders. "I want you to kill Lucifer."

It hurt to laugh. "That's impossible."

He tapped the sword. "Not with this. It's already bonded to you—that's one of the reasons I let you keep it."

"*Let* me keep it? You couldn't get it out of the Institute."

His smile turned tolerant. "I would think by now you wouldn't underestimate me."

"Ditto."

A tight sigh issued through his nostrils. "All I have to do is give you a bit of my power, and between that and the sword, you'll be able to take him."

I shook my head, an idea already brewing, but I still couldn't let him win me over too easily. "No."

Michael made a face. "Don't be a spoilsport, Kali. Think of the fame you'll receive in the supernatural community if you pull this off. The power you'll have—everyone will fear you."

I pretended to consider it. "The sword showed me...your power."

"That was just a taste. I knew it would suck you in. Wait until you feel the full dose. I can give that to you, Kali. Power beyond your wildest dreams."

Licking my lips, I canted my head back to stare at the blue sky. My ribs were mending but still painful. My back and neck as well. I looked at Michael once more, pretending I was a druggie after the high he promised. "You're sure I can kill him if I have enough of your magic?"

The spider smiled, believing he was luring the gullible fly into his web. "Do you see what I did here today? That's child's play. I have the power to wipe out everyone on this planet if I want to. I never would, mind you. My job is to protect humans. They call on me to help them and keep them safe. I would never destroy them."

*Right.* He would do anything that served his purposes. "Then why don't you kill Lucifer if you're so powerful? Why do you need me to do your dirty work?"

"Archangels cannot kill other archangels."

I coughed again, more blood flooding my mouth. I spit it out. "Not even with your sword?"

"It's not a matter of the sword's Heavenly power. It's the

order of things. We cannot destroy each other, much like you cannot take revenge for yourself."

The laws of magic were few, but they were inviolable.

I took my time rolling the possibilities around in my tired brain, letting Michael think I struggled with my choice.

As if I had one. "I do this for you, and you'll bring every one of my companions back to life?"

A pleased look crossed his features. "I'll even let you keep your memories as a bonus."

"I'll keep my memories, but that's not my bonus."

He sensed I was about to ask for something big. His hand went to his sword, believing that was the pawn I sought. "You cannot keep the sword. Once your assignment is complete, you will return it to me."

"I don't want your sword," I said, licking blood off my bottom lip. That was a lie, but I intended to pry the sword from his cold, dead fingers after I killed him.

"What do you want then?" Tabriss asked.

I met her gaze and then his. "Once Lucifer is gone, Hell will need a new ruler."

Michael's brows shot up. "You think to become queen of the Pit?"

"Not queen." Lilith already held that title, and whether in Hell or on Earth, I was learning that the title of queen wasn't enough for me.

My demon buzzed with renewed energy at the prospect. "I want to be the ultimate authority. God of Hell, if you will. If I destroy Lucifer for you, Hell is mine, and all mine."

Michael's hesitation lasted less than a heartbeat. He held out a beefy mitt. "Deal. You'll bring Lucifer's head to me on a platter."

"And I want the Fallen," Tabriss said.

I questioned Michael with my eyes, but I spoke to her. "What for?"

"To wipe them from existence. They cannot enter Heaven, no matter the prophecy about Lucifer's child. They are tainted with sin and deserve Hell."

There was a definite us-versus-them vibe. "You're Fallen, Tabriss."

"No." She shook her head adamantly, her violet eyes fierce. "Lucifer forced me out. I never would have betrayed Michael or our Father."

Michael seemed to be buying this story. Maybe he was the one who'd fed it to her. "You took her back to Heaven, didn't you?" I accused.

He shrugged as if it made no difference. "Kill Lucifer and let Tabriss have the Fallen. Hell will be yours."

"Not so fast. I want my friends back."

He looked bemused. "You don't trust me to abide by our agreement?"

Not particularly. "Call it a show of faith."

"Once you have your friends back, what guarantee do I have you'll perform your side of the deal?"

"Trust me, I want Hell," I said. "And I have no more love for your brother, or his Fallen, than you do."

Tabriss nodded. "I can attest to that. She barely tolerates the them. Besides, like you said, she's not stupid. Careless now and then, but she knows what you'll do to her and her lover if she doesn't comply. He's her weakness."

My healing ribs allowed me to breathe easier. "I need to remain as head of the Institute if I'm to get close to Lucifer and bring you the Fallen. It's the only place he visits regularly without worry for his safety."

"She has a point," Michael said to Tabriss. "It would be best for her to continue on as if nothing has changed."

The female angel rolled her eyes, but her scorn did not dissuade him. He was the true master the outcasts had referred to. Not Tabriss.

But not for long if I had any say about it.

"Bury your dead, demon," Michael said. He laid a hand over my chest at heart level and a surge of magic zapped me, locking up my heart for a moment and making me arch slightly. "Like you, I'm not easily misled. Once you've taken care of Lucifer and handed over the Fallen to Tabriss, I will bring back your friends, but not until then."

He released me and I slumped forward, my heart once again beating to a somewhat different rhythm. Before I could argue, he and Tabriss disappeared in a flash of light.

I sat motionless for a long moment, clouds gathering over the sun and throwing the destroyed building into shadows.

Crawling on hands and knees, I made it to Rad and grasped him by the lapels of his coat, pulling his upper body into my lap. Tears fell from my eyes, the agony in my chest so ferocious I wailed my heartache into the darkness.

## 33

$\mathcal{B}$ ent over Rad's body was where Lucifer, a dozen Institute demons, and the entire Chicago House of vampires found me when they arrived. My army had come, but much too late.

"What happened here?" the king of Hell asked, looking around at the devastation.

I had no energy for explanations and my anger at Michael quickly morphed into anger at him. "What the fuck does it look like? I took on your brother and lost."

A muscle in Lucifer's jaw jumped. "The world believes Chicago experienced an earthquake. Humans felt this from northern Canada to Texas. Even the underworld felt this."

"Just wait until I get your brother in Hell with me. Chicago won't be the only place feeling the tremors."

"He is quite good at pissing people off."

I was more than pissed, but if my plan was to work—f I was to save Rad and the others from eternal damnation—I had to keep my hate in check.

So I did what I had to and gave Lucifer and the shocked vampires the gist of the showdown. The only part during which Lucifer showed any emotion was about Tabriss's betrayal.

Staggering to my feet, my demon and vampire blood having healed the worst of my wounds, I handed out orders for the Chicago House Undead to administer to their king, Brianna, and Maddy. I put my fellow demons in charge of returning Cole, Rad, and Arman's bodies to the Institute.

As the two groups disappeared, only Lucifer and I remained, facing each other in the growing twilight.

"I want your Fallen out of the Institute by morning," I told him.

He didn't so much as cock a brow. "They're not ready."

"Not my problem. You and the Fallen are no longer my circus or my monkeys. Any angel who isn't out by sunrise will be escorted off the premises. If they put up a fight, I will kill them personally."

Lucifer narrowed one dark eye at me. "What did Michael promise you for your cooperation?"

"This isn't coming from him. This is all me. I've denied my true nature long enough. It's cost me everything I care about. I'm done. No more catering to the whims of you and your angels. No more protecting humans. You want Damon in Hell working for you? Good, keep him. The Institute is no longer an angel sanctuary and I'm no longer your errand girl, and I'm no longer your errand girl." I took a step closer, letting my demon shine through my eyes. "Let's see your child fix this vicious, immoral, and monstrous world. I no longer care about good and evil or who wins that fight. There's only one thing I care about now."

Lucifer didn't fear my demon any more than he feared a miniature spider. "What is that?" he asked, almost sounding bored.

"Destroying your brother."

"You can't destroy an archangel."

I saw a pale glow under a pile of debris and walked over to it, kicking the splintered wood and cement aside. The glow went megawatt, and Michael's sword brightened the entire area around my feet. Without even having to command it, it flew into my hand. I wondered if he had a name for it, as I did for my whip.

I held the sword high for Lucifer to see. "Wanna bet?"

The slightest show of surprise crossed his face. "How did you get that back?"

I would have smirked if I'd had the energy. Running my fingers along the blade, I simply started walking away. "Sunrise, Lucifer. Get your Fallen out of my Institute by then, or I'll start using this on them."

Swallowing down the bile in my throat, I made my way through the woods to the church. Inside, I let the sword fall to the ground in the living room, my knees following suit.

I'm not a crier. Ever. Yet, for the second time in an hour, I bawled like a human baby.

My parents had died because of me. My sister, too. Now Rad, Cole, Maddy, Arman, Dru, and Brianna. All gone.

Rage followed on the heels of despair. Rage and a need for vengeance.

My mind cleared after long minutes and I realized this might not be the end of it. I would have to play my part well. The only effective strategy available was to pit one archangel against the other.

This type of situation was all too familiar, and I hadn't been lying when I'd told Lucifer I was done. I had to bring my friends back, whatever it took, and then I was walking away from everything.

Wiping my eyes, I picked myself up, stripped, and bathed, shutting down the memory of their lifeless bodies, the images rolling like an old-time movie reel in my head. A numbness overtook my thoughts, and I went through the motions of cleaning off the grime.

I was braiding my wet hair when Di appeared in my bedroom.

"My god, Kali." She crossed into the bathroom, where I stood in front of the mirror, not at all awkward over the fact I was naked, and caught me in a hug. "I'm so sorry. What can I do?"

Lest Michael find out, I couldn't share my plan with anyone. Everyone had to believe I was going after Lucifer, just like Michael wanted, but I would need someone on the inside with me. Someone who wasn't susceptible to archangels.

Aphrodite was the only supernatural with enough power who fit that category.

I removed myself from her hug, dressed in my closet, and rejoined Di in the bedroom.

The church wasn't warded enough to keep Michael from eavesdropping, so I needed to communicate with her in two ways. "You can't help me."

Even as I said the words, I motioned at the heavens and then at my eyes, conveying that Michael was watching me. She nodded her immediate understanding. "Of course I can. Just tell me what you need."

"What I need is for you to go back to the Institute and round up the Fallen. They're to be gone by sunrise."

She cocked her head. "Where will they go?"

"That's for Lucifer and Damon to figure out. I don't care. I have a job to do for Michael."

She gave me a *what the hell* look. "What kind of job?"

"I can't talk about it." I motioned that I would tell her later. "Go back to the Institute and inform the Fallen."

She nodded and gave me the okay sign. "Lucifer won't be happy."

"I've already spoken to him," I said deadpan. "He's not."

"You're still doing it? Kicking them out?"

I had put on a special belt with a sword sheath. Michael's blade slid into it nicely. "I'll escort every one of them out personally if necessary."

Di shrugged and rose from the edge of my bed. "I never cared for them much, anyway. A bunch of whiners."

I tried contacting Damon through our mental link since I figured it was secure from Michael's prying ears, but he seemed to be ignoring me. What a time to go AWOL. I had planned on his assistance to get a message to Lucifer about the double-cross I had laid out in my head, but it looked like I might be on my own. If Lucifer had already informed him of his protégé's insurrection, Damon may have decided it was better to cut all ties.

I couldn't blame him, but it hurt, realizing he didn't have my back when push came to shove.

A half-hour later, I ignored Sal and the other *vitiums* at the Institute, drawing only Di and Kirill down to the warded dungeon. "One minute," I told them as we passed Vicky's cell.

I went back and entered the witch's quarters. She was on the floor meditating again.

"Your cloaking spell didn't work, bitch. You won't be helping me take down Michael."

"Didn't work?" She looked honestly surprised. "I don't believe it."

"Play dumb, but you cut off your own foot. The spell worked the first couple of times I left the Institute, I had no trouble with Michael. After that, when I really needed it, it failed. You've lost your mojo, Vicky, and that failure cost me dearly, so you can kiss any freedom you were counting on goodbye."

She sneered. "You stupid demon. I told you it was only good for twenty-four hours. If you went out after that, it wasn't the spell that failed. It was you."

Damn. For some reason, even after my memories had returned, I'd forgotten the particulars of that. But then, I'd been under just a little stress.

"Do it again. Now. Perform the cloaking spell, and I'll test it again."

She rolled her eyes but raised her hands and began chanting. I'd left the sword upstairs in my office, but Volante and my demon both welcomed the rise of magic.

Like pepper under my nose, Vicky's magic made me want to sneeze. Still, she was right—the spell had worked as intended when I'd visited the church the first time, keeping me hidden from Michael, although not from the outcasts. I needed that cloaking again.

Once she finished, I ordered the guard to bring her a decent dinner. She laughed and told me the next spell would cost me more than that.

"Trust me, witch, your time will come. I still need help with Michael, and you're going to be key in sending him back to Heaven empty-handed."

She eyed me with speculation and a bit of wariness. "Your magic feels different. What happened to you?"

*Everything.* "Nothing." I left her cell, closing it behind me and kicking up the wards on it. Down the hall, I caught up with Di and Kirill, leading them into an empty one. I used my magic to expand Vicky's cloaking, mixing in my superpowers with it.

Kirill looked around and screwed up his nose. "What the hell is going on? Why are we down here? Why are you kicking the Fallen out?"

Without Damon to help me, I had to look at my next best options. I wasn't sure I could count on Kirill, but between him and Di, they were my only hope. "Michael doesn't want to possess me in order to kill Lucifer's child. He wants me to take revenge on Lucifer."

Kirill's mouth dropped open as the words sank in. "You said no, right?"

"If I do the job, Michael will bring Rad and the others back to life."

Kirill started to argue, but Di stopped him. "She defeated Lilith when that bitch wanted revenge on Lucifer. She can handle Michael." She turned to me. "What's your plan?"

She's my best friend for a reason. "Lucifer has to believe I'm coming after him. I need you to leak it to the Fallen before they leave."

"Lilith was a different story," Kirill interjected. "She's a demon. Lucifer Morningstar is an *angel*. One of the archangels. God's favorite."

I looked at Kirill. "Thanks for clarifying that, but in the long run, it makes no difference."

"How can you say that?"

"Just listen. I'll get Lucifer and Michael in the same room—or at least within proximity to each other. Once they're together, I'll force Michael to bring Rad and the others back to life, and then we'll either return Michael to Heaven or take him out with Lucifer's help."

"Oh, Kali." Kirill shook his balding head. "This is a very dangerous game you're playing, pitting archangel against archangel."

"I can handle it."

They teach humans about non-verbal language, but it comes naturally to most of us. Kirill's body language clearly stated he didn't trust me in the least.

His cynicism was expected, but his lack of belief in me hurt. "After all the things I've done for the Bridge Council, after all the things I've done to save humans, you may not fully trust me, but you should, at the very least, have confidence in me. I do what I say I'll do. I may not do it your way, but I handle whatever needs handling. Every. Damn. Time. That,

Kirill, is why Damon put me in charge of the Institute instead of you."

He made a face and crossed his arms over his bulky chest. "For your information, I never wanted to be in charge. I have more interesting pursuits than shuffling papers and babying supernaturals. I just want it put on record that I am against this plan of yours."

"If you're not up for it, you can leave—as in, leave the Institute. I need my allies on board one hundred percent."

He drew back as if I'd hit him. "You can't force me to leave."

"Try me."

Di shifted so she stood shoulder-to-shoulder with me, Kirill looking panicked as his gaze ping-ponged between us.

I petted Volante, who slithered with eagerness around my arm. "You're either onboard, or you're gone, Kirill. Those are your choices."

"This is insane. You can't destroy an archangel."

"Michael shared some of his angel power with me and left me his sword to smite Lucifer. He claims that combo will do the trick."

"And if he's lying?"

"I'm sure he has no qualms about lying to a demon, but what will he gain if I fail? Lucifer will destroy me, and he'll still be around to bug Michael."

"You're going to use Michael's own magic and sword against him." Di nodded, calculating my odds. "Smart."

"It's not smart!" Kirill paced, sweat beading on his forehead. "It's the most asinine plan I've ever heard!"

"First," I spoke to Di, ignoring him. "I have to get Rad and the others back. The timing is the tricky part, getting Michael to raise them before I take care of him."

Kirill rubbed the top of his head, the back of his neck. "If this backfires, we'll go straight to Hell."

"Got that covered too," I told him. "If I end up forced to

destroy Lucifer, Hell is mine. Michael promised. Not that I trust his word on that, but you never know. It's not like Michael wants the Pit for himself."

"Hell is...*yours*?" Kirill blinked, flabbergasted. "Do I want to know how you pulled that off?"

I grinned, even though I didn't feel like it. "In or out, Kirill?"

He sighed dramatically and looked around the tiny cell as if the answer might be written on the warded stones. "Oh, all right," he said after a moment. "But if this goes sideways, I'm looking out for myself."

"Fair enough, but if you try to stop me, I'll kill you."

He nodded, demon to demon. I was stronger than he'd ever be, and he had enough self-preservation to know that defying me here, after I'd confided in him, could send him to Hell prematurely. "I won't try to stop you."

I had one chance to pull this off and only a few hours before sunrise. "Here's what I want you two to do."

# 34

*D*esperate times call for desperate measures, or sometimes just plain old sucky ones. While I wanted to be upstairs with the bodies of my friends, making sure Kirill and Seraphina put them in a proper stasis until they could be brought back from the dead, I had to trust the demon doctor to do his job while I did mine.

"You said you could handle this." I poked Vicky's bare foot with the tip of Michael's sword, giving her a goose of angelic energy. She snarled and the cell pulsed from the magic she and I were trying to work together while it was still warded and cloaked. No easy task. One of the Fallen, bound and gagged, both physically and magically, lay between us. "Do you need an amplifier? I have the human Noctifector next door if you need extra juice."

I said this to aggravate her, knowing a mere human would do nothing to help her powers, but still enjoying the idea of giving up Parker to be used as a sacrifice.

All in the name of the greater good, of course.

"I'm hungry." Her fangs showed. "I need your blood, not some worthless human's."

Ah, yes. The problem with blood slaves—they always want more of you. "I'll have someone bring you a pint after you perfect that spell."

The extra motivation would do her good.

The showdown that was about to happen would put everyone at the Institute in danger. Everyone who was left, anyway. I'd pleaded with Neve to leave town and visit relatives in Pennsylvania. She had refused so Di had knocked her out and taken her there anyway, courtesy of the Goddess Express. I expected Neve to no longer consider me her best friend, but her safety was paramount. The other *vitiums* were helping the angels pack for their mass exit, and Gor had taken over for Cole, doubling up on the already maximum-security measures in place.

Di had done the job I'd asked of her, carefully leaking the word to the angels about my assignment from Michael. A small contingent was hunting me, thinking to take me out and save Lucifer, but I was a ghost in the walls. Not many knew the Institute and all of its hidden rooms and tunnels the way I did. Plus, I could sense the angels coming from a mile away, so I made sure to stay ten steps ahead of them.

Lucifer knew he was on my hit list by now. The sniveling angel at my feet—the same one who'd challenged me in the stairwell a few days ago—had been the first to send him the message.

With sunrise an hour away, I awaited Lucifer's visit. Hell, I'd still take Damon at this point.

Unfortunately, neither had had the balls to show up.

The fear of failure ate at me. As Vicky worked on the spell I needed, I tried not to count the minutes until the sun rose. Had Lucifer found a new place for his Fallen? There was no way they were ready to fight yet, but he might have procured a new, secure training ground and knew a way to move them from here to there without exposing them to Michael and Tabriss. If he'd figured out a new place for them to hide out, he had no reason to show up and demand I let them stay.

The one contingency I hadn't prepared for.

*Damon! Answer me! Get your boss here, pronto!*

"Keep working at it," I told Vicky, leaving her cell.

I caught sight of the end of the hallway where Rad and I had exchanged words and bodily fluids the previous day. My heart pinched and I shut it down. It served no purpose. I had to stay focused.

I'd taken two steps toward the stairs when I felt the slithering heat of Lucifer's magic up my spine. I pulled up short, one booted foot on the bottom step.

"About damn time," I said, turning to face him.

I hoped that Damon was with him. Instead, I found him flanked by two other angels.

*Merde.* Lucifer had brought backup, just not Damon. Another contingency I had not planned for.

I twirled the handle of Michael's sword in my hand, lifting it in a protective gesture. "You brought reinforcements, I see."

Lucifer didn't fear anything, not even his older brother's sword. "Lower that thing and meet Raphael and Arial. This is the vengeance demon I told you about," he said to them.

More archangels. Oh goodie. "How did you get them through the wards?"

Lucifer raised a brow as if I were stupid. "Damon knows you and your magic well."

"*Faccia di culo.*" Of course he would know how to break through my wards.

"Raphael and Arial are here to heal you."

"Heal me?"

Raphael was as tall as Lucifer with long, brown hair that curled at the ends. His skin was olive-toned like my own, and his brown eyes probed my face and down my body as if I were an insect under glass. His X-ray vision lingered on my forehead for a moment before meeting my eyes. His wings were visible, a rainbow of colors and stark in contrast to the dark, drab walls. "I am here to remove Michael's curse from your brain."

Ah, yes, Raphael was the healer, wasn't he? "My nose is back in working order, and I have all of my memories again. I don't need healing."

"For now," Arial said, her voice beautiful as a melody. Everything about her was soft and delicate, including the pink roses she'd placed in her hair. Or maybe they were growing *out* of her hair, I couldn't quite tell. Either way, she looked as completely out of place in this cold, dank, evil environment as Raphael did.

Her wings shimmered pink and gold, rippling when she spoke. "It won't last."

"Why not?"

Lucifer huffed, impatient. "Until Michael's magic is totally removed from your brain matter, it will continue to infect you. You're only in remission at this moment because he wills it."

Great, but in the end, what did I care? Once Rad and the others were topside again, I wasn't hanging around. I would clear out and disappear, and none of them, including Michael, would find me.

But I sensed Lucifer wasn't offering me a cure out of the goodness of his heart. "If Raphael clears that magic, it removes the power Michael gave me as well."

I saw the confirmation on the king of Hell's face even though nothing about his features actually changed. I shook my head. "That would render me unable to complete the job he gave me. That's the real reason you brought your siblings here."

Again, not even a flicker suggesting it was true. "You no longer need to worry about my child," he said. "Azaria is safe from Michael."

He spoke as if the baby were here in the flesh. "Amy gave birth?"

A dip of his head. "Through a series of unfortunate events, Michael is now my daughter's guardian."

"What?" The irony hit me and I laughed out loud. Humans usually create their own storms, but angels? "You're kidding. How in the world did that happen?"

"Amy prayed for Azaria's protection hours before she was born. God granted the request."

"He sent Michael?" It was the best laugh I'd had in days, probably weeks. "No wonder your big brother changed his mind about who he wanted me to go after."

"Changed his mind?" Lucifer's steady gaze bore down on me. I saw the wheels turning in his angelic brain. If not Azaria, then... "We've been here before, demon, haven't we?"

"We have, and I don't care for it anymore this time than last. But like when Lilith hired me to take vengeance on you, I'm the one in the middle of a fight I have no dog in."

"If you go after my wife, I will end you."

Wife? "You married her? You've been busy, haven't you?"

"Our souls have always been bound, but she wished to be married in the ways of humans."

And he couldn't say no. Real love there, folks. Why, in the name of Hell, would God kick him and Amy out of Heaven?

Not my circus. What I really wanted to know was did Rad and I have that kind of love? Would I have the chance to find out?

A part of me wished Amy *was* my assignment, but it didn't make any difference. While she might be easier to take care of than Michael or Lucifer, doing so would bring Lucifer's sour attitude to new heights. When he said "end you," what he meant was to chain me to his wall of fire and let his minions torture me for all eternity. I don't mind torture, but eternity's a long time without chocolate, wine, or Rad. "If you want to make this go away, bring my friends back to life, and I'll tell Michael to go screw himself."

"It doesn't work that way."

"Why not?"

"Michael extracted their souls," Raphael said, continuing to eye me like I was a novelty. Maybe he'd never been close to a real demon before. "He holds their souls now and is the only one who can return them, besides our Father."

"I was afraid of that." But there was the technicality I was ready to exploit.

"He will not bring them back, even if you kill Amy," Lucifer warned when I started to say more.

*No, but he might if I kill you.* "Why do you say that?"

The three archangels exchanged a look. One I didn't particularly like.

"As you can imagine," Raphael said, crossing his arms over his chest, "Michael has no use for supernaturals of your kind. Or pretty much any that are not angels. He considers you all an abomination."

"I suspected his promises were worthless, but..." I toyed with Volante's handle as my brain ran through various scenarios I'd been working on. "How do I know I can believe *you,* either? You could be lying as well."

Arial snorted. "We don't lie."

"Says every entity who's lying," I countered. "Prove it."

"How?" Raphael asked.

I looked at Lucifer. "Cole is a demon, so he has no soul, and that means he's in Hell. You rule there, last I checked, and all who exist there are under your control. For now, anyway."

He narrowed his eyes, silently questioning the last bit of that statement. "And?"

"Bring him back."

"No."

"The king of Hell can't raise a lowly War demon and send him back to the earthly plane?"

Lucifer never gives anything away. I felt the eye roll over my taunting even though he didn't move a muscle. "It is possible."

"Good. Let's go upstairs where the bodies of my friends are, and you can bring Cole back." If I was making deals with the devil, I might as well go all the way. "Throw Damon in, too, and I won't go after your witch."

He seemed to consider it. "Damon is still needed to help with the Fallen."

I stepped forward. "Damon is needed here. Find someone else to do your bidding."

Raphael and Arial took my demand as aggression and closed rank around Lucifer. Raphael glared down at me. "Watch yourself, demon."

"How cute," I mocked. "Taking care of your little brother, who, from what I've seen, possesses far more power than either of you."

Arial actually smiled. "You're right, Kali. Lucifer doesn't need our protection." She stepped directly in front of him and got in my face. "But that doesn't mean we won't send you to Hell on his behalf."

"Hellfire and damnation," Lucifer swore. He rubbed a hand over his face. "That's the last thing I want or need. The vengeance demon stays here, and she can have her proof of our intentions." To me, he said, "I thought you didn't care anymore about the Institute, so why do you want Damon back?"

"Soon, I won't be here to run things, and those left behind will need him."

"Kali?"

The familiar voice came from the top of the stairs. I whirled and saw my friend and bodyguard standing there, looking completely shocked. "Cole!"

Taking the steps two at a time, I reached the top and grabbed him by the shoulders. "Are you okay?"

He rubbed his head and then his chest. "What happened?"

It might take a bit for his brain and magic to get back in the game. "Michael killed you, Lucifer brought you back."

"I'm sure there's more to that story, and you'll tell me later over a beer."

I smiled and patted his shoulder. "You got it."

I returned to the angels. "What about Damon?" I asked Lucifer.

He shook his head. "Not him, but your vampire friends are once again among the living. Or Undead, I should say."

My eyes widened, even though I tried to stay as neutral as the fallen archangel in front of me. "Thank you."

"You'll leave Amy alone, and you'll allow the Fallen to continue to reside here in exchange."

Changing the agreement on me. How devil-like. "Yes to leaving your wife alone. No to the Fallen staying."

"I gave you back the Undead in good faith."

"And I've been a loyal subject to you. Need I remind you that I took on Lilith to prevent Amy's death not so long ago? If it weren't for me, you'd have no wife or child at this moment. It was also me, along with my friends, who took on the Four Horsemen to save the earth and all who reside here, again, saving your witch. It's no skin off your back to raise a demon and a few vampires from Hell, but it means everything to me."

"Why do you take issue with the Fallen?" Raphael asked.

"They annoy me."

He believed that but knew it wasn't the real reason. "You don't strike me as the petty type."

I shrugged, not giving him anything more.

Lucifer eyed me with that intense stare. "When the Fallen walk out the front gate," he said, quicker on the uptake than his brother, "Michael will be able to sense them."

I touched the tip of my nose. "Winner, winner, chicken dinner. I've heard he's not a fan. What a shame for you to have found so many of your followers only to lose them again."

"We can cloak them," Arial said.

Raphael shook his head. "If we use our powers en masse to do that, Michael will sense the disturbance in the earth's energy field. He'll know what we're doing and come after them anyway."

I raised my hand. "I might know how to save them."

Arial squinted at me. "You're the one throwing them out. Why would you...?" She trailed off as she realized the trap I had led them into. "You're doing this on purpose! To trick us."

"I don't know why that surprises you. I *am* a demon."

She made an exasperated sound. Lucifer asked, "How can you cloak them so Michael will not notice?"

"I have a witch who can do it. Her magic is dark, not light, so Michael won't sense any disturbance in the energy around here since dark magic is *de rigueur*. My witch is here and ready to do what I ask, but if you want the Fallen to be safe, you have to help me get Rad and Arman back."

"I told you," Lucifer said. "I cannot bring them back to life."

"You can't personally, but if you want to save your Fallen comrades and don't want to be looking over your shoulder all the time wondering if your new wife is safe, I suggest you help me force Michael to undo what he's done. I believe the key is Tabriss."

"Tabriss?" Arial looked at Lucifer. "You found her?"

"Damon found her, I rescued her," I corrected. Lucifer obviously hadn't filled them in. "She's a real peach. Apparently, she and Michael are best buds once more, and she's got a jones for wiping out the rest of the Fallen."

"She was always his favorite," Raphael said. "I'm not surprised, but wipe out her brothers and sisters? Why?"

"No clue, but that's what she wants." I glanced at the large, ticking clock on the wall. "Sunrise is thirty minutes away. If we're going to cloak the Fallen before they're kicked out into the world, we need to get this show on the road. Are you going to help me get Rad and Arman back or not?"

Raphael and Arial glanced at Lucifer. He stared daggers at me, but I heard the faintest bit of awe in his tone. "You're more clever than I gave you credit for."

"Don't be too hard on yourself," I said. "Most angels underestimate me. Demons too. I'm surprised Damon didn't warn you."

"He did. I didn't believe him. Now I understand why Amy likes you so much."

I shrugged nonchalantly even though my veins hummed with anxiety. Lucifer wasn't one to mess with, and although he probably wanted to take the easy way out and let me cloak his Fallen, he was just as likely to strike me down and send me to Hell.

I had the sneaky suspicion it wouldn't quite work that way, however, with Michael's magic inside me. Neither of us knew for sure how effective I'd be at fighting back if Lucifer tried to end me.

I was ready to find out. Lucifer, not so much. After all, I wasn't an archangel, but I had some pretty righteous archangel powers at the moment.

"I did it!" Victoria yelled from her cell. "The spell works!"

Lucifer glanced toward the witch's prison cell, then at Michael's sword. "I assume you have a plan to blackmail Michael into raising your friends from Hell?"

It was really more of a statement than a question. "Yeah, and you're not going to like it."

"Silly me. Here I thought it would be fun."

The devil making a joke? "How do you feel about torture?"

One tiny section of his right upper lip tweaked. His eyes flashed with evil. "Tell us what you want us to do."

I looked at his cohorts. "You two helping?"

They exchanged some eye contact, then Raphael nodded.

"As long as you're not going to kill Michael. He is our brother, after all."

I sighed. "You guys are no fun."

"Swear to it, demon," Lucifer said. "We don't want to destroy him, only send him back to Heaven. Can you do it?"

*Oh, my dear king of Hell...* "You might be surprised at what I can do."

## 35

The graveyard behind the church I called home was eerily quiet in the early morning twilight. The sun was rolling over in bed, not ready yet to break the horizon, but inching closer, the shadows in and around the cemetery edged with purple and gray. In my mind, it was the perfect horror movie setup—I could imagine zombies, vampires, and serial killers all emerging from the woods to close in on me.

I'd take zombies, vampires, and serial killers any day over angels.

But angels seemed to be my lot in life these days, so angels it was.

The stage was set: Lucifer was on a tall Celtic cross inside the cemetery, bound, gagged, and beat up. Cole, next to him, kept a wary eye on the perimeter. I had no idea where Raphael and Arial had disappeared to, but I knew they were watching, ready to help their favorite little brother when the time came. I'd confirmed that Dru, Brianna, and Maddy were all amongst the Undead again but had asked them to stay away. I doubted Dru would abide by my wishes, so I hadn't told him what was going down or where. If he did as I suspected, he would go to the Institute looking for me. By the time he figured out I was here, I hoped the showdown was over.

Vicky was in the deeply shadowed northern corner, her magic cloaked. She kept the spell on him, and Di, Nemesis, and Athena watched over her to make sure she didn't screw up my presentation. The presence of the three goddesses wouldn't make Michael happy, but then, I'm not in the business of making archangels happy outside of my own interests.

Kirill and the other *vitiums*, minus Maria, laid Rad and Arman just inside the cemetery gates. I couldn't look at their lifeless forms, their bloodless lips. If I did, one of two things would happen – either I would go into rage mode and loose my demon again, taking out another couple blocks of Chicago, or I would cry.

Hell take me if I broke down and cried one more time.

Although I knew neither Rad nor Arman would blame me for what had happened, I still hated myself for letting Michael get the upper hand. My friends depended on me to protect them, and if I couldn't keep my own blood slaves safe, how could I protect all the others who worked and lived inside the Institute? How could I act as the Chicago House Queen? How could I continue to lead the Bridge in protecting humans?

I'm no victim, nor am I a martyr. I simply saw the logic behind my becoming a liability rather than an asset due to my increasing magical powers and prominence in the supernatural community.

I had no cloaking spell on me now as I paced around the king of Hell, who was strung up like Jesus on the cross. Symbolic and ironic all at once, don't you think? I did, and I enjoyed giving Volante free rein to do her damage.

The crack of the whip echoed in the air, which was heavy with magic and spirits. Lucifer cried out, the sound muffled against the ball gag in his mouth, kept there with powerful dark magic. His shirt and pants hung in strips, blood ran freely on the ground below his feet, and his face was a mass of purple and black bruises.

"Oh, Michael," I called in a sing-song voice. "Look who I have. Wanna say hi? May be your last chance."

He was no doubt watching. I hoped to goad him into joining the party.

No response, so I administered a few slaps and tickles just for good measure. The angel on the cross didn't like it, his angry magic straining to break free from the restraints Vicky and I had put on him.

"I thought for sure you'd want to look into Lucifer's eyes and say your peace," I called to Michael. "That's what makes true vengeance worthwhile, but..." I shrugged my shoulders, teasing the sharp end of the sword along Lucifer's neck and drawing a fine line of blood. "If you don't want to tell him off, tell him why you hate him so much and why you hired me to destroy him, I guess he'll die never really understanding the depth of your—"

A wave of angelic energy hit me so hard I nearly toppled over.

"I have something to say."

I turned to find Tabriss at the rickety iron gate.

Not Michael, but hey, this was even better.

Stepping aside so she could get a better view of the tortured soul on the cross, I eyed her as if suspicious. "What do *you* want? This isn't your affair."

Her gaze was glued to Lucifer, eyes firing with righteous anger. "I fell for you. I believed in you. And what did you do? Abandoned me. Abandoned all of us in your quest to find Amo."

Amo being Amy, his new wife. Apparently, in Heaven, she'd been named Amo, which meant love.

Gag.

Tabriss marched forward and got in his face, forcing me

back a few inches. "You spoiled, self-centered, heedless scapegrace. How dare you think that *you* of all angels can right the wrongs you have done to us?"

Lucifer's eyes rolled back in his head, wild with pain and urgency as he tried to communicate with her. While she ranted on and he made funny sounds against the ball gag, I mentally commanded Volante to slither down to the ground, snake-like, and make her way toward Tabriss's feet. At the same time, I touched my finger and thumb together, raising a barrier of magic around her, Lucifer, and myself.

When the ring of magic locked together, Tabriss felt the change in the air, stopping in mid-rant to look at me. "What was that?"

Pure innocence, that was me. "What was what?"

Realizing I was up to something, she snarled and tried to disapparate. My spell held her in place.

Which made her snarl morph into shock. And then she lunged.

Tabriss had been in a human body for a long time, and although she had plenty of street smarts, she was still getting used to her powers. Powers she could have used against me, but her natural instinct was to come at me physically.

Good thing I'd expected exactly that reaction.

She hit the wall of my protective shield; at the same time, Volante—already wrapped around her ankles—pulled taut.

With a loud gasp, Tabriss went down, doing a lovely belly flop on the ground at my feet.

You can take an angel out of Heaven, but you can't take Heaven out of the angel. Her powers instinctively kicked in, as they had in the training room, and she rose from the ground via levitation. Volante stayed secured around her ankles.

And then she did something that pissed me off even more than her grating attitude and the fact she'd finked out on Lucifer and ran to Michael.

She hit Volante with a burst of angelic magic and blew my beloved whip into a thousand pieces.

The burst of light and magic made me flinch, and then the pieces of my truest friend, a weapon that was as much a part of me as my inner demon, rained down around me.

Di gasped. Cole swore. On the cross, Lucifer stiffened.

Let me tell you, Hell hath no fury like an enraged vengeance demon.

Volante was not a being per se; she was a magically enhanced weapon. *My* weapon—one that had been with me since I'd been eight years old, through everything, protecting me as much as she could, and relishing every command I gave her.

In the blink of an eye, my demon rose, and I had Tabriss by the throat with one hand, the tip of the sword cutting into the skin under her chin. Her eyes went wide as I brought her levitating body back to the ground to face me.

"That was a mistake," I said through gritted teeth, clamping her throat hard enough she grabbed at my wrist and my fingers, trying to pry them loose.

She kicked and flailed like a two-year-old having a tantrum. Her magic was strong, stronger than mine on a normal day, but this wasn't any average, normal day. I was juiced up on archangel magic and I held the sword of Michael, ready to do my bidding.

*Throat to brainstem.* I could cleave her angelic head right off her shoulders.

But then I felt pressure inside my head and heard a familiar voice.

*Stop, Kali. Remember your end game.*

Damon.

*Fine time for you to show up*, I shot back and squeezed harder, enjoying the way Tabriss's eyes bugged out of her head. *Now, fuck off.*

A startled silence filled my head. Damon had taken offense.

*Seriously? I needed you, and where were you? You abandoned me. It's too late now to ride in on your magic horse and act pompous about saving me from my demon.*

He regained his composure. *Be careful what you do in the coming moments. Choose wisely.*

And then he was gone.

*Choose...* His voice from my dreams began an annoying, repetitive chant. Choose between saving Rad and condemning him to die? Choose between what Michael wanted and what I wanted?

I'm conniving, devious, sly, and underhanded. I've never been accused of being wise.

My demon demanded blood for Volante. I was about to run Michael's sword through Tabriss when Michael himself stopped my hand.

"Let her go."

I didn't. Nor did I look over my shoulder at the archangel that had started this fucking mess. His presence, with its angelic glow illuminating the cemetery, grew brighter and sent the evil, restless spirits scurrying back to their graves.

Smart angel that he was, he hadn't crossed into the graveyard like Tabriss, his hovering aura staying just outside.

The benefits of the graveyard being over a portal to Hell are many. The reason I'd wanted to hold this little business meeting here was to have a direct highway to the place no angel ever wants to go.

I smiled at Tabriss, still in my grip, as I spoke to Michael. *Show no fear. Act like an equal.* "Bring Rad and Arman back to life or Tabriss goes straight to the Pit."

Her already wide eyes grew wider.

It didn't take the archangel more than a heartbeat to put two and two together. "You would double-cross me?"

The disbelief in his voice, the sheer incredulousness, made

me roll my eyes. His ego was bigger than Lucifer's. I hadn't imagined anything larger than that.

"Isn't that what you planned to do to me?" I asked. "Get me to kill your brother, and then you'd kill me, right? I'm just a bothersome, evil demon, after all. You need someone to do your dirty work, but you never intended to keep me around or bring my friends back to life."

"Lower the sword from Tabriss, and your friends will be returned to full health."

Now *this* was a choice of epic proportions. He wanted to save Tabriss. I wanted to save Rad and Arman. Who would flinch first?

I tightened my grip on Tabriss. Her legs swung, kicking at me, but continued to bounce off my shield. "How do I know that once my friends are walking the earth again, you won't come after them in the future? Or me? I want protection for all of us, just like you're giving to Lucifer's brat."

Behind Tabriss, Lucifer shook his head violently, still making guttural noises that no one could understand.

Michael's glow intensified ever so slightly as if he were getting antsy. "I give you my word that I will not come after you or your friends. You will be Hell's new leader, and your friends will be safe from me."

"Your word doesn't mean jack squat right now. I want your promise in blood. I want your mark on my them, so no one messes with them."

"I have no such mark."

I sliced a bloody line down Tabriss's chest. She barely flinched, her eyelids fluttering. The lack of oxygen was getting to her. "Better make one up quick, then."

I heard a muffled sigh. "Is there no limit to your evil, demon?"

"This is just the tip of the iceberg, *archangel*." I spit the word at him. "Go ahead and test me. You won't like the results."

"I could wipe you and everyone here off the face of the planet. Do you think it wise to cross me?"

The three goddesses, who had been utterly quiet and watchful up until now, pulsed with intensified hate. I had warned them Michael would try to bluff his way out of my charade, and I'd told them to remain detached. They were not to move or interfere unless I gave them the signal.

"If you could, you would have done it already," I goaded. "You can't kill Lucifer, but I can, and I'm the only one willing to do it, so go ahead. Wipe us all out. Lucifer will still be here. The goddesses will still be here. And let me tell you, they'll all be really, really pissed off. But most of all? I'll take Tabriss to the Pit with me, and you'll never see her again." I stroked her hair with the blade of the sword. "The two of us will have so much fun together."

The fallen angel in question had gone completely limp. I knew she wasn't dead, but this was a nice preview for Michael. I lowered her so her feet dragged the ground, but I didn't turn loose of my chokehold.

I finally faced him. "Why didn't you protect her? Save her from this retched life she's been living all these centuries as an immortal? You love her, don't you?"

His cold eyes softened to a passionate orange as he gazed at her limp body. He moved to stand in the cemetery's open gates but didn't cross the threshold. "She was the first. The most special."

The *first*? Meaning his first love?

Eww.

He glanced at Lucifer. "She and I had what Lucifer has with Amo. Once Tabriss was gone, I..."

Silence hung, his attention returning to her.

"You wanted her back," I finished for him.

"She was reincarnated as a human, and her angelic spirit was hidden from me. I knew not why until Jesus cast all of you"

—he motioned to the other *vitiums*—"out. Later, I thought I had found her, but God had other plans."

Cue the violins. "A long, sad story." By now, my arm should have tired from holding up Tabriss's dead weight, but I was drawing on her magic, feeding off it, and combined with all the other magics in my system, I felt stronger than ever. "But killing Lucifer now, after he *did* find her, seems rather...petty." I figured Raphael was smirking somewhere as I used his term. "His brat can reunite the Fallen with Heaven. Why would you not want that? She could come home."

Michael didn't appreciate being questioned or chastised. "She wasn't just reincarnated like Amo. She is an immortal human."

I shrugged. "So?"

"Her human body cannot die and release her spirit, so no matter what Azaria accomplishes to reunite the Fallen with Heaven, Tabriss can never return there."

"Because she can't escape her human body? Tragic." I tsked and used the sword to point skyward. "You don't want to be here, and she can't go up there. At least not permanently."

His gaze once more returned to the icy hue I recognized. He held out a hand. "Give her to me."

*When Hell freezes over.* Which might actually happen soon.

Tabriss stirred, enough oxygen back in her system to bring her out of unconsciousness. "Mi...chael?" she half-whispered, her throat raw from the strangulation.

"My friends first," I said to the angry archangel. "Then I'll let her go and finish my assignment because, whether you believe it or not, I always finish the job."

He hesitated, weighing his options. Unknown to him, he really didn't have any.

A second later, Rad and Arman stirred. Just like that—without Michael so much as moving a muscle or blinking an eye.

His blade hummed in my hand. My absolute, gut-wrenching relief at seeing Rad sit up and look at me was so strong that I nearly crushed the handle.

"Kali?" Rad looked down at himself before his gaze bounced around at the audience watching him. His eyes then checked out the cemetery and Lucifer's unfortunate predicament. "What's going on?"

I gestured at him and Arman with the sword but spoke to Michael. "What about the protection mark?"

Michael, exploitable at this moment, crossed the threshold to lay a hand on both Rad and Arman. Arman swayed as Michael forced him into sitting. Rad jerked away from the archangel, so I had to reassure him. "It's okay. Let him touch you."

A flash of iridescent light illuminated the graveyard for a moment, blinding me. Instinctively, I tightened my grip on Tabriss, pulling her close and expecting Michael to try and take her by force.

He didn't disappoint. A second later, blinking my eyes rapidly to clear my vision, I found the archangel standing right in front of me, a towering hulk of magic and passion. My demon wanted to lunge, but I held back, hoping my shields held against whatever he was planning.

He once again reached for Tabriss, her hand automatically going to his. "Release her," he said to me, their fingers intertwining. "And do your job."

I whistled, and like magic—pun intended—Raphael and Arial appeared, whisking Rad and Arman out of the graveyard – a little backup protection in case Michael was messing with me.

Raphael, as instructed earlier, closed the iron gates behind them, sealing the energy around us before he and the others disappeared in a flash.

The change in the air when the gates closed was like a lock

clicking into place. My sensitive hearing could almost pick up the distinctive sound of a deadbolt. *Ka-chunk.*

Michael glanced back but saw nothing. Raphael and Arial had already disappeared with Rad and Arman. "What did you just do?" he demanded.

Surprise, surprise. Satisfied that my friends were safe for now, I decided to let Michael in on my plan. "I love this graveyard because it's over a portal that goes straight to Hell."

He narrowed his eyes. Tabriss, still held in my clutches and starting to strain to break free, stopped squirming and whipped her head around to glare at me. "You can't..."

"Wanna try me?"

"I gave you what you wanted!" Michael's porcelain skin flushed with anger as he realized I might not fulfill my end of the bargain. His gold-tipped wings vibrated with rage. Spittle flew from his lips. "You're like every other lousy, bottom-feeding demon that ever walked the earth. I'll have no mercy on you or your friends."

He raised his free hand.

My shields heated instantly from the laser he sent my way, but they held, thanks to the magic I drew from Tabriss, combined with his sword. The blade was an instrument of righteousness, of protection, and certainly seemed to hold a vengeance streak, but as the current holder of said weapon, its protection against the archangel's anger kicked in due to the fact that I was, in fact, in need of it. He'd willfully given it to me along with the power in which to use it. Any direct attack on me, even from him, was thwarted.

Phew.

I chuckled with relief, which served to piss him off even more when he realized I hadn't been reduced to ashes. "After dealing with you, Hell is going to be a cakewalk when and if I ever land there."

Looking slightly confused, he lowered his hand and blinked in disbelief.

"We both need to work on our trust issues," I said, "so I'll take the first step."

In one deft movement, I swung around and stabbed Lucifer through the heart.

# 36

The angel on the cross went rigid, body seizing.

For one horrible second, his gaze pinned me. The cross trembled, the ground shook. Everyone struggled to keep their footing, and as the sound of thunder rent the air loud enough to make us all flinch, the sun broke over the horizon with a blinding flash.

A scream went up from everything—the birds, nocturnal animals, even the trees. The spirits in the graveyard wailed. Engulfed by the screams and the sun, the intensity was so severe it felt like my eyes were being burned out of their sockets and my eardrums would burst.

A heartbeat later, the light receded. Everything fell silent. The ground no longer quaked. As the rest of us blinked our vision back to normal, Michael staggered, his fingers breaking from Tabriss's. He clutched his chest and reached toward Lucifer's body. "No!"

Lightning came out of nowhere and struck the cross. In its wake, nothing but charred, smoking wood remained.

Lucifer Morningstar. Gone.

"Sweet," Vicky murmured from the corner of the graveyard.

Tabriss's knees went out, and I let her sink to the ground. Michael seemed to suffer the same problem, dropping to the tainted soil of the graveyard.

"What have you done?" he cried, staring at the cross in horror.

"Me?" I shook my head, not at all surprised. "You told me to finish my assignment. I did." I waggled my fingers at him. "Pony up."

He seemed to have trouble breathing. His hand clutched his chest, and he gasped in and out frantically. Angels didn't need to breathe as far as I knew, so I assumed it was more of an issue with his soul realizing he'd committed the ultimate sin, whether I'd pulled the trigger—or hefted the sword, in this case—or he had.

Michael, the most revered of archangels and God's right-hand son, wept.

As his tears hit the ground, they sizzled and tiny crystals formed. A shocked silence hung in the air, broken only by the sound of his sobs. The Celtic cross that had supported Lucifer's body slowly disintegrated, forming a pile of ash. I sunk the tip of the sword into the ground, using it to brace myself.

What, indeed, *had* I done?

Tabriss crawled to Michael, rounding over his back to comfort him. I gave them a moment, looking to the east and the rising sun, mourning my own loss.

There would never be another Volante.

Powerful magic still surged in my veins, but a bone-weariness weighed on me. I was tired mentally and emotionally. If I could have sat down without appearing weak, I would have.

Cole moseyed up beside me, his shoulder grazing mine and his quiet strength wrapping around me. I took what comfort I could in it.

A part of me wanted to walk away. Take Cole, Di, and the others and leave Michael and Tabriss in the graveyard. Let them deal with the fallout. What was done was done, and there would be consequences for all of us. At that moment, I didn't care.

I wanted a steak. And a hot cup of espresso. Maybe a side of pasta with Alfredo sauce.

And Rad. I wanted Rad.

But there was one last thing to take care of. Two, really, but one wasn't my place to reveal.

Michael raised from his crouch, unsteady on his feet, his eyes bloodshot. He stared at the pile of ash, then glanced up at the heavens. "I can't believe he's gone."

For such an egotistical ass, he seemed completely dismayed. As if he were truly shocked I'd actually *smote* his brother for him.

"You blackmailed me into killing him," I said. "Did you really think I wouldn't go through with it?"

"I...I..."

Tabriss snarled, tough and self-righteous again, but her tone became almost happy. Gleeful. "Of course he did. But ending Lucifer's existence is monumental. It changes everything! Surely even *you* can understand that."

I flicked my tongue against my teeth. "Seems like he should have thought of that a little sooner."

Michael clamped a beefy paw on her elbow. "We must go." He looked at me, the tears now dried up. "Hand me the sword."

I leaned on it, the tip still buried in the ground at my feet. "Tabriss is not going anywhere. She belongs to me."

Tabriss cocked a brow. "I certainly do not."

Michael puffed out his chest. "No more games, demon. I will leave you and your kind alone for now, but unlock the gate. Release the magic holding Tabriss here."

"The games have just started, Michael, and you would do well to remember you cannot outsmart me." I flicked my fingers at the gate. "You may go."

The iron gates unlocked, both literally and magically. I pulled the sword from the ground and used it to slit the inside of my forearm. Blood welled, and my demon licked her lips. "But Tabriss stays," I added.

The fallen angel, once the embodiment of the seven sins, flared her nostrils. Her gaze dropped and zeroed in on my blood as it ran down my arm and onto the ground. It coated the crystals Michael's tears had formed, and the spirits sprang from their hidey holes and rushed to lap it up.

Michael knew instantly what had happened. Tabriss's hunger pangs. Her ebbing strength.

He seemed to teeter, understanding the consequences. "Tell me you didn't," he whispered to her.

So focused was she on my blood she didn't hear him. Her tongue snaked out and licked her lips.

I lifted my arm, teasing her. "I fed her my blood before I knew who she was. *What* she was. She's my blood slave, so regardless of her nature or the fact she's my spiritual mother, my blood is in her veins. Demon blood. Vampire blood." I stepped forward and offered him the sword. At the same time, I offered her my arm. "She's more like me now than she'll ever be like you again. She belongs to me."

He cried out and went to smack me, but a sudden wall of angels appeared between us. Raphael, Arial, and...

Lucifer.

The real Lucifer, not Yael, the imposter who'd given his soul on the cross in place of the king of Hell's.

Vicky's spell had worked a minor miracle on the fallen angel, but it had still taken a bit of angelic mojo from the three angels now protecting me from their big brother to make his essence pass the Michael test. Not one of the three of them had shied away from using the angel as a sacrifice, so I figured my initial impression of Yael had been accurate. He'd been a troublemaker—there's one in every bunch—and he would not be missed by his fellow Fallen.

Plus, Raphael had assured me the angel would not be destroyed permanently. While Raphael could not bring his soul back to life as an angel, his soul would be reincarnated somewhere down the road.

Heaven is big on recycling.

Michael's face fell at the sight of Lucifer. Then he clenched his jaw, his features growing hard, unrelenting, as he shot daggers at me from his icy eyes.

"You tricked me," he snarled at me over Lucifer's shoulder.

"And good thing she did," Arial said. "Michael, what were you thinking?"

He snatched the sword and pointed the tip at Lucifer's face. "You have caused our Father nothing but pain."

"He's caused *you* pain," I corrected. Tabriss dropped to her knees and sucked greedily at my arm. "But if you didn't love him, you wouldn't have wept over his death."

Seething, Michael took one last look at Tabriss and turned, heading for the gates. "I will be back for you, demon."

"Promises, promises," I called, wondering if he was going to leave me with some of his mojo. "Just remember, I have Tabriss. She'll be in a cage for safekeeping. Anything happens to me, she'll be destroyed. I've already made the proper arrangements."

"See you back in Eden," Lucifer called as Michael left the enclosure before disappearing.

Eden, Illinois, a few hours west of Chicago, is where Lucifer lived with his new wife and child. "You should go home," I said to him. "Be with your family."

He turned and gave me a brisk nod. "The Fallen are allowed to stay at the Institute for now?"

"Of course."

"Let Raphael heal you, and then enjoy your friends."

A wink, and then he was gone.

"Did the Devil just...wink at me?" I asked the others.

Arial smiled. Raphael sighed. Beside me, Cole chuckled.

I'd made a deal with the Devil, and it wasn't over yet, but at least Rad was alive. Arman was alive. Everyone was safe.

Time to go home and enjoy what time I had left.

# 37

*T*he art of delegation is a tricky one, but during the early morning hours of the new day, I got damn good at it. The key was having the proper resources.

Di and her goddess buddies took care of Vicky and the Fallen, Kirill brought Arman and Rad in for a checkup. Maddy was waiting at the Institute by the time I arrived, Brianna with her. They were already handling Neve's normal duties and making sure I had a hot bath and a big meal waiting for me. I put Sal in charge of our new *vitium* think-tank I created on the spot to better handle the coming problems I knew we would encounter with the angels, both those currently living at the Institute and those with Michael in Heaven. I handed Tabriss over to them as well. It was time for her to get on board with her new mission in life – helping humans. Satiated and high from my blood, she agreed without issue.

I spoke with Dru on the phone and reassured him that all was well. He invited me to a midnight dinner to celebrate my success. For a moment, I hesitated, but in the end, I decided I deserved one last meal with my friend. He was going to need a new queen soon, and I had a few ideas for him.

By the time I finished my bath, Rad was done with Kirill's tests. He entered the bathroom just as I stepped out of the tub.

"Are you okay?" he asked, and I fell in love with him all over again.

"Are you?"

"Kirill gave me the all-clear. What you did..."

Words were inadequate, and I knew we would get to them later. I crossed the few feet between us and wrapped my wet arms around him. He lowered me to the plush rug on the floor, where I helped him undress in between long, lingering kisses before he slid inside me.

Our lovemaking was slow and gentle for once. I guess death and resurrection can do that to you—make you want to savor the moment. For me, it was bittersweet, knowing that when I disappeared into the world hours from now, he would try to come after me. Try to stay with me or convince me to come back.

But we were liabilities to each other now, just like we had been three hundred years ago in Maria's court. Our love would only bring us tragedy in the end.

We eventually moved to the bed and enjoyed a day of sleeping, making love, and talking. He played his guitar and sang to me as I inventoried my personal stash of weapons and silently mourned for Volante once more.

I gifted him a dagger with a ruby inset in the handle. "It will darken if danger gets near you," I told him.

He knew I was keeping things from him, and this put him even more on edge. He didn't even glance at the weapon as I held it out. "What kind of deal did you make with Lucifer, Kali?"

"The kind that's one-sided and only favors the Devil," I said lightheartedly. "He got to live, his wife and child are safe, and the Fallen still reside inside these walls. Meanwhile, I pissed off another archangel and nearly didn't get you back."

He rose from his seat on the bed, coming to stand in front of me. He brushed aside a strand of my hair, tucking it behind my ear. "But you did get me back, and I know there's more to it than you're admitting. Being in league with Lucifer always comes with a price."

"The house always wins," I agreed. "But I'd rather be in league with him than Michael."

"Both are more dangerous than I can fathom. Lucifer will expect something from you in the future."

I didn't have to lie about this. "Maybe. I honestly have no idea. I didn't kill him, obviously, which I think should be commended, nor did I throw out his precious Fallen, but he wasn't too happy about my tactics. Funny how angels think nothing about using blackmail, coercion, and extortion to get what they want, but they don't enjoy having the tables turned on them."

"Maybe Damon—"

"No," I cut him off. "Damon cannot help me with Lucifer or anything else."

He cupped my shoulders with his strong hands and squeezed. "You have the rest of us, *mon couer*. Don't forget that."

"Never."

I DIDN'T MAKE it to my midnight dinner with Dru.

Once the sun went down, I made the rounds, checking in on everyone, and saw that things were running well. Cole had training sessions going on in the gym, Tabriss was resigned to helping the *vitiums*, and Neve was back, bossing Di, Maddy, and Brianna around. Arman followed Maddy around, and although she complained loudly about him, she loved every second of it.

I spent time with each of my friends, and bequeathed my favorite throwing stars to Cole, who frowned and started asking questions like Rad had. I reassured him that all was well. "I was inventorying my weapons now that Volante is gone and came across these. Thought you might like to use them."

He accepted the throwing stars, dipping his head as he stared at them for a moment. Then he stepped forward and dropped his voice low as he spoke next to my ear. Behind us, the clang of metal and the grunts of hand-to-hand combat echoed under the high ceiling. "Wherever you're taking off to, I'm going with you."

Cole, a warrior through and through, and also a friend who actually knew me better on some levels than all the others.

I played dumb. "I'm going to the Chicago House for dinner with Dru at midnight. Not really your thing, but you're welcome to come."

He stepped back, rolling his eyes. "I'll be watching you," he said, walking away.

Hmm. If anyone could catch me in the act, it was him. I'd outsmarted an archangel, but Cole might be harder to dupe.

Good thing I like a challenge.

I returned to Damon's office—I was back to thinking of it as his— and kicked my feet up on the desk. The new one Neve had secured. It was missing a few nicks and scratches the old one had accumulated over the years, but by the time Damon came back, there would be plenty of wear and tear on this one. He would never know the difference. The one thing that seemed to be missing was Michael's sword.

Ironic that I had hated the thing, but ended up growing fond of it. It was truly powerful, and like Volante, seemed to possess its own personality and temperament.

I leaned back in the chair and took a good look around, wanting to remember everything that had happened here. Good memories and bad. Things that made me laugh, and a few that didn't. The Institute would continue to survive, just like it had for centuries. I was simply another spoke in the wheel. Once gone, someone would take my place.

Keeping my escape covert would be challenging. I considered putting it off for another day or two. My heavy heart lifted at the idea, but all I was doing was delaying the inevitable. I already knew what weapons I would carry, what clothes I would wear, and a general idea of when and how I would slip unnoticed into the night, but I needed some contingency plans.

I was working on those when Rad and Cole burst into the office, Dru on their heels. The three imposing males stood shoulder-to-shoulder and glared down at me.

"What's up?" I asked, but in my heart, I already knew. My plans had taken a turn. There would be no sneaking off tonight.

Dru, in the center, leaned on the desk to get in my face. "You're a coward."

I have been called many things in my life. Coward was not one of them. "I beg your pardon?"

"Did you really think we wouldn't realize what you're up to?" Rad asked.

Shame on me, I'd miscalculated my stealthiness. "What exactly am I up to?" I asked, playing the innocent card.

"Come on, Kali." Cole tossed one of my throwing stars on the desk. "Give us some credit. You want to ditch us, don't you?"

"Of course not." I didn't *want* to ditch them. I had to. "Why would I do that?"

Dru resumed the cross-examination. "Because of some misguided thought in your head that we're in danger if you're around."

I leaned back. "You are, as recently proven when Michael took out all of you in order to get me to do his bidding."

"Collateral damage." Rad poked the top of the desk with a finger. "That's all we were, and that could happen no matter who we're around or who we work for. That wasn't your fault, and you know it."

"Besides," Cole added. "You suck at the martyr shit, so knock it off."

So much had happened in the past few days, I felt the pressure cooker finally releasing. Not like it had with Michael and my demon cutting loose, but in a way I hadn't realized I'd been holding back equally well.

For years after escaping Maria's court, I'd been on my own. Even once I'd begun working for the Bridge Institute, I'd kept to myself as much as possible. Did my job, ran my own agency, and went home at the end of every night. Since Rad had come back into my life and Damon had given me more responsibilities, I'd been forced to accept friendships I'd never dreamed of. I'd been put in charge of supernaturals that made my skin bristle, and I learned to like the position anyway.

So part of me wanted to laugh off my plans to leave, but another knew that was risky business. "I appreciate the intervention, guys. I really do, but you know as well as I do that my presence here has become much too dangerous for everyone. There were plenty of entities who didn't like me before, but now there are more and more gunning for me. It won't stop. It will get worse."

Cole shrugged. "We're in this together. Always have been. What comes, comes. A good commander doesn't bail when under attack."

"Maybe I'm not a good commander. I can't ask you to sacrifice yourselves for my benefit."

"It's not up to you," Dru said, drawing up to his full height. It's our choice. Besides, you're Queen of Chicago's Undead. You have a blood allegiance to me and your subjects. If you walk away, I will be forced to come after you and return you to your post—by force if necessary."

He could probably do it too, since I'd given him my blood once to save his life. I know, I know, I have to stop doing that. Rad was my blood slave, and between him, Arman, and Dru, they could pick up my trail if I wasn't careful.

But I *was* careful. I had Vicky's cloaking spell and had

tweaked it to keep most all supernaturals from being able to find me.

And while a halfbreed and a cheetah weren't as good at tracking as say a wolf, Dru was a vampire. He was better at tracking his prey than any wolf or trained scent dog would ever be.

"You guys are acting emotionally, and I appreciate the love, go figure, but you have to be realistic. I outsmarted Michael once. I doubt I can do it again."

"You told him you could," Cole challenged.

"I might have been bluffing." I grinned, but none of the posse smiled back. "He knows my moves now. He won't be as easy to trick next time."

"You have Tabriss," Rad said. "I thought she was your ace in the hole."

"He left her without a backward glance when he realized she had my blood in her. She's tainted beyond his comfort zone now. Eventually, he'll forget he was ever in love with her. He'll sacrifice her without hesitation."

"So you'll use the cloaking spell Vicky gave you," Cole said. "That's what you were planning to do to get away from us, wasn't it?"

I'm not the only cunning and clever demon inside the Institute. "You know me far too well."

He grinned then, just one corner of his mouth lifting. "Don't you ever doubt it."

I sighed, halfway resigned to their combined wills. "I won't leave tonight, but I won't promise to stay forever either. I have to consider all the options. I have to make the tough choices, that's what Damon keeps telling me."

"If you leave, I'm going with you," Rad said, "so don't even think about sneaking out."

"Same." Cole took the throwing star back and slid it into a pocket. "I'm sure as hell not staying here without you."

He started for the door. Dru, still glaring at me, sniffed. "I'll expect you at 11:30 sharp."

"I thought our dinner was at midnight."

"We have House business to discuss. Victoria has petitioned me for a cell."

"She doesn't like her current one? What a surprise."

"Since she is a vampire, I must consider her request."

"We don't need half an hour to discuss that. She's all yours."

He rolled his eyes. "I'll see you at 11:30."

Rad lingered as the other two started to leave, but before they were out the door, the air near the desk shimmered, and I felt an unwelcome wave of heat.

"*Merde*," I swore under my breath, and sure enough, Lucifer appeared. Damon was with him.

"Miss me?" I asked the king of Hell. "It hasn't even been twenty-four hours."

My three companions froze, suspecting as I did, that this was no social call.

"You wanted Damon back," Lucifer said, pointing at the archdemon.

Damon didn't look happy. Solid and not ghost-like anymore, but definitely not pleased to be back.

Something wasn't right.

I vacated the office chair and held out a hand to motion him to it. "She's all yours, boss."

I had hoped for a flicker of relief to cross his face. Instead, he clasped his hands behind his back. "I trust everything here is back in working order?"

"Better than ever," I assured him, taking a step away. "Everyone will be thrilled you've returned."

"Good," Lucifer said with a nod. "Shall we?"

He was looking at me. "Shall we what?"

"You said you wanted Damon back running the Institute, and I should find someone new to take his place."

Gooseflesh rose on my arms. "Yeah...?"

"He's back, and I've found his replacement."

Still looking directly at me as if his meaning were obvious.

It was.

"No, no, no." I retreated another step. A giant one, finding a filing cabinet against my back. "I wasn't volunteering."

Rad closed the distance and grabbed my arm. Cole and Dru moved closer as well.

Lucifer ignored them. "I didn't ask for a volunteer. You'll be taking Damon's place in helping me find the Fallen."

"But I..."

Before I could finish, a sensation like being pulled through water hit me. I wobbled, felt Rad's grasp tighten.

"What are you doing to her?" I heard him ask, but his voice was muffled, as if I were truly submerged under water.

My joints softened, my muscles relaxed. I steadied myself, and the liquidy feeling went away. "I'm okay," I told Rad.

But Lucifer wasn't done yet. He hit me with another wave.

Except this one wasn't water.

It was fire.

The burning started at the base of my spine, running down my legs and into my feet. The moment it hit the floor, a new flame surged up my spine, all the way to my head. My back arched, my head flew back.

Rad's hands were the only things that kept me standing.

There was yelling, but I was too busy with my own nuclear problem to worry about what was being said. I jerked, I gasped, and my demon rode the fiery flame with glee. Hellfire is her natural state.

Something snapped – I felt a strange separation, and for a moment, I thought my demon had left my meat suit. But as the inferno inside me subsided, I looked down at myself, and I was still...well, me.

My heart still beat, and my demon, encased next to the organ, was happy and content.

And yet, something was definitely different.

Gone was my sharp vision, everyone staring at me seemed slightly opaque. The sensation of viewing them through a watery film took root in my mind.

Rad's hands were on me, but they weren't. They suddenly passed right through me.

He took another swipe, trying to grab my arm, but his hand cut through my bicep as if nothing was there.

"Shit," I murmured, looking at Lucifer. "You made me a ghost?"

"Not a ghost," Damon corrected. "You're simply more spirit than carbon and bone at the moment."

"This embodiment makes it easier for you to pass back and forth through different realms." Lucifer curled two fingers at me. "Come. We have work to do."

Arguments erupted from Rad, Dru, and Cole.

"You can't take her."

"She belongs here."

"This was never part of the deal!"

Rad had once warned me not to get in the middle of Michael and Lucifer's pissing match with each other. To let them duke it out and keep my backside intact. Instead, I'd been sucked into the fight, and now look what it had garnered me.

I'm cursed. Definitely cursed.

But every curse hides a blessing. If I *were a spirit traveling between* Earth and Hell, I wouldn't be a danger to my friends or the Institute. I would be invisible to Michael and any other supernatural who wanted to hurt me.

I looked at my three guardians, realizing things could be worse. "I'll be okay," I tried to reassure them. I glanced at Damon. "I can come here whenever I want, right?"

Damon gave me a half-nod. I'd take that as a yes.

"It won't last forever," I added, growing more confident. I'd worked for Damon for centuries. Working a few weeks, maybe a month or two for Lucifer – how hard could it be? "There aren't many Fallen left to find, right? We hit forty already. There's probably, what, another dozen or so?"

Lucifer's top lip moved in that reaction I'd learned was his version of a smirk. "There are one hundred and forty-four thousand barred from Heaven. Along with Amy and another Fallen residing in Eden, and the forty you have living here, we still have one-thousand forty-three, nine-hundred and fifty-eight. Give or take."

My mouth dropped open. I should have listened to Rad last year when he'd voted for us to hide away in the Oak Park stronghold I owned but never visited. "You're joking, right?"

Damon cleared his throat. "One hundred and forty-four thousand angels were kicked out after the Great War in Heaven, Kali. There are still many more for us to find."

"For *you* to find," Lucifer emphasized.

He hadn't been kidding when he'd once told me there were a thousand Fallen.

I panicked slightly, my gaze going to Rad. He stepped forward. "I volunteer to help."

"I'm going too," Cole added.

Damon shook his head. "Just Kali."

I heaved a deep breath, letting it out slowly. *Don't take it personally*, I reminded myself. *Stay detached.*

I gave Rad the best smile I could work up. "Don't worry. I'll be way faster at finding the Fallen than Damon was." Damon arched a dark brow but didn't argue. "I'll be back before you know it."

And then I looked at my new boss—blessing or curse, I still hadn't decided. "Let's go. I have a job to do."

. . .

\*\*\*

D𝐄𝐀𝐑 𝐑𝐄𝐀𝐃𝐄𝐑, I hope you've enjoyed deep diving into Kali's world once again! Sweet Shadows is coming soon. If you'd like to read early chapters (unedited as I write them), join my Unlimited Subscription community and watch for the first new episodes in the Kali Sweet Chronicles to drop Fall 2024!

Like your VIP backstage pass at a concert, my subscription gives you VIP access to me and my stories. Early access to books, exclusive stories, and bonus content. Get that ultimate experience today.

**Give me more Kali, Rad, Cole, and Lucifer!**

# GLOSSARY OF TERMS

Glossary of Terms

Alciscor – vengeance demon, based on Ulciscor, the Latin term for *to take vengeance for, avenge.*

Cupiditas – demon

Dominus vobiscum, et cum spiritu tuo – The Lord be with you, and your spirit also

Erinyes – Greek earth deity of vengeance

Errore colossale – colossal mistake

Fermati – that's enough

Giganto – gigantic, enormous

Giuro davanti a dio – so help me God

Il pistolino – dick, prick

Khanda – Indian double-edge straight sword used for hacking and cutting

Merde – shit

Noctifector – demon slayer belonging to the Roman Catholic Church's secret organization; slang term Slayer, Noct

Porca miseria – miserable pig

Psuhke – Greek derivation of Latin term "psyche" and means breath, life, soul

Spiritu sancto – by the Holy Spirit

Straordinario – exceptional

Stretchers - Titans, deities that overstretched their powers to screw with lesser gods and goddesses as well as humans

Tempter – demon who tempts other supernaturals

Testa de cazzo - dickhead

Ti voglio bene – I love you

Tortura – torture

Vitiums – vices

Volante - flying

Vaffanculo – fuck you, fuck off

# VISIT MY STORE

Did you know you can buy directly from me? When you do, the retailer doesn't take a cut and I can pass on the savings to YOU!
https://mistyevansbooks.com/shop

**Benefits:**
You can find ALL my books in one place
SAVE money
EARLY access to new releases
Special Collections, Boxed Sets, and Limited Editions
Support a small business (and support a dream!)

**Why Buy Direct?**
When you purchase a book by your favorite author, electronic or print, on retailer platforms, the company keeps 30-70% of the sale, leaving the author with little to no profit (after the company deducts delivery fees, taxes, and other fees).

Buying directly from the author means that more goes to them so they can keep turning out stories for you. Every published story, every book, requires cover art, editing, and hours and hours of the author's time simply to create it. Not to mention overhead costs, such as websites, newsletters, writing software, graphics programs, advertising, taxes, etc.

In addition, one of the big-name retailers requires exclusivity, and all of them have terms of service and rules and regulations that make it challenging and time-consuming for an indie author to navigate the publishing world.

Most of us would MUCH rather spend our time creating more stories for YOU, rather than trying to jump through the hoops at the retailers. Buying direct from your favorite authors (where available) helps ensure that an author you love is not subject to unexplained account closures, withholding of royalties, censorship, and other issues that can affect their livelihood.

I've experienced ALL of these. By buying direct, you help put control of my work back in my hands - and I can continue to write more.

Either way, thank you for supporting me! I understand buying direct doesn't work for everyone and even if you use the retailers to buy my books, I appreciate you!

Happy reading,

Misty

https://mistyevansbooks.com/shop

# YOU'RE INVITED!

Do you have a passion for my stories?
Want more from my characters?
How about early access to ALL my new releases?
My reader community is for YOU!

Try my **Magic Bites reader community** at www.mistyevansbooks.com for a month! It's ONLY $5 - you're buying me a coffee - and in return, you get all these perks:

    **Writing Updates** so you know what's in the works and how soon you can get it

    **Special Content**, including chapters in new and upcoming stories

    **FREE Access to new books** - Read all of my new paranormal and urban fantasy releases for FREE before they're available at retailers

**Don't miss out on this opportunity! Join my Thrill Rides reader community today.**

*You're Invited!*

**I'm in! Give me more stories!**
https://mistyevansbooks.com/membership-levels

# PNR & UF BY MISTY/NYX HALLIWELL

### The Accidental Reaper Series

**Grim & Bare It, Book 1**

**Reaper's Keepers, Book 2**

**In too Reap, Book 3**

**Killin' It (short story for newsletter subscribers only)**

**The Vampire's Kiss** (an exclusive short story available in Misty's Store. *Intended for mature audiences 17+*)

**Grave Girl**

**Grave Magic**

**Grim Vows**

---

### The Kali Sweet Series

*Revenge Is Sweet, Kali Sweet Series, Book 1*

*Sweet Chaos, Kali Sweet Series, Book 2*

*Sweet Soldier, Kali Sweet Series, Book 3*

*Sweet Curse, Kali Sweet Series, Book 4*

---

*Witches Anonymous Step 1*

*Jingle Hells, WA Step 2*

*Wicked Souls, WA Step 3*

*Dark Moon Lilith, Witches Anonymous Step 4*

*Dancing With the Devil, Witches Anonymous Step 5*

*Devil's Due, Witches Anonymous Step 6*

*Dirty Deeds, Witches Anonymous Step 7*

*Wicked Wedding, Witches Anonymous Step 8*

---

*Soul Survivor, Moon Water Series, Book 1*

*Soul Protector, Moon Water Series, Book 2*

---

COZY MYSTERIES (WRITING AS NYX HALLIWELL)

**Sister Witches Of Raven Falls Mystery Series**

*Of Potions and Portents*

*Of Curses and Charms*

*Of Stars and Spells*

*Of Spirits and Superstition*

---

**Confessions of a Closet Medium Series**

*Pumpkins & Poltergeists*

*Magic & Mistletoe*

*Hearts & Haunts*

*Vows & Vengeance*

*Cupcakes & Corpses*

*Tea Leaves & Troubled Spirits*

*Haunted Honeymoon*

*Wedding Bells & Psychic Spells*

*Phantoms Are Forever*

**Sister Witches of Story Cove Series**

Cinder

Belle

Snow

Ruby

Zelle

**Sister Witches of Story Cove Complete Set**

\*\*\*

**Witchy Candy Shop Mysteries**

**Tricks and Treats**

**Candy and Creeps**

**Gum and Ghouls (releasing 2025)**

# THRILLING ROMANTIC SUSPENSE & MYSTERIES

Don't want to miss a single release? Sign up for my newsletter at www.mistyevansbooks.com!

## SEALs of Shadow Force Series

*Fatal Truth*

*Fatal Honor*

*Fatal Courage*

*Fatal Love*

*Fatal Vision*

*Fatal Thrill*

*Risk*

---

## SEALS of Shadow Force Series: Spy Division

*Man Hunt*

*Man Killer*

*Man Down*

*Covert Affairs*

*Covert Tactics*

*Covert Obsession*

---

## The SCVC Taskforce Series

*Deadly Pursuit*

*Deadly Deception*

*Deadly Force*

*Deadly Intent*

*Deadly Affair, A SCVC Taskforce novella*

*Deadly Attraction*

*Deadly Secrets*

*Deadly Holiday, A SCVC Taskforce novella*

*Deadly Target*

*Deadly Rescue*

*Deadly Bounty*

*Deadly Betrayal*

*Deadly Threat*

---

### The Super Agent Series

*Operation Sheba*

*Operation Paris*

*Operation Proof of Life*

*Operation Lost Princess*

*Operation Ambush*

*Operation Contraband*

*Operation Sleeping With the Enemy*

*Operation Heist*

---

### The Justice Team Series (with Adrienne Giordano)

*Stealing Justice*

*Cheating Justice*

*Holiday Justice*

*Exposing Justice*

*Undercover Justice*

*Protecting Justice*

*Missing Justice*

*Defending Justice*

---

**SCHOCK SISTERS MYSTERY SERIES w/Adrienne Giordano**

1st Shock

2nd Strike

3rd Tango

---

**The Secret Ingredient Culinary Mystery Series**

*The Secret Ingredient, A Culinary Romantic Mystery with Bonus Recipes*

*The Secret Life of Cranberry Sauce, A Secret Ingredient Holiday Novella*

# MEET MISTY

**USA TODAY Bestselling Author Misty Evans** has published over ninety novels, as well as nonfiction inspirational journals. She loves writing urban fantasy, paranormal romance, and mystery/suspense. Under her pen name, Nyx Halliwell, she also writes supernatural cozy mysteries.

When not reading or writing, she enjoys music, movies, and hanging out with her husband, twin sons, and three spoiled rescue dogs. She's a crafter at heart and has far too many projects to finish.

**Visit www.mistyevansbooks.com to check out her online store and sign up for her newsletter.**

# LETTER FROM MISTY

Hello Beautiful Reader!

Thank you for reading this story! It is an honor and a privilege to write books for you. I'm an indie author and every fan is important to me. I pour my heart into each story and do my best to bring you an escape from the real world.

Readers are the key to my success - not a traditional publishing deal (had four), an agent (had two), or a publicity team (yep, you guessed it, had several of those as well.)

Those of you who read my books, love my characters and worlds, and then tell others about them are the best of friends. I adore you and will keep writing if you keep reading!

If you'd like to learn about my other books, sales, and special promotions, please sign up for my newsletter at **www. mistyevansbooks.com.**

You'll get coupons to download starter packs for FREE, whether you love my suspense or my paranormal.

Support me directly (no retailer taking their cut), grab special edition box sets, and get new releases before they are out at retailers by visiting my store **https://mistyevansbooks. com/shop.**

I have sales and offer NEW RELEASES early! Check it out.

Last but not least, if you enjoy clean, cozy mysteries, visit my pen name **www.nyxhalliwell.com** to see those books.

Thank you, and happy reading!

Misty

www.ingramcontent.com/pod-product-compliance
Lightning Source LLC
Chambersburg PA
CBHW020227260626
47156CB00002B/573